Kelvin knew what he must say—"Miss Stratton, it is time you knew the truth about me. My name is not Anthony Forrest. I am Kelvin Rainham, the man who wrought your brother's ruin." The words, abrupt and brutal, were in his mind, but his lips refused to utter them. So for a space they faced each other in silence beneath the apple trees.

"Dorothea," he said at last, and in his voice was passion and tenderness and desperate longing, overlaid by a note of unutterable pain. Almost of its own volition his hand went out towards her, and wordlessly, in answer to that desolate cry, she went into his arms and surrendered her lips to his.

"Anthony," she whispered tenderly, "beloved!" With her cheek against his, she did not see the sudden agony in his eyes at the sound of the murmured name.

SYLVIA THORPE

Beggar on Horseback

A FAWCETT CREST BOOK

Fawcett Publications, Inc., Greenwich, Connecticut

To Velvet,
my cocker spaniel,
whose place can never be filled

BEGGAR ON HORSEBACK

THIS BOOK CONTAINS THE COMPLETE TEXT OF
THE ORIGINAL HARDCOVER EDITION.

A Fawcett Crest Book reprinted by arrangement with
Hutchinson Publishing Group.

ISBN 0-449-23091-0

Printed in the United States of America

10   9   8   7   6   5   4   3   2   1

CHAPTER I

THE VICTOR

The candles had burned low and, since no one had troubled to snuff them, were guttering and smoking in their heavy, silver holders. In the six-branched stand upon the table one of the tiny flames had already flickered out, and each candle had melted and run, shrouding itself in coils and folds of wax. Winding-sheets—the macabre name given to such waxen cloaks passed with a sense of chill foreboding through the mind of the young man who, white-faced and haggard, was slumped in a nearby chair, and with an uncontrollable shudder he averted his eyes from them. His lips twitched and he put up an unsteady hand to tug at his lace cravat.

The room was very quiet, for the night's play was over and though a number of the gentlemen who patronized this exclusive gaming-house had lingered to see the end of a game which, even in an age of reckless gambling, involved a fantastic stake, they clustered in silent or softly whispering groups about the table where the two men sat. On five consecutive nights had they sat thus, young Sir David Stratton and his quiet, self-possessed opponent, facing each other across the cards while a fortune changed hands. Each night Stratton had appeared more distraught, his blue eyes wilder and his hands less steady; each night he drank more deeply and played more recklessly as his losses mounted and ruin stared him in the face, but not once had the other's cold calm faltered. Even now, when he found himself master of the Stratton lands and fortune, he sat silent and unsmiling, idly shuffling the cards between his hands.

Young Sir David was watching those hands now, staring at them in fascinated dismay, for to his overwrought imagination it seemed that they possessed a malignant life of their own. They were beautiful hands, long and slender and of a whiteness which many fine ladies might have envied, yet in spite of this, and the ribbon-tied ruffles of lace from which they emerged, there was nothing effeminate about them. Rather was there an uncanny suggestion of strength in the tapering fingers, on one of which gleamed a gold ring wrought into an heraldic device.

With a supreme effort he forced himself to look higher, into the face of the man opposite, and found that he was watching him with an unfathomable expression. His face, too, was pale, the features finely chiselled, the lips austere; his dark grey eyes, just now fixed so inscrutably upon David, regarded the world with an expression of cool indifference, and in defiance of fashion he wore no periwig but his own auburn hair, which fell in heavy waves over his shoulders. A strange, cold, passionless man, this Major Rainham, who had come from devil knew where to win a fortune from a weak and reckless profligate.

It was as he looked into those aloof and faintly mocking eyes that the first full realization of what had happened swept over Stratton, hitherto sustained by wine and by the feverish excitement of the game. He was ruined. His fatal passion for gaming had cost him the noble patrimony to which he had succeeded only two years ago, for in five nights of play—during which he had plunged ever deeper in a desperate effort to recover his losses—his wealth, his lands, and finally even the old house of Hope

6

Stratton in Worcestershire, the home of his family for generations, had passed from him into the hands of a stranger. A groan which was almost a sob broke from his lips, and his head went down upon his arms outstretched across the table.

Those who watched him turned awkwardly away, torn between pity and contempt, and the groups broke up, some of the men going out and down the stairs, the rest drifting to the far end of the room, where the embers of a fire still glowed on the wide hearth. There were hostile glances towards the unheeding figure of the Major, but no suggestion that the game had been aught but fairly played. Sally Cheriton's gaming-house was above suspicion, and she herself had vouched for Kelvin Rainham, introducing him as a friend of long standing.

She stood now, the only woman in the company, midway between the group about the fire and the table where the two men sat, a tall, middle-aged woman in a fashionable gown, with a head-dress of stiffened lace and ribbon on her modishly-curled grey hair. Her heavily-painted face, with its strong, humorous mouth, was handsome still, but just now there was a frown on her brow and trouble in her shrewd brown eyes. She did not relish incidents such as this, which brought unwelcome notoriety upon her establishment, but greater even than her anxiety for her house was her concern for the stricken boy huddled across the table. His face was hidden by the tumbled black curls of his periwig, but his hands gripped and wrung each other in an agony of despair. She was relieved when a stocky, fair-haired young man detached himself from the group about the fire and came forward to lay his hand on Stratton's shoulder.

"David," he said quietly. "David, come away."

Stratton lifted a ravaged face and looked blankly at the speaker for a moment before he obeyed the pressure of the friendly hand and got slowly to his feet. Grasping his arm, his friend propelled him towards the door, but on the threshold David paused and looked once more at Rainham, who, as though conscious of his regard, raised his eyes from the cards with which he was still toying. For a long moment the blue eyes and the grey

7

met across the width of the room, and then with a gesture half menacing, half desperate, the ruined man passed through the doorway and out of sight. His companion was turning to follow when Mrs. Cheriton's voice checked him.

"Mr. Ashton," she said in a low voice, and went forward, her trailing skirts rustling across the polished floor. "Stay with him, sir. Do not allow him to be left alone."

He nodded, and she saw in his face the confirmation of her own fears of what Sir David, in his present despairing mood, might seek to do.

"I will not, madam, rest assured of that," he replied, and with an abrupt bow turned on his heel and followed Stratton down the stairs. Mrs. Cheriton went back into the room, where chairs had been thrust untidily back from tables on which cards and dice were scattered, and which looked oddly forlorn in the light of the guttering candles and the dying fire. At her approach the low-voiced group about the hearth broke up, and in twos and threes bade her good night and departed, but no word was spoken to the silent man at the table, nor did he look up as they went past him on their way to the door. His utter indifference was like a shield upon which their open hostility made not the slightest impression.

When the door had closed behind the last of them Mrs. Cheriton moved slowly forward to the table and stood, resting one hand upon the back of a chair, to look down at her companion.

"May you be forgiven, Kelvin," she said slowly, "for what you have done to that boy."

He glanced up at her, raising his brows in faint amusement.

"A pious hope, my dear," he replied carelessly. "Am I expected to say 'amen'?"

She continued to regard him, the trouble in her eyes deepening.

"You have beggared him," she said, "and in such circumstances stronger men than he have killed them-

8

selves. Can you reconcile your conscience to that possibility?"

He shrugged.

"Do you know so little of me, even now? Is my conscience to irk me because, for the first time in seven years, Fortune has stood my friend?"

"Fortune—and your own wits." The words fell softly upon the silence, and Rainham looked up sharply, his lips tightening and a flash of anger in his eyes.

"One might almost suppose," he said coldly, "that you were accusing me of cheating him."

She sighed and shook her head, moving to seat herself in the chair which Stratton had lately vacated.

"I know that there was no dishonesty in the game," she replied, "but 'tis not only marked cards and loaded dice which can give a man so great an advantage over his opponent that the conclusion is foregone. Oh, I have watched you these five nights past, driving the lad to distraction with your devilish calm and bitter tongue, goading him on every time some glimmer of prudence warned him of the road he was treading. He was no match for you, and you knew it from the first."

She paused to look irritably at him, but the Major was occupied in erecting a fragile structure of playing-cards and continued to do so with unimpaired calm. Mrs. Cheriton's annoyance increased.

"I would not have blamed you for winning a large sum from him, but to carry it to such lengths! You could have stopped after the third night's play and still been the richer by thousands of pounds, but you were not content until you had stripped him of everything he possessed. In God's name, Kelvin, why?"

"The poet tells us," Rainham replied dryly, "that there is a tide in the affairs of men which, taken at the flood, leads on to fortune. My affairs have been at low ebb these many years, but when the flood-tide came I knew it for what it was and took all it offered." He laid another card carefully upon the erection before him. "Only a fool would have neglected such an opportunity."

"There are worse things than to be a fool," she retorted. "What name should be given to a man who deliberately reduces a weak-willed youth to abject poverty?"

The straight brows lifted; there was a faint contempt in the fine grey eyes.

"My dear Sally, this persistent picturing of Stratton as the innocent victim of an adventurer is absurd, and you know it. He has, I am told, spent the past two years in a wild pursuit of pleasure, and if his career has been less vicious than that of most young men of fashion, it has exceeded theirs in its extravagant follies."

"He'll be guilty of extravagance no more, poor boy," Mrs. Cheriton said sadly. "Would to heaven I had never made you known to each other. Could I have foreseen the consequences I would rather have ordered you both from the house."

With a flip of his finger Major Rainham demolished the frail structure he had built, and for a few seconds regarded the ruins with sombre and unseeing eyes.

"Many of us would act differently could we be granted a glimpse of the result of our actions," he said in a hard voice, "but regret, my dear, is worse than useless. There is no second chance."

He rose to his feet and sauntered across to the fire-place, a man above the common height and with the erect bearing of the professional soldier. As Sally pondered him from her seat by the table the irritation faded from her eyes, to be replaced by an expression almost maternal, for her affection for him was deep and sincere. They had been friends for years, and she was one of the very few who realized how reserved and lonely a spirit dwelt within the armour of his almost impenetrable calm, and she knew, too, of the tragedy which, seven years before, had blasted his life and sent him, an ambitious young officer for whom a brilliant career had been prophesied, into dishonoured exile as a wandering soldier of fortune.

He turned at length to face her, leaning his shoulders against the mantel and folding his arms across the breast of his dark blue velvet coat. The feeble light from the candles above and behind him glowed on his tawny hair, leaving his face in shadow, but his voice was calm and faintly ironical as he continued:

"It may surprise you to learn, Sally, that I have grown

weary of being a homeless wanderer, roaming from one country to another and selling my sword to the highest bidder. When you told me two years ago in Paris that you had done with exile and were coming home to England, I laughed at you. Later I came to realize your wisdom."

"I came home because my brother had left me this house," Mrs. Cheriton replied prosaically, "and when I found that he'd not left me also the means of maintaining it I turned it into a gaming-house." She shrugged. "Well, I have prospered. Today it is the most fashionable hell in London."

"Tomorrow its fame will be doubled," Rainham assured her cynically. "Good lack, Sally, do you imagine that any harm can come to you through this night's work? When the story becomes known every noble fool in town will be clamouring for admittance, and those who come to satisfy their curiosity will remain to play."

She rose and curtsied to him in mock gratitude, saying sarcastically:

"So 'twas done for my sake, was it, Kelvin? The profit to yourself was a mere accident? Oh, I am vastly in your debt, but I should prefer to prosper by some other means, believe me."

He laughed softly, and though she could not see his face clearly she could guess its expression, the eyes glinting with mockery, the mouth cynically curved.

"Growing squeamish, Sally?" he inquired. "I assure you that your sympathy is wasted upon that young man. Drink or the cards would have been his ruin eventually, and as well sooner as later."

Mrs. Cheriton shook her head.

"You are mistaken, I think. I have watched him during the months that he has been coming here, and I believe that there is little real evil in him. He is young, and has probably been indulged more than is good for him. Women have flattered him for the sake of his handsome face, and men for his money. Always he is surrounded by a crowd of sycophants."

"That, at least, he will be spared henceforth," Kelvin replied indifferently. "Friends are few when the purse is empty." He observed his companion's troubled frown and laughed again. "Oh, console yourself, my dear. If he has the qualities you think to perceive in him—though I take leave to doubt it—misfortune may well be the making of him."

Mrs. Cheriton had resumed her seat by the table and was looking at him searchingly. Presently she sighed.

"You are hard, Kelvin, damnably hard," she told him. "Sometimes I wonder whether they are right who say that you have no heart at all."

He made an impatient movement.

"Because I have no sympathy for a young wastrel who squanders a rich inheritance at cards? 'Pon honour, Sally, I had not suspected you of such sentimentality."

"I cannot forget the look in his eyes when he realized what he had done," she said in a low voice. "Laugh at me an you will for a sentimental old woman, but I will own to a liking for the lad. So young, and ruined! Faugh, sometimes this life sickens me!"

"Men are ruined every day." Rainham's level voice was suddenly harsh and bitter. "Some, unlike Stratton, through no fault of their own, but because, poor fools, they choose to follow the path of duty."

Startled by words and tone out of her preoccupation with Sir David's misfortune, she remembered the speaker's own tragic history and was silenced. If ever a man had cause to rail against fate, that man was Kelvin Rainham, and yet it was but rarely that the bitterness and frustration within him broke through his cloak of cynical indifference.

"When I sat down to play against Stratton for the first time," the angry, bitter voice continued, "my entire fortune amounted to less than a hundred pounds. From past experience it seemed probable that even that would be gone before I rose from the table, but by some miracle the luck was with me and I won. The next night he challenged me again—for his revenge, he said—and by chance I discovered that a few mocking words so discomposed him that he scarcely knew what he was doing. I realized then that fortune had elected to favour me at last, and I resolved to win every penny I could while the luck lasted, even if I had to beggar him to do it. Yes, I goaded him to desperation, taunted him into flinging not only gold, but lands and home into the game, but do you look to see me shamed therefore? Does not life owe me some recompense for the blows it has dealt me in the past?"

He broke off, passing one slender, beautiful hand across his eyes in a weary gesture, and for a space there was silence. When he spoke again his voice had resumed its note of cold self-possession.

"Forgive me," he said quietly, "I had not thought myself so easily unmanned, but 'tis not every day that one wins such a prize."

He moved forward to the table as he spoke and picked up some of the scattered cards, looking down at them with an expression of mingled contempt and amusement, while Mrs. Cheriton regarded him curiously.

" 'Tis a strange thing," he remarked musingly at length, "but not once had it ever occurred to me that I might become a rich man by such means as this. If ever fortune came to me, I thought, 'twould be by way of some service rendered by my sword, for I am a soldier, not a gamester. But all that my sword has brought me is wounds and hardship and a few valueless foreign orders, while these—" With a sudden movement he spread the cards face upwards on the table. "Look at them, Sally! In a few short nights they have brought me wealth undreamed of in all my years of soldiering. Faith! 'tis a sobering thought."

"Here's one more sobering still," Mrs. Cheriton replied somewhat grimly. "There was an occasion once when the cards cost you more than a few hard-earned guineas. You realize, I hope, what would result if that story became known."

Rainham shrugged, perching himself on the edge of the table and idly swinging one elegantly-shod foot.

"Small chance of that, I fancy," he replied easily. "Who in London save we two is likely to know of something which happened four years ago in an obscure foreign city? Even at the time it occasioned no great stir. Such incidents are common enough in the tail of an army."

"Nevertheless, it would go hard with you if it became known that the man who won the Stratton fortune was once convicted of cheating at cards. Oh, Kelvin, what a fool you were to shoulder another's guilt in that crazy fashion—and a bigger fool not to make known the truth after Anthony Forrest's death. Mad enough to shield a living man, but to continue to do so now passes all bounds."

"By the time that Anthony died the matter was forgotten. Would you have me drag the whole sorry affair into the light once more when the only result would be to tarnish the memory of a brave man? I challenged Dacres and killed him because he knew that 'twas Anthony, and not I, who cheated that night."

She sighed and shook her head, looking up at him with exasperated affection.

"How loyal you are to your friends, Kelvin," she said. "How foolishly, fanatically loyal."

A faint smile touched his lips.

"Perhaps because my friends have been so very few," he replied. "Only yourself and Anthony—and he is dead." He thrust his hand into the breast of his coat and drew out a slim volume bound in worn and faded leather. "Do you remember this, Sally? 'Tis the book of verses of which he was so fond. I never knew why, for he had no love of poetry, but he carried it always, and since his death I have done the same."

He opened the book at the fly-leaf, where the name 'Anthony Forrest' was inscribed in a flourishing hand, and for a space they both regarded it in silence. Sally Cheriton frowned, for the memories it evoked were not, to her, pleasant ones. Though she and Rainham had been friends for over ten years, during much of that time they had met only at intervals, when the erratic paths they followed converged for a while, but at one such time, now four years past, the incident had occurred which unjustly branded him a cheat.

He and Forrest were comrades-in-arms, an oddly-assorted pair in all conscience—the mad, merry, fatally-charming Anthony, and Kelvin, remote and aloof, embittered by past misfortunes—but true friends in spite of these differences of temperament. Sally had never liked Forrest, though she tolerated him for Rainham's sake, and when he played a coward's part and allowed his friend to shoulder the dishonour which rightly was his, she felt her mistrust justified. Forrest, knowing her antipathy towards him and her affection for Kelvin, wrote a letter full of specious excuses for his conduct and entreaties to her not to reveal the truth, a letter which she did not deign to answer but which she had kept ever since, realizing its value either as a weapon or as proof of Rainham's innocence should need arise. She referred to it now.

"At least," she remarked, "I still have his letter. You may use it whenever you will to show where the true guilt lay."

He looked up, his brows drawing together in a frown.

"I have asked you many times to destroy that letter," he said. "You know that I would never make use of it to blacken the name of my friend."

"Your friend!" Her voice was scornful. "A man who stood aside and watched you dishonoured in his stead."

"And who died in my arms on the field of battle, having taken a thrust intended for me." He shook his head, and glanced again at the scrawled signature, his face softened by a smile which few were privileged to see. "Poor, foolish Anthony! Whatever debt he owed me was paid in full at the last."

"But if someone accused you——" she was beginning, when he cut her short.

"I have said that there is little fear of that." The finality in his voice convinced her that it was futile to argue further. "Scandal concerning me may well be remembered, but I fancy 'twill not be that."

"Ah!" Understanding was in her voice and eyes. "You fear that it may be remembered that you are that Major Rainham who——"

"Who was cashiered seven years ago for striking a superior officer, and who was suspected of an ugly crime?" he supplied calmly as she hesitated. "It is possible, I think, but I do not fear it. There have been many changes since then, and now, moreover, I have a powerful shield. I have observed that the world generally permits a man to forget his past if he is able and willing to pay for the privilege."

"From this I gather," she said after a moment, "that you intend to step completely into David Stratton's shoes, and take his place in fashionable circles. Well, you never lacked for boldness."

He had closed the little book and returned it to his pocket, and now he looked at her with laughter glinting in his eyes and softening the sternness of his lips, and she thought, as she had often done before, what a pity it was that so few people ever glimpsed that swift, transfiguring smile.

" 'Tis boldness that best will serve me now," he said. "Stratton is popular, and there may be some feeling against me. It will not last, of course. He will drop quietly out of society and in a few weeks his existence will be forgotten."

"While the place which he vacates, you intend to fill." Reluctant amusement dawned in her eyes as she pondered the difference between the two men. "Faith, it may well have its entertaining aspect, after all."

"Later," pursued the Major, "I shall visit the estate of which, overnight, I have become the master. Hope Stratton, is it not, in the county of Worcestershire? It has a pleasant sound."

"It has, indeed. I doubt not 'tis a fair estate." Mrs. Cheriton spoke lightly, but her eyes were fixed with curious intentness upon his face. "Wealth, lands, a home—faith, Kelvin, there is but one thing you lack!" She hesitated, and then added quietly: "It now behoves you to take a wife."

She saw the fine mouth harden again, the grey eyes grow bleak.

"That," said Major Rainham in a voice of ice, "is one folly of which I shall not be guilty. Seven years ago my honour was blasted and my military career ruined by a woman's perfidy, and I swore then that never would I love a woman, and so place my life in hands which would in all probability prove false. Well, I have kept that vow! Dalliance has never amused me, and as for marriage——"
He shrugged, and, rising abruptly to his feet, went to stand again before the hearth, resting both hands against the mantel and staring down at the grey ashes of the fire.

With her gaze upon that straight, uncompromising back Mrs. Cheriton said quietly:

"You cannot bid love come and go at will, Kelvin. Were it to come to you not all the vows on earth would prevent it—no, nor the memory of the betrayal which you suffered at Catherine Manville's hands."

"Catherine meant nothing to me," Kelvin replied levelly, without turning his head, "but when I learned what manner of woman she was, and the way in which she made use of those—and they were many—who did love her, I resolved that no woman should ever have such power over me. None has, and none ever will."

"Have a care, Kelvin," Mrs. Cheriton warned him dryly. "That sounded remarkably like a challenge, and when a man flings down such a gauntlet, destiny is apt to take it up."

At that he turned to face her, completely master of himself once more, a mocking smile hovering about his lips.

"When I fall victim to a pretty face," he said lightly, "I will take it as proof of your wisdom and confess myself mistaken, but I assure you that 'twill be long before bright eyes hold any lure for me. I am past the age of such youthful folly."

"I wonder?" Sally's voice was sceptical. "One thing at least is certain. The bright eyes you so despise will not fail to look kindly upon you."

"Upon the Stratton fortune, rather," he retorted, "but be easy, my dear. Though I have been a poor man for many years, the sudden acquisition of wealth will not cause me to lose my head to that extent."

Mrs. Cheriton leaned back in her chair and studied him thoughtfully.

"That you are uncommonly level-headed I know," she said. "However, there is a proverb which says 'set a beggar on horseback and he will ride to the devil.' "

He raised his brows; the mockery about his mouth became more marked.

"My dear Sally," he said, "ride thither I may, but by your leave I will ride alone."

CHAPTER II

THE VANQUISHED

He lay prone and fully-dressed on the great, canopied bed, so still that he might have been sleeping, save for the violent shudders which from time to time shook his slight figure, and the way in which his hands constantly clenched and unclenched upon the silken coverlet. So he had lain, motionless and silent, ever since his return to his lodgings in the first grey light of dawn. So he had lain, while the sun rose and the city woke to life and movement beyond his curtained windows, and in bedchambers and boudoirs, in clubs and coffee-houses, the story was whispered how young Sir David Stratton, the spoiled favourite of fashion, had lost all his great fortune and broad estates over the card-table.

In an arm-chair a little removed from the bed sat the man who had accompanied him home from the gaming-house. Michael Ashton was a few years older than his friend and of infinitely stronger character, a thick-set young man of medium height, with a square, pleasant face marred only by an extremely hard mouth. He had kept his vigil at David's side for many weary hours, but now at last, in spite of all his efforts, fatigue had overcome him. His chin buried in the folds of his cravat, Michael Ashton slept.

For a space no sound broke the stillness of the luxurious room, but presently the huddled figure on the bed stirred and raised its head from among the tumbled pillows. Haggard, unshaven, blinking a little at the glimmer of sunshine which found its way between the heavy, brocade window-hangings, David struggled into a sitting position on the edge of the bed and pressed both hands against his throbbing temples, striving to cast off his stupor of despair and face the consequences of what he had done.

It was the first time in his five-and-twenty years that David Stratton had been called upon to face a disaster of any magnitude, for hitherto Fortune had chosen to shower favours upon him, until an originally generous and likeable nature had been overlaid by a veneer of selfish waywardness. Upon the death of his father two years earlier he had lost no time in taking up residence in London and plunging immediately into the life of gaiety and dissipation which had led to his present plight. His sister Dorothea, concealing her preference for a quiet, country life, had accompanied him reluctantly to the capital, but David, having bestowed her in the care of her godmother, Lady Norland—for their own mother had been dead for some years—and introduced her to the leaders of fashion, thereafter paid her scant attention. His duty, as he saw it, had been done.

In these circumstances it was inevitable that they should grow apart, but the process was undeniably accelerated by Miss Stratton's efforts to restrain her brother's recklessness and her frank criticism of the company with which he surrounded himself. Out of the host of well-bred young rakes and pleasure-loving women who were admitted to the ever-growing ranks of his intimates only one, Michael Ashton, gained her respect and liking, for the rest, she knew, were self-seeking flatterers eager to impose upon David's extravagance and lack of discernment.

His whole mode of life, and in particular that passion for gaming which amounted almost to an obsession, occa-

19

sioned her constant anxiety, but her remonstrances fell upon deaf ears. David, intoxicated by the heady wine of popularity, had no mind to be brought to book by his younger sister, and told her loftily that he was quite capable of ordering his own affairs. Dorothea, watching him go from folly to extravagant folly, was of a different opinion. She knew that the present state of affairs could not long continue, that her arrogant and headstrong brother was riding for a fall, and knew, too, that when it came he would look to her for sympathy and comfort. With the quiet humour characteristic of her she had resolved to bide her time, never guessing how complete and shattering the catastrophe would be. During the week when David was gambling away his fortune Dorothea was visiting friends in the country and knew nothing of this crowning folly. Had she not been absent from London, Major Rainham's victory might have come to him less easily.

It was of Dorothea that David was thinking now, as he crouched in abject despair amid the hollow grandeur of his bedchamber, wishing passionately that he had paid some heed to her warnings, and yearning in vain for the comfort of her presence. Throughout his boyhood, when fine plans went awry and events inexplicably refused to mould themselves to suit his pleasure, it was Dorothea to whom he turned; Dorothea, with her sweet serenity and clear, untrammelled judgment, who had ever seemed the elder and wiser of the twain; but he could never turn to her again. That was the bitterest thought of all in those hours of self-abasement—that, and the knowledge, which not even Michael yet shared, that he had wronged her beyond hope of forgiveness.

How long he sat there, elbows on knees and his hands supporting his aching head, he did not know, nor at what precise moment he remembered the loaded pistol in the drawer of the bureau and resolved to use it. Perhaps the thought had been growing in his mind through all the hours since he flung himself down upon the bed, perhaps it sprang to life full-grown as his glance rested for the first time that day upon the bureau where the weapon lay. He only knew, as he sat there staring at the closed drawer which held the pistol, that he had not the courage to confess to Dorothea nor to face the future penniless and alone.

He stole a furtive glance at Ashton, for he realized now his friend's reason for keeping so close a watch upon him since their return from Mrs. Cheriton's. Michael had not stirred; his head had fallen forward, the fair curls of his periwig almost hiding his face, and his breathing was deep and regular. David rose cautiously to his feet and stole across to the bureau, pausing, with his fingers about the handle of the drawer, to look once more at the sleeper. Gingerly, inch by inch, he eased it open, until the dim light glimmered faintly on the silver-mounted butt and long, chased barrel of the hidden weapon; for an instant he stood looking down at it, and then reached into the drawer and grasped it in a hand which, in spite of all his efforts, shook a little. As he withdrew it the barrel scraped against the wood, a slight sound, yet loud enough to break Michael's uneasy slumber. His head jerked upright, he blinked for a moment at the ominous scene before him, and then in a bound was out of the chair and across to David's side, his hand closing about that which held the pistol.

For some seconds they stood thus, breast to breast, in a silence broken only by their own quickened breathing, while the grip of Ashton's square, capable hand tightened slowly and ruthlessly, until with a gasp of pain David released the gun and it dropped back into the drawer. Then, with a lack of effort which seemed almost contemptuous, the elder man thrust him away and into a chair, and, picking up the pistol, proceeded calmly to unload it. David watched him apathetically for a moment, and then with a groan buried his face once more in his hands.

"My God, Michael, why did you stop me?" he muttered. "I should be better dead."

"You young fool!" Ashton's voice, though curt, was not unkindly. "Do you wish to be remembered as a coward who had not the courage to face the consequences of his folly? Gad'slife, you are not the first to lose a fortune over the gaming-table, nor, while cards and dice exist, will you be the last!"

"If it were only that!" David lifted a white, despairing face towards his friend. "Michael, you do not know what I have done! But I was so sure that the luck would change, that I would win back all I had lost, and more besides!" A sudden thought struck him and hope glimmered faintly in his eyes. "Do you think it possible that Rainham cheated me?"

"No," said Michael flatly. "I'm sorry, David, but I'll not give you false hopes. I am convinced that the game was fairly played." He thrust the unloaded pistol into the drawer, turned the key and withdrew it. Twisting it idly between his fingers, but looking narrowly at Stratton the while, he added: "What is it that you have done that makes the loss of your wealth of small account?"

" 'Tis Dorothea," David replied wretchedly. "That which I lost to Rainham was not wholly mine. I have made her as penniless as I am myself."

The key became suddenly motionless in Michael's hands and he stared incredulously at his companion.

"As Gad's my life!" he said in a stunned voice. "Has she nothing in her own right?"

David shook his head.

"Only a beggarly pittance which she inherited from her mother. You know how suddenly our father died, and he had made no provision for Dorothea. I meant to do it! As God's my witness I never meant to rob her! But there seemed no need for haste, and now——" he broke off and with a helpless gesture relapsed into silence.

"You contemptible scoundrel!" Ashton's voice was like the crack of a whip. His eyes had narrowed and there was an unpleasant expression about his mouth. "By your damnable folly you make your sister a pauper, and then seek to take your own life and leave her to shift for herself as best she may. How, think you, was she to live? Was she to go begging to Rainham in the hope that he would take pity on her, or was she to seek a protector elsewhere? 'Sdeath, I should have let you have your way just now! You are not fit to live!"

He strode away to the far side of the room and, flinging the curtains violently apart, stared down into the street. David, who had winced beneath the lash of his words, remained huddled in his chair and made no attempt to reply, and slowly the anger died out of Michael's eyes, to be replaced by an expression almost calculating. He turned and surveyed his companion for a moment, then, as though resolved, went forward and laid his hand on the bowed shoulder.

"Forgive me, David," he said quietly. "I was not prepared for what you told me, and spoke in the heat of the moment. This past night has tried us both to the limits of endurance. I ask your pardon."

Stratton lifted his head and looked almost incredulously at his friend, and in silence Michael extended his hand. Wordlessly, his face working, David gripped and wrung it, and then, rising to his feet, began to pace the room.

"Michael, what am I to do?" he asked desperately. "How am I to tell her? She will never forgive me."

Michael shook his head.

"Do you know your own sister so little that you can imagine for one moment that she will hold your folly against you? But she must be told at once, before the story is blurted out to her by some malicious scandalmonger. Take my advice and go to her at once."

"I cannot!" David halted and stood gripping the back of a chair until his knuckles shone white. "I have not the courage to face her. If only——" He broke off, looking at his companion. "Michael, will you do it for me? Please, I beg of you."

With something which might have been satisfaction flickering in his eyes, Ashton bowed his head in assent.

"I will do it, David, if I may have your word that you will make no further attempt upon your life. Promise me that and I will set forth at once."

"I swear it," Stratton replied eagerly. "You are right—'tis no answer. I cannot tell you how grateful I am that you will break the news to Dorothea."

"Spare your thanks until we are sure that I am first with the story," Ashton said dryly. "Where shall I find her?"

"I am not sure, but Lady Norland will know. Shall I send to ask her?"

"No, I will go myself. 'Tis quicker so." He went to the door, but paused there to look back at David. "You would be wise to stay within-doors until I return, and, above all, remember your promise."

When he left Stratton's lodgings, Michael Ashton went straight to Sir Charles Norland's house in the Strand, for he wished to learn without delay the whereabouts of Dorothea, so that he could make his preparations for the journey accordingly. On his arrival there, however, he was surprised and gratified to discover that Miss Stratton had returned unexpectedly the previous night and would, despite the early hour, receive him at once, so it was after only a brief delay that he was admitted to her presence.

Dorothea Stratton was at this time in her twenty-third year, a slender, graceful girl bearing a strong superficial resemblance to her brother. Her admirers—not least of whom was Ashton himself—acclaimed her as a beauty, but though her face with its broad, serene forehead and firm chin was fair enough, it was lifted out of the commonplace chiefly by its rare tranquillity of expression. Her mouth, though well-shaped and with tenderness and humour in its generous curves, was a fraction too wide for classical beauty, and her brows, low-arching over wide-set eyes, somewhat strongly marked. Somewhere far back in the Stratton ancestry there was Spanish blood, and to this Dorothea owed the gleaming, blue-black hair which clustered about her brow and lay in heavy curls across her shoulders, but the clear blue eyes between the black lashes were as English as the delicately-tinted complexion upon which, contrary to the demands of fashion, she scorned to use the artificial aids so popular with most women of her class.

That she was unmarried at the almost unprecedented age of twenty-two was a fact directly attributable to her devotion to her brother. Suitors she had had in plenty, country squires and town gallants, and might, had she so chosen, have borne one of the proudest titles in the peerage, but so far not one of these gentlemen had aroused in her feelings which prompted her to forsake her maiden state. David came first with her, as he had always done, and though he customarily took her affection for granted, and she was by no means blind to his many faults, she had never yet been tempted to grant to any other man the place which he had ever occupied in her heart.

When Mr. Ashton was ushered by the liveried servant into Lady Norland's drawing-room, he found to his surprise that, early though it was, Miss Stratton was already dressed for the street. She had a lace-bordered wrap of deep blue silk about her shoulders and a hood of the same colour over her black hair, the lace head-dress rising in front of it and making her appear taller than she actually was.

In silence she regarded him, and in silence Michael went forward and bent to kiss her hand. Dorothea's glance travelled over him, noting the general disorder of his dress and the fatigue in his grave countenance, and apprehension deepened in her eyes. Her free hand lifted unsteadily to her throat in a gesture of which she seemed unaware.

"There is something wrong," she said in a low voice. "I had the strangest conviction that all was not well, and that is why I returned so soon. Michael, what has happened to David?"

Ashton had retained his clasp upon her fingers and now he laid his other hand over them.

"Physically, he is well enough," he replied gravely, "but he has been guilty of a folly so great, so disastrous, that I scarcely know how to tell you of it." He led her to a chair, and when she was seated, added quietly but with much feeling: "I would to God that this task had not fallen to me, but 'tis best that you should hear the story from a friend."

Simply, and as briefly as possible, he recounted the tale of weakness and folly which had reached its culmination the previous night, and she listened quietly, her hands clasped in her lap and her clear eyes fixed upon his face. Dorothea Stratton was not the woman to swoon or weep at evil tidings, not even at the news that, without warning and through no fault of her own, she had lost her home and fortune to a man whose very name she was now hearing for the first time. Watching her, Ashton thought that he had never admired her more than at that moment.

"Thank you, Michael," she said, when at length the story was told. "That was no pleasant task, I know. David should have told me himself." She rose to her feet. "Now will you take me to him, please?"

He bowed his head in assent.

"I will summon your coach," he said, but Dorothea shook her head.

"It is already at the door. This presentiment of trouble had so wrought upon me that I was on the point of setting out for David's lodgings when you arrived." She sighed. "Would that I had acted upon it sooner."

"Would that you had," Ashton agreed soberly. "You might perhaps have prevailed upon him to desist. He would pay no heed to me."

He escorted her from the house and handed her into the waiting coach, and only once during the short journey did she speak. Then she said:

"Tell me again the name of the man who has done this thing."

"Major Kelvin Rainham," Michael supplied. "He has not been long in London. I know little of him, but I fancy that he has lived abroad for some years."

"I'll warrant he has," Dorothea retorted scornfully. "By choice or necessity, I wonder? Is his military rank of his own bestowing?"

"Perhaps, but he has the look of a soldier."

"A soldier of fortune, belike." She leaned back in her seat and turned her head against the cushions to look from the window, her lips taking on an unwontedly vindictive expression. "Major Kelvin Rainham," she repeated in a low voice. "That name is branded upon my memory, and some day, God willing, I will make him regret the wrong he has done."

When David's lodgings were reached they found him still in his bedchamber. He had flung himself down again upon the bed and was staring blindly up at the ornate brocade hangings, but when the door opened he glanced listlessly towards it and said, without moving:

"Back so soon, Michael? What is amiss now?"

Ashton made no reply, but merely stood aside to permit his companion to enter the room. Stratton stared unbelievingly for a moment and then started to his feet.

"Dorothea!" he said hoarsely. "Why have you come here? Do you not know what I have done?"

"Michael has told me, as you asked him to do," she replied gently. "Did you doubt that I would come?"

"You do not realize what it means," he answered wildly, "you cannot! I have lost everything. Money, lands, home, all are gone. We are beggars—aye, beggars, through my damnable folly—and like to starve in the gutter. Go back to Lady Norland. She will not turn you adrift when she knows that you are free of me, and I have brought nothing but trouble upon you. You should not have come here! For your own sake you should not have come!"

"David!" Dorothea's quiet voice broke in upon the hysterical outburst. "What nonsense is this? You cannot think that I would desert you now." She moved serenely to a chair and sank into it, extending one hand towards him. "Dear, foolish David, surely you know that nothing can ever come between us?"

For a moment longer he stared at her, and then with a choked exclamation flung himself on his knees beside her, his arms about her and his face hidden in her lap, while the pent-up emotions of the past few days found relief in racking sobs. Ashton saw her stoop and gather the bowed figure tenderly into her arms, and then he withdrew and softly closed the door, leaving brother and sister together.

CHAPTER III

AT GALLOWS FARM

Michael Ashton was an extremely shrewd young man. For many months he had been in love with Dorothea Stratton, but though he had striven to appear all that she would wish, and had even simulated a regard for her brother which he did not really feel, he could not flatter himself that his wooing had prospered. She honoured him with her friendship, but she had gently but resolutely forbidden any tenderer relationship. When David confessed the wrong he had done his sister, Michael, after his first angry outburst, had perceived that it might be turned to his own advantage. Upon Dorothea would the chief burden fall; she it was who would be obliged to build a new life for them from the wreckage to which her brother's folly had reduced the old; now, as never before, she would need a friend and counsellor upon whom she could depend, and to whom should she turn if not to Michael himself?

In this belief he was presently justified. Dorothea might comfort and reassure her brother, but for all her courage the thought of the future daunted her, and though her instinctive desire was to retreat from London, to find some quiet haven which the tide of gossip could not reach, where was such sanctuary to be found now that Hope Stratton had passed into Major Rainham's hands? She confided in Michael, and he, delighted at this new turn of events, at once placed his own country house, Dene End in Essex, at Miss Stratton's disposal.

So to Essex they went, David, Dorothea and Michael, to that remote and lonely house on the edge of the flat salt marshes, and if in those first difficult days, when Stratton's mood alternated between violent self-reproach and the apathy of complete despair, only Michael knew what it cost him to maintain a sympathetic and understanding attitude, he had his reward in the increasing kindness with which Dorothea appeared to regard him. Insensibly she came to depend upon him more and more, turning to him constantly for advice and comfort, and perhaps it was the very consciousness of her dependence, and the vague alarm it inspired in her, which prompted her to seek another sanctuary.

Michael had no suspicion of her intention, and it was David who dashed his friend's rising hopes by announcing one morning that the time had come for him and his sister to leave Dene End. All the tedious formalities resulting from the loss of his fortune to Kelvin Rainham were now at an end, they knew exactly how they were circumstanced, and they could no longer impose upon Michael's hospitality, which they had already enjoyed for a number of weeks. They had determined, he said, to make their home with an old servant, who was now the wife of a farmer in Kent. This woman had been their mother's personal maid, and owed the late Lady Stratton a debt of gratitude for giving her employment when she was left a widow with a child of weak intellect to support. Dorothea had written to her, and Mrs. Ashe had expressed her willingness to give them a home.

Michael, dismayed at the prospect of Dorothea's departure, and even more at the thought of the life to which her brother's folly had condemned her, was moved to protest, but all his objections were swept airily aside. David then announced his intention of seeking employment of some kind, and it was apparent that the injustice of this undeserved misfortune occupied his mind to the exclusion of all else. Finding him adamant, Michael abandoned his efforts to prevent the departure of his guests, and sought instead to delay it.

"What need for such haste?" he said. "You will always be welcome here."

"You're a damnably good friend, Michael," David replied feelingly. "Our one true friend, as misfortune has taught us. As it has taught me, rather," he corrected himself after a moment. "Dorothea cherished no illusions regarding my so-called friends, who are now, no doubt, fawning upon Rainham as once they fawned upon me." He laughed shortly on a note of bitterness. "I wish him joy of them."

" 'Tis not easy to deceive Dorothea," said Michael quietly. "She possesses some strange clarity of vision which pierces all shams and pretensions and knows the true from the false. You would do well to trust her judgment, David."

"Had I trusted it in the past I should not now be a penniless outcast," Stratton replied bitterly. " 'Tis cursedly unjust that a few hours of folly should ruin a man's whole life!"

Perceiving that he was still absorbed in self-pity Ashton said no more, but, excusing himself, went in search of Miss Stratton. He found her in the library, where she was writing a letter at a small table by the window, and though she looked up and greeted him with a smile, courtesy obliged him to wait until she had finished before embarking on conversation. He chose a chair from which he could watch her as she wrote, and wondered a little anxiously how he could best word that which he had to say to her.

At length she laid down her pen, read the letter through with an expression of faint dissatisfaction on her face, and then with a slight shrug sanded and folded it. As she sealed it she said, without looking up:

"I have been writing to Lady Norland. It occurred to me that Sir Charles might be prevailed upon to help David in some way, though I fear that his past conduct has done little to commend him. But our position is such that we can afford to neglect no opportunity of advancement."

"Dorothea," Michael rose and came to stand by the table, leaning one hand upon it, "David has just told me that you mean to leave Dene End."

She coloured faintly, but leaned back in her chair and met his eyes frankly enough.

"Yes," she replied, "everything is settled now and we know exactly what our resources are. We have the money which I inherited from my mother, and a little more which came from the sale of my coach and all my horses, and such jewels as were truly mine. Unhappily the most valuable gems were family heirlooms and went with all the rest to Major Rainham." A wry smile touched her lips for a moment. "David, you see, was prodigal in his recklessness."

"David was a damnable fool!" said Michael shortly, betrayed into hasty speech by the contrast between her bearing and her brother's. "He should be shamed beyond words by what he has done to you."

"But he is—can you doubt it?" The reproach in her voice was gentle but unmistakable. "What have we been struggling against all these weeks past but his shame and remorse?"

Michael, recalling the struggle to which she referred, suspected that the violence of David's feelings was due in great part to selfish concern for himself, but since he had no desire to wound or anger Dorothea he did not put the thought into words. Instead he asked:

"Why have you planned all this with never a word to me? I had hoped that your confidence at least was mine."

Miss Stratton seemed a trifle discomposed by the question. She picked up her pen again and twirled it between her hands, looking at it and not at Michael.

" 'Twas unhandsomely done, I know," she confessed, "but had you known of it you might have tried to dissuade us. David is"—she hesitated—"indolent, and as long as you were willing to keep him here as your guest he would make no effort to fend for himself. Now we have a home waiting for us with Janet Ashe and her

31

husband, and there is no longer an excuse for tarrying here."

"An excuse!" he repeated reproachfully. "Dorothea, has it come to that? Yes, you are right. I would have done everything in my power to dissuade you from going to these people, who, worthy though they may be, cannot give you the life which is yours by right. I would use any means to keep you here a while longer, in the hope that you would find it in your heart to remain for ever, as my wife." He caught both her hands and drew her to her feet to face him. "Oh, my dear, I do not ask that you should love me, but only that I may have the right to protect and care for you, and the happiness of serving you all my life long."

She had made no attempt to free herself, but stood quite quietly with her hands in his, and since they were much of a height her eyes, clear and serene, met his levelly and with no hint of embarrassment.

"Michael," she said quietly, "when I was wealthy I refused to marry you because I cared for you only as a very dear friend. You would think poorly of me if, still lacking those tenderer feelings, I accepted you now merely for the sake of the security you offer me."

"Think poorly of you?" he repeated feelingly. "Never!"

"But I should think poorly of myself," she told him gently. "No, Michael, it is not to be. I honour and thank you from the bottom of my heart, but I will not marry you."

"Think of David," he begged, despising himself even as he spoke for stooping to such a plea. "I have enough for us both, and 'twould spare him all fear of the future."

She shook her head.

"That is an ignoble thought, Michael," she said gravely. "I have no intention of letting David become your pensioner, for 'twould result in naught but harm for both of you. No, there is but one solution to our problem. The Strattons must vanish altogether from the world as we know it. Fortunately very few people know where we are at present, for I particularly asked Lady Norland not to make it known, and when we leave Dene End no one need know whither we are bound. We must make a new life

32

for ourselves, and David must learn to depend upon his own merits and not upon the benefits bestowed by wealth and consequence."

"Dorothea, you do not mean to leave me in ignorance of your whereabouts?" Ashton protested. "You would not be so cruel."

"Or so ungrateful," she added, smiling. "Of course, I did not mean that, but you will promise me, will you not, that you will not share the knowledge with anyone? I believe that the only hope for David is to ensure that he does not fall again into the company which has already cost him so much."

"You are probably right," he agreed. "'Tis a thousand pities that David has not even a small part of your wisdom. I will promise what you ask."

"Thank you, Michael," she said, "and for the rest, we shall never, I trust, turn our backs upon our truest friend, and you will always be welcome wherever we may chance to be."

He sighed, and, bending his head, pressed his lips to each hand in turn.

"It is something to be accounted your truest friend," he said. "With that I must perforce be content—for the present."

"For ever, Michael," she answered gently. "Believe me, my dear, 'tis better so."

Sir David Stratton, in his embittered declaration that the self-styled friends who had clustered about him in the days of his affluence would soon transfer their allegiance to Major Rainham, spoke no more than the truth. When the news of his misfortune first spread through the ranks of London society it occasioned a good deal of indignation, and it was agreed that if the villain who had ruined him presumed to come among them his reception should be frigid in the extreme. He should learn that the mere possession of a fortune—and a fortune, moreover, acquired in so dubious a manner—was no passport into London's most exclusive circles.

So it was determined and so, undoubtedly, it would

have come to pass, had Rainham shown the least hint of anxiety or diffidence. He showed neither. In those public places frequented by people of fashion he appeared as of right, self-possessed and supremely indifferent to the stir his presence created. A curled and perfumed beau who fancied himself a wit made some audible comment upon the Major's recent good fortune without disturbing a fraction of his calm; a great lady stared at him very hard and tittered scornfully, and he returned the regard coldly, with a slight but unmistakably contemptuous lift of his brows. Clearly it was impossible to discompose him. They were nonplussed, but when a gentleman who had made his acquaintance at Mrs. Cheriton's extended an invitation to him, the rest thankfully followed his lead, and Major Rainham was accepted.

It could not be said, however, that he became popular, for his manner alone discouraged any attempt at familiarity, and men who had been the boon companions of young Sir David found that in the new master of the Stratton fortune they had a very different man with whom to deal. He took their measure at a glance, and though he was willing to spend freely and extend a hospitality in keeping with his altered circumstances, it was not possible to impose upon him as they had imposed upon his predecessor. Always, too, there was that coldness in his bearing, a reserve which kept everyone, as it were, at arm's length. He made a host of acquaintances and no friends.

Among the fair sex his austere good looks and the aura of mystery which surrounded him—for no one knew with any certainty who he was or whence he had come—created something of a sensation, and the fact that one or two gentlemen declared that the name of Rainham struck a faint and elusive chord of memory merely added to the attraction. But to all efforts to captivate him the Major remained maddeningly indifferent, and not one much-courted beauty could boast that he looked kindly upon her. Even his compliments were spoken with a cold formality which rendered them completely meaningless.

Sally Cheriton, who sooner or later heard all the gossip of the town, learned of the havoc he had wrought and was amused. She referred to it laughingly one evening when he was taking supper with her. The meal was over and the servants had withdrawn, but Sally and her solitary guest were still facing each other across the fruit and wine on the candlelit table.

"I marvel," she remarked with assumed innocence, "that you should choose to sup with an old woman when half the beauties in London are pining for your company. Oh, I have heard rumours! 'Tis said that the Duchess of—well, no need for names, but that a certain young and lovely lady is eager to grant you favours for which many have sued in vain."

"But not, I think, that I am eager to accept them," Rainham retorted blightingly, and with no answering smile. "I have no desire to receive favours from her Grace, or from any other pretty wanton."

Mrs. Cheriton chuckled.

"That will not deter the lady," she said. "She, like so many others, is eager to unravel the mystery surrounding you." She hesitated, and then added more seriously: "You know that already there are rumours afoot?"

He shrugged.

" 'Twas to be expected. What are they saying?"

"Little enough as yet. One or two there are who declare that your name seems familiar to them, and one—Sir Walter Maddox—is convinced that he has met you before."

" 'Tis likely enough, though I do not recall it. What more?"

"That is all at present, but it cannot remain so for long. I am amazed that you have not been recognized ere this."

He shook his head.

"Seven years is a long time, Sally, and this"—he touched the heavy auburn hair which fell over his shoulders—"changes my appearance a good deal. I wore a periwig in those days."

"I know," Mrs. Cheriton's voice was troubled, "but even so your identity cannot remain secret for ever. Sooner or later the truth is bound to come out."

"Yes." Kelvin rose to his feet and began to pace

restlessly about the room. "Sooner or later——! 'Slife, I was a fool to come back!"

"Yet on the night you won the Stratton fortune you told me that you did not fear such discovery."

"Fear it?" He shook his head. "No, sins as great as that laid at my door have been condoned ere now, and everyone who was closely concerned in the affair is dead or far away. But 'tis the thought that I must go through it all again. The stares and whispers, the half-veiled taunts, the scurrilous lampoons which, because they are anonymous, may not be flung back in the writers' teeth. Oh, I have faced it all before, and I am not sure that I can endure it again! Yet, if the tale be remembered, endure it I must if I am to retain the place I have won for myself in London." He paused, and leaning his arms on the back of a chair, stared sombrely at the candle-flames. "What evil stars, I wonder, were in the ascendant when I was born? Even now, with my fortunes mended at last, I find that seven-year-old tragedy rising again in my path like a mockery from Hell itself. God! was it not enough to have thrust upon me the choice I had to make that day? The memory of it will go with me to my grave."

He lapsed into silence, gazing before him with eyes which saw nothing of his surroundings, but looked back across the years to that black day when he had taken the decision which eventually ruined him. Mrs. Cheriton watched him with troubled eyes, for even she, who knew him better, perhaps, than any other living soul, could not bridge the gulf between them and bring him comfort. Even before tragedy had darkened his life he had been solitary; friendship had touched him but rarely, and love never, but now he dwelt apart in a terrible loneliness which grew with the passing years. Somewhere, surely, there must be one with the power to capture that bitter, lonely heart, but she had begun to fear that if ever such salvation came, it would come too late. The fortune he had won, bringing in its train the self-seeking flattery of those who hoped to profit by his newly-acquired riches, was serving to increase rather than lessen his cynical indifference, and it seemed that her lightly-spoken warning concerning the beggar on horseback would prove to be a true prophecy. When she remembered the brilliant promise of his early career, the high hopes and brave ambitions so wantonly laid waste, she could have wept for the pity of it.

She was aroused from her sorrowful reverie as Kelvin stood erect again and said, in a tone which suggested that he had just reached the decision:

"I have had a surfeit of London and London ways. I will away into the country for a while, and learn what manner of home I have acquired along with my riches. Perchance the life of a country squire will suit my humour better than that of a town gallant."

" 'Twill have novelty at least," Mrs. Cheriton agreed. "When will you go?"

"As soon as may be, before the year is too far advanced, and if I find it to my liking I shall remain there until the spring." He smiled at her, raising his brows inquiringly. "What say you to visiting me there?"

Sally shook her head.

"Not in winter, Kelvin," she said firmly. "I am too old to go wandering down miry roads unless 'tis from dire necessity. Go establish yourself as master of Hope Stratton, and ask me again when summer comes."

Major Rainham would undoubtedly have carried out his intention to make an almost immediate journey to Hope Stratton but for an incident which took place on the day after his conversation with Sally Cheriton. He had been bidden to a rout at the house of my Lady Lansmere, and among his fellow-guests was that Sir Walter Maddox who from the first had been so loudly insistent that the name and features of Kelvin Rainham were familiar to him. It was in vain, however, that this gentleman had racked his brains, and urged his friends to do likewise, to recall the exact circumstances of any previous acquaintance—in vain, that is, until that evening at Lady Lansmere's rout. He was standing with two or three other gentlemen, but instead of joining in their conversation was staring fixedly across the room to where the Major was listening with distant courtesy to something his hostess was saying. Suddenly Sir Walter's gloomy gaze quickened; he let out a triumphant oath and slapped himself exultantly on the thigh.

"Gad'slife, I have it at last!" he exclaimed. "I knew I had seen him before, but that damned tawny hair of his misled me. He was wont to wear a periwig in those days. Rainham!" he added, as his companions broke off to stare at him with mingled surprise and perplexity.

That caught their attention, for everyone was anxious to discover the Major's antecedents, a desire obviously unlikely to be gratified by Rainham himself. The gentlemen regarded Sir Walter impatiently.

"Well?" one of them said shortly. "You saw him—where?"

"Here in London, seven years ago," Maddox transferred his gaze to the speaker, "though I did not know him well. No one ever did, I fancy, for he was a secretive, cold-hearted young devil even in those days. His regiment was one of those ordered to the west at the time of the Rebellion, and after Sedgemoor—Somerset being his native county—Rainham used his authority to settle a few private scores."

"Damme, you're right!" another member of the group broke in. "I remember now. He was cashiered for it a few months later."

"No, no, no!" Sir Walter replied testily, annoyed at being thus robbed of the climax of his story. " 'Twas not that way at all." He glared at the speaker and continued hurriedly, before the other could intervene again: "There was a woman concerned, I'll stake my life on that! There was a quarrel over her, and Rainham struck his superior officer. Drew on him, too, and tried to force him to fight. Devilish stir it caused at the time. They broke him for it, of course."

The other man, though willing to admit that Maddox was right in the main, persisted in regarding the introduction of a lady into the story as a deliberate fabrication, but as no one, not even Sir Walter himself, could recall with any accuracy the details of the seven-year-old scandal, this point could not be settled.

It was not long, however, before the tale became common knowledge, and within a few days the town was ringing with it. Rumours of this reaching Major Rainham's ears occasioned him no alarm; he fancied that he had established himself too firmly to be dislodged by the first breath of scandal, though he judged it prudent to postpone his journey to Worcestershire. To leave London now would savour of flight and perhaps make a return impossible, for only by carrying matters through with a high hand could he hope to survive the tide of gossip which Sir Walter's inconveniently long memory had unleashed.

Survive it he did, partly by reason of his assumption of utter indifference to the stares and whispers which for a while greeted him every time he appeared in public, and partly for that reason with which he had once cynically answered Mrs. Cheriton's misgivings on that score— that a man who could pay for the privilege was generally permitted to forget his past. He was amused to find his confidence justified, but it was an amusement tinged with bitterness, for the memory of that old dishonour was a wound which had never healed, and to find it tolerated, and even condoned, by the people of his acquaintance merely increased the contempt with which he regarded them.

So Kelvin Rainham stayed on in London, surrounded by all the comfort and consequence that wealth could bestow, yet knowing as little peace of heart or mind as in the days when as a mercenary soldier he had wandered through Europe, and meanwhile the brother and sister whom he had supplanted set out for their new and humble home at Gallows Farm.

Ashton went with them into Kent, for he felt that he could not rest until he had seen for himself what manner of place Dorothea's new home might be. Its very name had an ominous ring, and he pictured it as a ramshackle hovel crouching in the shadow of a gibbet.

His fears, however, proved groundless, for Gallows Farm was a pleasant place, standing remote from the road at the end of a winding lane, in a hollow between two gently-sloping hills. It was a fine, rambling old building as large as many a manor-house, with a fair garden behind it, and upon one side the farmyard with its great thatched barns and byres and stables. On the other, orchards of apple and cherry trees clothed the hillside and stretched to the very walls of the house.

The inhabitants of the farm were equally reassuring. Thomas Ashe, the master of the house, was a man of good yeoman stock, deeply attached to the land which his family had farmed for generations; Janet, his wife, stout, grey-haired and sharp of tongue, but kindly withal; and Will, her son, a flaxen-haired young giant slow of speech and thought, but far from being the idiot which David's careless description had led Michael to expect.

He remained at Gallows Farm for more than a week, and when he returned to London he carried with him letters which David had written to such of his acquaintance as might conceivably use their influence on his behalf. It was Ashton himself who had suggested this, for he feared that if David were left to his own devices he would remain indefinitely at the farm, living on his sister's slender income and making no effort to fend for himself.

With Michael's departure the Strattons felt that their one remaining link with the old life had been broken. Dorothea found herself missing him more than she would have thought possible, while David, as soon as he was deprived of his friend's companionship, fell prey once more to depression and self-pity, until Dorothea wondered almost desperately what she would do if no employment for him was forthcoming.

This thought was uppermost in her mind one day a little more than a week after Michael's departure, when they were together in the parlour. They were sitting on the roomy window-seat, Dorothea sewing and David idly casting dice, right hand against left, his handsome face disfigured by an expression which even a loving sister could not deny was sulky in the extreme. The weather, which had been fine, grew suddenly overcast, and almost before Miss Stratton had time to remark upon this fact it began to rain heavily.

Suddenly they heard the noise of approaching hoofbeats, and two riders swept at a gallop round the bend of the lane. They had barely observed that the foremost of the two was a woman when she put her mount at the high gate giving on to the yard. Dorothea gasped and David started up with an oath, but their concern proved to be needless and in a moment the intrepid horsewoman had disappeared round the corner of the house. Her companion, whom they now saw to be a groom in livery, entered the yard more soberly and followed her, leaving the pair at the window to look at each other in strong perplexity.

Their mystification was short-lived, for soon they heard hasty footsteps, the door of the room was flung open, and the lady came quickly in. When she saw them she stopped short in an astonishment as great as their own, and so for a space they regarded each other in silence.

Observing her thus at leisure, Dorothea saw that in spite of her riding-dress of russet velvet and modish, wide-brimmed hat, the newcomer was very young, scarcely more than a child. She was small and slightly built, with a merry, vivid little face framed in light brown curls, and large brown eyes alight with laughter. A nut-brown maid indeed, for her complexion was of a warm, golden tint and her tip-tilted nose unmistakably freckled. For a moment she looked at them uncertainly, and then she said:

"I beg your pardon. I did not mean to break in upon you, but I was looking for Mrs. Ashe."

She was turning to go when David, who had been staring at her with a bemused expression which could not be wholly due to the unexpectedness of her appearance, came to himself with a start.

"Pray do not let us drive you away, madam," he said gallantly. "I've no doubt that Mrs. Ashe will be here directly, and meanwhile may not my sister entertain you in her stead?" He fixed a commanding eye upon Dorothea, who had also risen to her feet.

"Yes, please stay," Miss Stratton said with a smile. "You must forgive our incivility, for we were as surprised as I think you must be. May I present my brother, Sir

41

David Stratton? I am Dorothea Stratton."

The young lady turned back very willingly, acknowledging the introduction with a smile which betrayed a fascinating dimple.

"I am Clarissa Spencerwood," she informed them. "I should not have walked in on you in that fashion, but I have been used to come here very often and I did not expect . . . that is . . ." she broke off in some confusion.

"We, too, are guests of Mr. and Mrs. Ashe," Dorothea said helpfully. "But will you not be seated? I fear that you must be very damp and chilled—perhaps it would be wise to light the fire."

"Oh, pray do not put yourself to that trouble," Clarissa replied cheerfully, pulling off her hat and shaking a shower of raindrops from it. " 'Tis nothing, I assure you. Had I not known that there would be an outcry at home I would not have sought shelter at all." She tossed the hat on to a chair and smiled sunnily up into David's dazzled and delighted eyes. "But I am so glad that I did."

Their visitor, the Strattons discovered later from Janet, was the only daughter of the Earl of Ardely, whose country seat was situated only a few miles from Gallows Farm. Lady Clarissa was a merry, wilful creature, much pampered by her five elder brothers but blessed with the happiest of natures and the gift of making friends, and since at their first meeting she conceived a sudden and violent affection for Miss Stratton it was not long before she paid another visit to the farm. This time she was accompanied by her brother Andrew, an amiable young man of about David's age, in whom Stratton was delighted to discover a congenial companion, and in spite of Dorothea's protests, and her conviction of the folly of such a course, it was not long before a close friendship had sprung up between the Strattons and the Spencerwoods.

Although Dorothea had insisted that Lord Ardely should be told the true reason for their presence at Gallows Farm, his lordship, a jovial, easy-going man, made no objection to the association, and Miss Stratton was obliged to give in, which she did the more readily since she had grown fond of Lady Clarissa. David was once more bent upon pursuing pleasure with the same thoughtlessness which had led to his downfall, and as she watched him jesting with Andrew, or going off with him to a cock-fight or a bull-baiting, she knew that it troubled him not at all that no hint or hope of employment had been offered.

So passed the golden days of St. Martin's summer, while the leaves reddened and fell and the harvest fields stood stripped and bare, and presently Dorothea discovered a new cause for disquiet. David and Clarissa were too much together. In vain she reminded herself that Clarissa was but fifteen, that David treated her as her own brothers did—the doubt refused to be stifled, and one day towards the end of October she learned how well-founded it was.

The three of them were together in the parlour at Gallows Farm, and Clarissa was holding forth on the folly of those of her brothers who preferred to live in London rather than in Kent. She had no such desire, she declared, but added regretfully:

"Of course, I shall be obliged to live there when I am married."

"Is that so certain?" David's eyes, resting upon her, were teasing and affectionate. "In any event, that day must be some way off."

"No, for I am to be married next year." Clarissa sighed heavily, then, becoming aware of a sudden silence, added in some surprise: "Did you not know?"

Dorothea had been looking at her brother as Clarissa spoke, and she saw him go white, as though he had received a mortal blow. With a sensation of sick dismay, but conscious of the need to distract her ladyship's attention, she said hastily:

"No, we were not aware of it. You must permit us to felicitate you and . . . and the fortunate gentleman."

"Viscount Jevington," Clarissa supplied helpfully. "I suppose 'tis no wonder you did not know, for it has been settled for years and is taken so much for granted that no one speaks of it, but it is understood that we shall marry next spring, as soon as I am sixteen."

"Do you wish to marry him?" David said abruptly, and his voice was so unlike his normal tones that Dorothea looked warningly at him. Fortunately, Clarissa did not appear to find anything odd either in tone or question, and gave the latter her consideration.

"I have grown accustomed to the idea," she said cautiously at length, "though I own it has taken time. When we were betrothed—it was on my eighth birthday—he called me a puny brat, and I kicked him." She dwelt pleasurably upon the recollection for a moment, and then continued: "But last time he visited us he said that I had improved out of all knowledge and he had not made such a bad bargain after all."

David's chair rasped violently across the floor as he got suddenly to his feet. For a few seconds he stood looking down at Clarissa, then with the air of a man who can endure no more turned on his heel and went out of the room. Clarissa turned to Dorothea, her eyes filled with surprise and a growing distress.

"Pay no heed to David," Miss Stratton said hurriedly, before the younger girl could make any remark. "He ... he is worried about a private matter. Tell me about your betrothal. I had no notion that you were to be married so soon."

Clarissa told her willingly enough a story all too common in those days, of a marriage arranged between two children as a matter of policy between their respective families, with no regard whatsoever for the feelings of the young people concerned. Clarissa was probably more fortunate than some, for she had been granted plenty of opportunities to become acquainted with her future husband, who was a frequent guest at Ardely Place. Lord Jevington, Dorothea discovered, besides being wealthy in his own right, was the nephew and heir of a rich baronet, Sir Edward Amberstone, and these facts made quite clear to her the reason for the betrothal. Lord Ardely, with five sons to provide for, would not be able to give his daughter a very large dowry, and had obviously seized upon the first opportunity to secure for her a rich husband.

David did not put in another appearance before Clarissa left the farm, but though she seemed a little hurt at this defection, Dorothea felt justified in thinking that she had not guessed the cause of his extraordinary behaviour. She watched her friend ride away down the lane, and as soon as she was out of sight went in anxious search of her brother. When Clarissa first spoke of her imminent marriage Dorothea had realized with a sudden shock that David's true feelings far exceeded her gravest forebodings, and she wondered uneasily what effect this fresh misfortune, coming so soon after the first, would have upon him.

She found him at last in the apple-orchard, seated on a moss-grown log with his face buried in his hands. Dorothea sat down beside him and laid her arm across the bowed shoulders.

"David," she said quietly. "My dear, I had not realized! I did not know how much you cared for her."

He raised his head at that, clasping his hands between his knees and staring before him with haggard eyes.

"I scarcely knew myself," he said unsteadily, "until I realized how completely she is beyond my reach. I suppose that I have been mad to dream of winning her, I, a broken gamester! But she is so young, and some miracle might have happened. Somehow I might have regained my fortune in time to ask for her in marriage, but if she is to be wed within the year——" he broke off. "Did she speak of it again?"

"Yes," Dorothea replied slowly, and recounted to him, briefly, all that she had learned from Clarissa. "David, she is prepared to marry him. She has not guessed the truth, nor must you let her. If she should come to care for you it would be too cruel."

"I could make her love me," he said, half to himself, and a smile touched his lips. " 'Twould be sweet to teach her. A consolation in some part for all the rest."

Dorothea drew away from him, looking at him with disbelief and something akin to disgust.

"You think of no one but yourself," she said in a

low voice. "They are right who name you spoiled and selfish, and if you can entertain such a thought, even for a moment, then 'tis not love you feel for Clarissa. Would you teach her to care for you, knowing that she must marry another man? David, for shame!"

A dark flush stained his pale cheeks and he shifted uncomfortably beneath the reproach in her eyes.

"No," he muttered, "I would not. Pay no heed to what I say. I am mad, I think! I cannot bear to think of her married to Jevington. You do not know him! God knows I am no saint, but his excesses are a byword in London, and that though he is not yet four-and-twenty! What can her father be thinking of to promise her to such a man?"

"David, is this true?" Dorothea was staring at him in dismay. "Surely you must be mistaken. Lord Ardely would not——"

" 'Tis unlikely his lordship is aware of it, for Jevington will have been at some pains to keep such tales from him, I make no doubt."

"Yes, of course, and they were betrothed as children. Moreover, his lordship will be anxious to avoid raising any obstacle to the marriage, for Lord Jevington is rich, and will be richer yet when his uncle dies, and Clarissa's brothers must be provided for. There is nothing that we can do!"

"I was rich once," said David bitterly. "It seems I lost more than a fortune across that damned gaming-table. Oh, curse Rainham, curse him, curse him!"

"Of what avail are curses?" Dorothea said wearily. "They will not help us nor harm him. Something must be done about this new problem. We must leave the farm, of course, but where are we to go?"

Though she had spoken aloud it was more to herself than her companion and she expected no reply, but the words, or perhaps the unconscious wistfulness of her tone, penetrated even David's armour of self-absorption. He turned to look at her, realizing for the first time how great a burden she had taken upon herself, and how little he had done to share it. No word of reproach for the irreparable wrong he had done her had ever passed her lips; what little money she possessed she had willingly shared with him; through her endeavours they had found asylum at Gallows Farm, and now for his sake she was preparing to leave that safe and happy sanctuary. A flood of genuine shame and remorse surged up within him, and on the crest of it he caught her hand in his and spoke with sudden earnestness.

"No," he said firmly. "There must be no thought of leaving the farm, for you at least. I have brought trouble enough upon you as it is, and now that you have found a measure of peace here I will not take that from you as I have taken all else."

Dorothea's fingers tightened upon his. Moments such as this, when her brother's true nature broke through its veneer of selfish indolence, erased all memory of the innumerable occasions when she had been hurt by his thoughtlessness and folly.

"There is no need for us to leave the farm," he continued. "It cannot now be long before I find some sort of employment, and meanwhile I give you my word that I will say nothing to Clarissa of my feelings for her. She will not guess. If, taken unawares as I was today, I did not betray myself, I am not like to do so henceforth."

Dorothea regarded him searchingly.

"I do not doubt your purpose, David," she said gently, "but are you certain that you can continue to see her almost daily, and not go back on your word? To abide by such a resolve will not be easy."

"Perhaps my life has been too easy hitherto," David replied ruefully. "Too easy, too pleasant—and too prone to folly! Would that I realized it earlier! No, I will keep my word, never fear. If she cared for me I would be less confident, but she does not, and I love her too well to cause her needless pain. For that reason, if for no other, you may trust me."

"I do trust you, my dear, and I wish with all my heart that it were in my power to remove all obstacles between you and Clarissa. If only you could have met a year ago!"

"I have been wishing that since the first time I saw her," he replied with a sigh, "but I have no one but myself to blame for the fact that I dare not approach her now. 'Tis easy to curse Rainham as the cause of my present plight, but I see now that only my own folly and conceit made his triumph possible."

Dorothea was silent, too surprised to reply. His love for Clarissa had undoubtedly wrought a miracle in making David perceive, and frankly admit, that his downfall was due to his own weaknesses and not to a malignant destiny. Perhaps, even though he could never win her, Clarissa's influence might be the means of saving him from himself.

For a while they sat without speaking, their fingers still entwined, and in the silence the familiar sounds of the farmyard came to them faintly from the far side of the house. A fiery sunset was fading in the west, and a blue mist gathered in the hollows and between the trees. Above the massive chimneys of Gallows Farm a single star glittered frostily. At last David said abruptly:

"Dorothea, why did you refuse to marry Michael?"

Taken by surprise, she stared at him for a moment before replying.

"Because I regard him only as a friend," she said presently. "I thought you realized that."

"Yet he offers you security, comfort, a place in the world—all that I have taken from you. Does not that weigh with you?"

"I have security and comfort here, and no regrets for the world we have forsaken. These are not considerations to tempt me into marriage."

"There's another which might. He loves you dearly."

"A better reason, David, but still insufficient." Her tone was jesting and she rose to her feet as she spoke. "You see, I do not love him—no, nor any man. I doubt I've the nature for it."

David got up also. He took her other hand and held her so before him, looking down at her.

"That is false, and you know it," he said with a flash of insight. "You could love greatly, I think, so greatly that all else would be of no account."

Dorothea looked past him into the gathering shadows with a strange expression in her eyes, but what thoughts were passing through her mind David could not guess. After a little he added quietly:

"Be that as it may, of one thing I am certain. The man fortunate enough to win your love should give thanks for it every day of his life."

It was not to be supposed that David's mood of self-knowledge and self-contempt would be of any long duration, and his sister knew him well enough not to be disappointed when the following day brought a return of his habitual manner. She fancied, however, that the events of the previous day had left their mark upon him, and was relieved to see that when next he encountered Lady Clarissa his bearing towards her was as it had always been. How long this rigid self-control would last she did not know, and grew more anxious than ever that he should find some employment which would necessitate his removal from Gallows Farm.

Opportunity presented itself at last from an unexpected quarter. On a visit to Ardely Place came that Sir Edward Amberstone whose nephew Clarissa was to marry, with his wife, and the Strattons naturally became acquainted with them. Lady Amberstone, herself childless and cherishing for her husband's heir an incurable dislike, took a strong liking to David, and it was due to her influence that Sir Edward, a few days before his departure, offered him the post of secretary. David had the good sense to accept the offer. He was finding it increasingly difficult to conceal his true feelings for Clarissa, and knew that in departure from Kent lay his only hope of keeping the promise he had made to Dorothea.

On the eve of his departure with his employer for the latter's home in Hampshire, the Strattons went together to Ardely Place. Since the travellers were to set out early on the following morning, the Countess had invited Dorothea to spend the night at the Place so that she might enjoy her brother's company until the last possible moment. It was an unusually mild day for the time of the year, and in the afternoon David and Dorothea, accompanied by Clarissa and Andrew, went out into the gardens. Even then all would have been well had not her ladyship tired of strolling sedately along the gravel walks and sought to relieve her boredom by a childish prank. As they drew near the entrance to the maze she touched David's arm with one hand, laid a finger of the other on her lips, and, slipping past him, disappeared into the labyrinth, glancing over her shoulder with a smile which was an unmistakable invitation to him to follow. This he immediately did, while Miss Stratton and Mr. Spencerwood continued on their way unaware of the defection.

That Clarissa was bent upon some mischief David was certain, and though he knew it to be a dangerous pleasure as well as a doubtful one, he could not resist the temptation to spend a short while alone with her on their ordinary, friendly terms. This would be their last informal meeting; his duties were unlikely to permit him to return to Gallows Farm for months to come, and when he saw her again she would be the wife of Lord Jevington.

He plunged recklessly into the intricacies of the maze, but though he had been conducted through it on several previous occasions, he found that he had overestimated both his memory and his sense of direction. Clarissa disappeared from view almost immediately, and thereafter the only intimation of her presence was a flash of her saffron-coloured gown at a turn of the path, or a ripple of laughter from the far side of the hedge.

At the centre of the labyrinth, which he eventually reached, was a small open space bordered with flower-beds, containing two stone seats and an ancient sundial, but no sign at all of a small lady in a yellow gown. David strode purposefully across it and into the first path which offered on the opposite side, but at the end of ten minutes, when for the third time the miniature pleasance presented its emptiness to his wrathful gaze, he owned himself defeated. For that length of time there had been neither sight nor sound of his quarry, and he was forced to the unwelcome conclusion that he, and not, as he had supposed, Dorothea and Andrew, was to be the victim of a practical joke. Angry, disappointed, and somewhat out of breath, he sat down on the nearer of the two seats and glared at the inoffensive sundial; next moment there was a faint, rustling sound behind him and two small, soft hands were clapped over his eyes.

Involuntarily his own went up and drew them away, and then he sat rigid, staring at the little, captive hands and fighting an insane desire to press his lips against them. Then, because the temptation was so great, he released her somewhat abruptly and, rising to his feet, said without turning to face her:

"I trust your ladyship is sufficiently amused. I should be grateful, no doubt, that I am not left to find my own way out of the labyrinth."

Even to himself the words sounded churlish, but when he turned to see what effect they had upon Clarissa she flitted past him and went to stand beside the sundial with her back towards him, tracing with one finger the legend inscribed about its pedestal.

" 'Twas foolish, I own," she admitted in a small voice. "Pray forgive me, Sir David."

He stared at her, deliberately goading himself to anger as a barrier against more tender emotions. The words were meek enough, but her voice, in spite of a palpable effort to steady it, quivered with laughter. He moved to her side and with elaborate ceremony proffered his arm.

"May I suggest, madam, that we return to the house? Our absence will occasion remark."

There was no response to this but a small, indistinguishable sound. He looked suspiciously at her, saw the glitter of tears on her averted cheek, and let ceremony go by the board.

"Clarissa!" His resolution forgotten, he caught the hand nearest to him in both his own. "My dearest, what is it? Why are you weeping?"

"I cannot help it," she said pathetically, turning towards him. "I have tried so hard to be good, but it's no use. I know that I am wicked and unmaidenly, but I never wanted to be betrothed to Jevington. Oh, David, David, don't go away! I cannot bear it!"

CHAPTER IV

PORTRAIT OF DOROTHEA

It was mid-October before Major Rainham deemed it safe to retire from London and visit his strangely-acquired home in Worcestershire. By that time the old scandal concerning him, which Sir Walter Maddox had revived, had once more returned to the realm of things forgotten, and the Major was so completely accepted by London society that he was no longer a conspicuous figure, and for this reason his absence from town occasioned little remark.

Behold him, therefore, one clear October evening, with a fine thoroughbred beneath him and two mounted servants at his back, riding in at the gates of Hope Stratton, between the tall pillars crowned by heraldic beasts supporting shields, and past the neat, ivy-clad lodge whence curious faces peeped. The lodge-keeper himself, who had hastened out to swing open the wrought-iron gates, bowed as his new master rode through, but not before Kelvin had glimpsed the scarcely veiled hostility in his face. He had expected this, however, and smiled coldly as his horse carried him at a brisk trot along the gently-curving avenue of chestnut trees which stretched across the park from the gates to the house itself.

A noble building, the house of Hope Stratton, set upon a slight eminence and commanding a fine view of meadow and woodland. Its lofty walls and slender, soaring chimneys had been raised when Elizabeth was queen, and now, mellowed by more than a century of sun and rain, surrounded by smooth lawns and formal gardens, it stood like a jewel in as fair a setting as England could show, and Rainham, looking about him, marvelled anew at the folly which could fling down such a heritage as the stake in a game of chance.

Word of his coming had been sent before him, and so the old steward who stood at one of the windows flanking the main door had no doubt whom this mounted stranger might be. For a few minutes he watched the approach of that erect and soldierly figure which rode with such easy assurance beneath the chestnut trees, and in his eyes was the same hostility as the lodge-keeper had shown. Then, as Rainham emerged from the avenue on to the broad space before the steps, he turned away and signed to one of the waiting lackeys to open the door.

Kelvin dismounted, tossed the reins to one of his men and went slowly up the steps and into the house. As the servant closed the door, and another stepped forward to take his hat and cloak, the steward approached and in an expressionless voice welcomed the new master to Hope Stratton.

"Your name?" said Kelvin, looking at him keenly. He was an old man, with thin, stooped shoulders and silvery hair, and Rainham guessed that he had spent his life in the service of the Strattons. Guessed, too, the resentment which must be raging beneath that polite and formal mask.

"John Danvers, sir," the steward replied with a bow. "Will it please you to take a glass of wine after your journey?"

"Thank you, I will." Kelvin strolled across the wide hall towards the log fire which blazed in the great, hooded hearth and paused there to take stock of his new domain. Danvers gave an order to one of the lackeys and dismissed them both with a gesture, himself remaining quietly by the long table in the centre of the hall until it should please the Major to address him again.

Several minutes passed in silence. Kelvin looked about him, at the lofty ceiling where the ornate carving was lost in shadow, the panelled walls hung with antique weapons and trophies of the chase, and the wide oak staircase which rose at the far end of the hall. Lastly, turning, he surveyed the Stratton coat-of-arms which glowed in rich colours amid the carving above the fire-place, but though the steward watched him closely he could detect no change of expression in the pale, austerely-handsome face, which remained indifferent and a little forbidding.

The servant returned with wine and Danvers, taking the salver from him, carried it to the fireplace and set it down on a small table beside the chair in which Rainham had now seated himself. As he poured the wine he said:

"Your apartments have been prepared, Major Rainham, and a meal is ready when you desire it. The bell-rope is yonder, within reach of your hand. Is there anything further, sir?"

"No, thank you. You may go."

The old man bowed and withdrew, and Kelvin, glad of a period of quiet reflection, sat sipping his wine, his brooding gaze upon the fire. To one who for years had lived a roving life, who had known poverty, and squalid lodgings in many a foreign city; who had often lain down at night, wrapped in his military cloak and with a saddle for pillow, on the bare earth beneath the open sky, the events of the past few months had almost the strangeness of a dream. This was the life to which he had been born and bred, but he had turned his back upon it seven years before, disillusioned and dishonoured, thinking never to return. Now the wheel had turned full circle, and he sat of right in a home of his own.

A home! Involuntarily he sighed, knowing that he was deceiving himself, that this great house with the well-trained servants who watched him with hostile eyes was no more a home to him than any one of a score of houses where he had dwelt in the past. He might live out his life at Hope Stratton, but it would never be more than a roof to shelter him, and he the solitary stranger in another man's house.

He dined that night in lonely state in a large room where shadowy portraits looked down from the walls and the candle-lit table made an island of brightness in the surrounding gloom. Soft-footed servants waited upon him, the food and the wine were above reproach, but always he was aware that beneath the surface simmered a burning resentment of the stranger who had possessed himself of the home of the Strattons.

Next morning John Danvers conducted him on a tour of the house, through a succession of handsome rooms where their footsteps echoed strangely in the silence. At length, at the extreme end of the west wing, the steward opened the doors of a room which he declared to be the finest in the house.

"Not the largest, sir, you will understand," he explained, a trace of enthusiasm creeping for the first time into his voice, "but undoubtedly the finest. It was the late Sir Humphrey's favourite apartment."

He stepped aside and Rainham entered what was undoubtedly one of the most beautiful rooms he had ever seen, of perfect proportions, with two tall windows on either hand and a ceiling exquisitely moulded. Between the windows were bookcases filled with handsomely-bound volumes, and at the far end rose a great fireplace, magnificently carved from floor to ceiling and forming, as it were, a vast frame for a full-length portrait of a woman. The morning sun was streaming through the windows upon one side, and not until he had advanced well into the room was Kelvin able to discern the details of this painting, but when at last he could see it clearly he stopped short with the breath caught in his throat and every other thought driven out of his head.

She sat in an attitude of studied elegance which displayed to best advantage her brocaded gown with its embroidered petticoat and sweeping train, and the towering head-dress of lace and ribbon on the formal curls of her night-black hair, but this could be readily forgiven for the skill with which the artist had captured the very spirit of his model. A serene young face, with blue eyes which gazed tranquilly upon the world from beneath well-marked brows, and with just the hint of a smile at the corners of the beautifully-shaped mouth; a face in which tenderness and humour blended with a certain high courage. Danvers was still talking, but his voice was a meaningless drone in Kelvin's ears and the only reality in the world was that pictured face.

"Whose portrait is this?" he heard himself ask at length, and marvelled to find that his voice was still calm and only mildly interested.

"That is Miss Dorothea Stratton, sir," Danvers replied. "Sir David's only sister."

So she was Stratton's sister! Yes, he could see a likeness now, a similarity of feature and colouring, but this girl's face had a strength and integrity which her brother's lacked.

"It was painted last year in London," the steward was explaining, "and when 'twas sent to Hope Stratton Sir David ordered that it was to be placed here and nowhere else. So it was done, and his great-grandfather, whose likeness had hung there these fifty years, banished to a corner of the gallery."

He broke off, as though remembering suddenly to whom he spoke, and closed his lips firmly upon any further loquacity, but Rainham was unaware of his companion's sudden forbidding silence. Standing there before Dorothea Stratton's portrait he was conscious for the first time of remorse for what he had done, remorse as sharp as physical pain. He who had faced unmoved the critical stares of fashionable London found himself unable to meet the tranquil gaze of the painted eyes, and turning abruptly he strode quickly from the room.

During the days that followed, for a reason which he himself scarcely understood, he avoided the beautiful room in the west wing and sought, by interesting himself in other matters, to drive the memory of the portrait from his mind. In company with the steward he rode about the estate, visiting farm and cottage with an eye keen to discover any sign of hardship or oppression, but found little of either. Sir Humphrey Stratton had been a just and careful landlord, and the men who had served him and, later, his son, followed still the precepts he had laid down. The Strattons had been not only liked, but loved, and no ill-will was felt towards the man who had flung away his birthright for a few nights of febrile excitement in a gaming-hell, all resentment being reserved for his successor. Though policy dictated an outward show of deference towards the new master, though men uncovered and women curtsied when he rode by, he knew that it was no more than an empty show, a cloak for an unreasoning hostility amounting almost to hatred.

With the neighbouring gentry he fared no better. Many avoided him from the first, and those not previously prejudiced against him were soon antagonized by his contemptuous self-assurance and cynical humour. For a century-and-a-half the Strattons had set their imprint on the countryside, and he was an interloper, shunned and resented.

Nowhere and at no time was he permitted to forget it, for their name or their crest faced him at every turn. Carved and painted above the hearth before which he sat, emblazoned upon the head-board of his bed, the colours of the heraldic device stared on him in mute reproach. It glowed in stained glass in the little church, and was repeated in faded colours on the creaking sign of the "Stratton Arms," the village's one inn, while the very name of his house was a constant reminder of the family he had dispossessed. He might have turned his back upon it all and returned to London had not pride forbidden it—pride, and some other emotion which he could not define.

One evening, some ten days after his arrival, he gave way to a sudden impulse and, taking up a branch of candles, went through the dark and silent house to the room in the west wing. Standing before the fireplace and holding the light above his head, he looked up almost defiantly to meet the only gaze which had the power to shame him, but the clear blue eyes looked back at him with sweet serenity, the generous lips seemed to hover on the brink of a smile, and in response a new emotion stirred in his heart. He became conscious of a sense of reassurance and comfort, and with it a growing certainty that it was no chance which had brought him to Hope Stratton, but that his destiny was in some way linked with that of this sweet-faced girl.

So strong was the illusion, and so persistent, that thereafter he abandoned the great hall in favour of the West Room, as it was called, and there he would sit for hours, a book open upon his knee but his eyes fixed upon the portrait, until its every detail was familiar to him and curiosity grew into a burning desire to learn more of Dorothea. He knew extraordinarily little about the Strattons and bitterly regretted that he had not obtained more particular information regarding them while he was in London, for even if he could bring himself to seek it from the servants, it was unlikely that they would be willing to discuss Miss Stratton with him.

At last, however, chance favoured him, for, losing his way while riding alone, he halted at a lonely cottage to ask in which direction Hope Stratton lay. The old woman who dwelt there informed him, with the garrulity of extreme age, that she had been nurse to Sir David Stratton and his sister, and—since she had no inkling of the identity of this courtly stranger—was only too ready to talk of her former charges. Thereafter it became his custom to visit the cottage, and though old Martha's memory played her false at times, Kelvin's overwhelming desire to learn all he could of Dorothea Stratton gave him the patience to unravel the rambling tales.

He did not know that in those weeks preceding Christmas, when from the portrait and from Martha's stories he was building his mental image of Dorothea, his eccentric behaviour was winning for him an odd reputation in the surrounding countryside. His solitary life—for no guests came now to Hope Stratton—and the cold aloofness which was his normal bearing, were beyond the understanding of these forthright countryfolk, and when the servants from the great house told how he would spend hours alone in a certain room, permitting no one to disturb him, or wander about house and gardens so absorbed in thought as to be unaware of their presence, instinctive dislike gave way to superstitious fear. It was an age of superstition, and before long all manner of wild tales were told of the stern, proud, lonely stranger who had lately come among them.

When at length rumours of this reached Major Rainham—his source of information was once again the old nurse—his only reaction was a faint, contemptuous amusement. Let the rustics believe what they chose, so that they left him in peace; let them marvel at the solitude in which he chose to dwell, not knowing that for him the house and gardens of Hope Stratton were filled with the presence of the serene and gracious woman whose pictured face had captured a heart he had thought invulnerable. So real to him had Dorothea become that she possessed his mind to the exclusion of all else. The embittered, disillusioned man who, seven years before, had sworn that no woman should ever have any power over him had fallen desperately, hopelessly in love with a girl he had never met, whom he knew only from a portrait and from the vague stories of an aged servant.

There were times when with a sudden revulsion of feeling he told himself that he was a fool, that probably Miss Stratton in no way resembled the ideal he had created, but these moods were brief and transient. His conviction that she was all he dreamed her was as deep as its origin was inexplicable, though as yet no thought of wooing her had entered his head. Not only was that which had passed between her brother and himself barrier enough, but his love for Dorothea was a reverent and spiritual emotion which set her far above all earthly passions. It needed some chance words of Martha's to startle him out of his curious world of fantasy and make him realize that after all Dorothea Stratton was a mortal woman with a very human capacity for suffering. It was now that he learned for the first time how completely his own good fortune had spelt ruin for the Strattons. He had never doubted that Dorothea was well provided for, but it was apparently common knowledge that, thanks to her brother's indolence, she, too, had been reduced to penury. At first Kelvin could not believe the truth of what he heard, but when at length conviction came he left the cottage with no word of farewell, nor did old Martha ever see him again.

That evening he sat as usual in the West Room, his frowning gaze bent upon the portrait while unanswerable questions echoed in his mind. What had become of her? How was she living, she who had never known anything but the security of great wealth? Months had elapsed since the night when the Stratton fortune had passed into his hands, and in that time what hardships might she not have endured? She was young, beautiful and un-protected—for that weakling of a brother was no adequate guardian—and his mind shrank from contemplation of the harm which might have befallen her through his own uncanny luck in that fateful game. That was the bitter, the fiendish irony of it, that he, who loved her now with a love akin to worship, should have been the one destined to reduce her to such straits. With a groan he covered his eyes with his hand, shutting out the fair, tranquil face above him and the blue eyes which seemed suddenly accusing.

Next day the news spread through the neighbourhood that Major Rainham had left Hope Stratton, departing as suddenly as he had come and with no hint of when, if ever, he would return. His servants told in awe-struck whispers how he had spent the previous night in the West Room, in a solitude they had not dared to disturb, but that when at dawn he emerged he had the look of a man hag-ridden, or haunted by evil visions. After only the scantiest preparation he had mounted his great black horse and ridden away as though possessed. The story, repeated in farm and village, occasioned its hearers no surprise. "Who sups with the devil——" they said, and nodded wisely at each other, accounting themselves well rid of him.

Kelvin reached London late on a cold December night, and, dismissing the two servants who had ridden with him from Worcestershire, made his way at once to Mrs. Cheriton's. The servants, who knew him well, admitted him without question and conducted him to their mistress's drawing-room, while one went to fetch her from the gaming-rooms, which at that hour were at their busiest.

When she came in Kelvin was standing before the fire with both hands resting upon the mantel, looking down at the glowing embers. As he turned to greet her Sally came forward with outstretched hands.

"Kelvin!" she exclaimed. "My dear boy, I had no notion that you were in London." She became aware of his look of fatigue, and the mud which caked his spurred boots and spattered the skirts of his coat, and added anxiously: "Something is amiss! What is it?"

"I have just reached London from the west country," he replied. "Forgive me for coming to you in this state, Sally, but I need your help."

Mrs. Cheriton regarded him with growing concern, for the look in his face reminded her strongly of that other time, years before, when he had come to her in great trouble. She said gently:

"You know that if 'tis in my power to help you, you have only to tell me how. What can I do?"

"You can discover for me," he replied, "the present whereabouts of Sir David Stratton."

She was startled by the request, but dissembling her surprise, moved to a chair by the fire and, sitting down, asked simply:

"Why, Kelvin?"

He turned to face her, resting one arm along the mantel.

"I have been to Hope Stratton," he said, and paused. Sally nodded.

"I know," she said, "you wrote to me upon your arrival there. One brief letter, and then for weeks no word at all. Kelvin, what mystery is this?"

"There is no mystery," he said. "I made a discovery there which makes it imperative that I learn what has become of Stratton. Did you know that he has a younger sister?"

"I have heard so," Mrs. Cheriton agreed, looking at him rather hard. "Well?"

"I have learned that she was left in his care," Kelvin

explained slowly. "It was for him to see that she was adequately provided for, but he did not do it. Instead he flung down his whole inheritance as a stake in your gaming-rooms. Flung it down and lost it."

"Then his sister is penniless also!" Sally's voice was incredulous. "But are you sure? Could he indeed be guilty of conduct so base?"

"He was guilty of it. Without compunction he gambled away that which was not his—and this is the man you pitied as an innocent dupe in the hands of an adventurer!"

"It seems that I was mistaken in him," Mrs. Cheriton agreed. "But, Kelvin, if you wish to make provision for the girl out of the estate, it is the lawyers who best can help you."

"I had thought of that," he replied, "but I fear 'tis not so simple. The Strattons are a proud race, and she—Dorothea—devoted to her worthless brother. Would she accept my help?" He shook his head, a smile at once bitter and sorrowful touching his lips. "No, she would starve rather than take charity from me."

Mrs. Cheriton studied him in some perplexity, for the situation was still a trifle beyond her. She said in a matter-of-fact tone:

"You have already approached her, then, on that subject?"

"No," he said impatiently. "I do not know where she is. Nobody seems to know, for the Strattons left London for an unknown destination immediately after their loss. I learned that from the lawyers at the very first, but they would tell me no more than that. I did not press them, for it did not matter to me then."

"But it matters now?" Sally prompted hopefully.

"Yes, it matters," he said in an odd tone, staring down at the glowing coals. "It matters damnably. Sally, there was a portrait of her at Hope Stratton, painted a year ago. A wonderful face, serene and lovely and unafraid—then! Now, who knows?" His voice broke suddenly, and his head went down upon the arm outstretched along the mantel. "My God, Sally, I must find her, or run mad!"

Mrs. Cheriton rose to her feet, and if her reply was

mocking both her voice and the hand she placed upon his bowed shoulder were very gentle.

" 'No woman has any power over me, and none ever shall,' " she quoted softly. "My dear, I warned you 'twas dangerous to cast such a challenge at fate."

He lifted his head, and though his face was haggard a smile touched his lips.

"And I laughed at your warning," he replied. "Well, now the tables are turned. Does it not afford you infinite amusement to see me, at my age, behaving like any callow youth?"

She chuckled, but her eyes rested upon him affectionately.

"Oh, infinite amusement, thou greybeard!"

He shook his head ruefully.

"My dear Sally, I am five-and-thirty, and I have fallen in love with a dream, a portrait—and a portrait, moreover, of a woman whose dearly-loved brother I have ruined. If that is not the quintessence of folly, I know not what is."

" 'Tis a folly, my dear, which may well prove your salvation if when you find her your Dorothea proves kind."

"No," Kelvin answered with a sigh. "A fool I may be, but not fool enough to imagine that I may ever go a-wooing. That is not my purpose in seeking her."

Mrs. Cheriton raised her brows.

"What, then, is your purpose?"

"To assure myself that all is well with her. She was born to wealth, but now, through me, she is poor, perhaps even in actual want, and necessity is a hard task-master. 'Sdeath, Sally, you know your world! How are they living? What may she not do for the sake of that pampered weakling of a brother? Ever since I learned the truth that fear has haunted me! I tell you I will not rest until I have found her!" He paused for a moment, and when he resumed his voice had regained something of its former calm. "Sally, you hear all the gossip of the town. Surely some whisper of their whereabouts has reached you?"

Mrs. Cheriton shook her head, frowning in an effort of memory.

"I can recall nothing," she said, "but I will do my best to find out. Young Ashton, I think, is the most likely source of information. Leave it in my hands, Kelvin, and if I discover aught I will send word to you."

So Major Rainham returned to his lodgings, and for four days waited in a fever of impatience for a summons from Mrs. Cheriton. At length it came, and he hastened to her house, only to be told that such information as she had gathered was vague in the extreme. Sir David and his sister had stayed for a time at Ashton's house in Essex, but were now living with an old servant at a farm in Kent. The name of the farm, and its situation, she could not discover.

"You are a friend in a thousand, Sally," said Kelvin when she had finished. "Thank you, my dear. A farm in Kent, you say? Well, 'tis little enough in all conscience, but any information is better than none. All that remains is to find the farm."

"All?" Mrs. Cheriton stared at him. "Heaven defend us, there are hundreds of farms in Kent!"

"But few, surely, which shelter a lady and gentleman of fashion? That is in itself a fact remarkable enough to occasion talk among the rustics." He rose to his feet, drawing a deep breath. " 'Slife, I am glad that this damnable waiting is over."

"Kelvin!" Mrs. Cheriton rose also, looking at him with an expression of grave misgiving. "What do you mean to do?"

"Do, my dear Sally?" he repeated calmly. His manner had recovered all its old self-possession. "Why, I am about to set forth upon an exhaustive and probably prolonged journey in the county of Kent, in the hope that sooner or later I shall stumble upon the farm which has the privilege of sheltering Dorothea Stratton."

"At this time of year?" she exclaimed. "You must be mad! You know now that she is safe, so why in the world can you not wait until the spring?"

He shook his head.

"I cannot wait, Sally. Thanks to you I know that she

has found a haven of a sort, but I shall know no peace until I have seen for myself what manner of place it is." He broke off as his glance met and held hers for a space, and then with a sigh and a gesture of resignation he turned away. "Ah, why do I pretend? Why seek to deceive either myself or you? I go because I must, because I hunger for sight of her as the devout yearn for a glimpse of Paradise. I long to hear her voice, see her smile, look into her eyes. I can no more tarry here until the spring than a river can withhold itself from flowing to the sea."

For a moment she pondered him with troubled eyes, startled and dismayed by the deep feeling in his voice. At length she said hesitantly:

"Kelvin, you have created an image of her which may bear no resemblance to the real woman. You are like to be grievously disappointed."

"Do you think I have not told myself that?" he said with a wry smile. "Aye, a score of times, but this is something which goes beyond mere logic and cold reasoning. Whether she is all that I dream her, or spoiled and foolish like her brother, matters not at all. I love her and I must find her—that much I know. For the rest—well, chance or destiny has drawn our lives together, and shall be my guide henceforth. I am content that it should be so."

Mrs. Cheriton, greatly agitated, took a turn about the room, while Kelvin, leaning against the table, watched her with faint amusement. At length, coming to a halt beside him, she said resignedly:

"I tell you frankly, Kelvin, I have no liking for this hare-brained scheme, but I know you too well to try to reason with you, though I trust you will never have cause to regret that I helped you in this mad business. Well, go your ways, and if your quest is successful send me word of it."

"I will," he promised, smiling, "and if fortune favours me it may be sooner than you expect."

Major Rainham remembered those parting words many weeks later, when he was riding along a narrow lane in the teeth of a February gale, and his lips twisted in self-mockery as he recalled their eager confidence. Fortune had not favoured him. For close upon two months he had roamed to and fro through the county of Kent, sometimes in deep, leafless woods, at others in richly-cultivated valleys of orchard and hop-field; he had breasted the high, bleak slopes of the Downs and traversed the inhospitable wastes of the marshes, but in vain. In village inn and wayside tavern he had listened and questioned in the hope that one day he would hear the tidings he sought, but the hope remained unfulfilled and was beginning slowly to fade, while his desperate desire to find Dorothea grew with the fading of his hopes.

Now, on this grey afternoon, he was riding somewhat aimlessly along a winding lane, with a fierce wind plucking at his cloak and driving icy rain into his face. The inclement weather, the bleak, wintry landscape and the apparent hopelessness of his quest combined to induce in him a lowness of spirit, and when a tumbledown hedge-tavern presented itself to his gaze he drew rein and, dismounting wearily, entered in search of warmth and food.

It was a humble place, dingy and rather squalid, and when Major Rainham entered the tap-room the landlord, a thin, depressed-looking man with a cast in one eye, gaped to see so fine a gentleman in his establishment. Then, spurred on by a nudge from his equally melancholy wife, he hurried forward to welcome this elegant stranger.

Having bespoken a meal and given orders for the care of his horse, Kelvin strolled across to the fire, glancing idly at the only other occupant of the room, a burly, ill-dressed fellow with a singularly unprepossessing countenance, who slouched on one of the time-blackened oak settles before it. The man returned his regard in an unfriendly fashion, then, averting his gaze, spat copiously in the general direction of the fire. Unmoved by this reception, the Major tossed his hat and gloves on to the table, cast his cloak over the back of the other settle and sat down. The other vouchsafed no remark, and as the host and his wife proved equally taciturn, and did no more than answer Rainham's questions as briefly as possible, the next hour or so passed almost in silence.

Kelvin had finished his meal when the door opened to admit a third guest, a small, brown-faced man with a huge pack on his back. The peddler, for such he obviously was, seemed well-known to the landlord, who welcomed him with a gloomy nod. The newcomer returned the greeting cheerily, doffed his battered hat to the Major and nodded to the surly occupant of the other settle, who responded with an inarticulate grunt. The peddler was a talkative fellow, and over a tankard of ale chatted in sprightly fashion to the landlord and his wife, promising to open his pack for the latter's benefit as soon as he had finished his drink.

Major Rainham, seated apparently lost in thought before the fire, was none the less attentive to the stream of trivial gossip, and at length his patience was rewarded in no uncertain fashion. The pack having been opened and its contents spread upon the table, the lady of the house expressed admiration for a cap ornamented in front with a large, upstanding ribbon bow.

"You buy it, ma'am, and you'll not regret it," the chapman assured her promptly. "Only four o' them caps I had, and could ha' sold ten times as many! See that there ribbon a-standing up in front so brave-like? That's how the fine ladies up in London wear 'em. Why, only this morning I sold a cap like that to Mistress Ashe, o' Gallows Farm over by Reppington, and she were maid to a great lady once, so 'tis said, Aye, and that's not the only reason she's got for knowing what the London fashions are. No, not by a long way it ain't."

The hostess, her curiosity immediately piqued by this cryptic remark, demanded an explanation. The peddler chuckled, closed one twinkling eye and laid a finger beside his nose.

"Because there's people o' Quality at Gallows Farm, ma'am, that's why," he replied. "Didn't I see 'em wi' me own eyes when I were at the farm last harvest-time? A lady in a silk gown, wi' a cap near a foot high on her head, and me lord her brother in his periwig and laced coat. Aye, ma'am, that I did, and what's more, I caught a glimpse o' the young lady at the window when I was at the farm this morning. A handsome, black-haired lass she is, wi' the finest pair o' blue eyes I ever saw in a maid's head."

With a stifled exclamation the tawny-haired stranger swung round in his seat to stare at the speaker, his face transfigured and the light of a great joy in his grey eyes. Had not the three been so intent upon the intriguing story, and had not the surly man fallen into a doze, they must have remarked this extraordinary behaviour, but they were not looking at him, and after a moment, recovering himself, he turned back to the fire and forced himself to resume at least an outward show of unconcern.

His thoughts were in a turmoil. At last, when he had almost abandoned hope, chance had brought him news of Dorothea. The peddler's words rang in his head—"Gallows Farm, by Reppington"! It was an odd, uninviting name, and surely such a place was no fit home for her? But she was found at last, and the end of his long search was in sight.

That last thought brought him to his feet, eager to set out on the final stage of his quest. He reached for his cloak, slipping it about his shoulders, and the movement woke his surly fellow-guest who sat up and yawned and scratched his head. Kelvin paid his score, asked the way to Reppington, and, on a sudden impulse, tossed a gold coin to the peddler who had been the unwitting bearer of such welcome tidings, bidding him drink his health. Then, smiling at the man's amazed and incoherent thanks, he went out to the ramshackle shed behind the tavern which served as a stable. There were two horses there, his own powerful black thoroughbred and a sorry-looking grey which the Major accorded no more than a passing glance. He saddled his own mount and a few minutes later was riding towards that which awaited him on the road to Gallows Farm.

The rain had ceased, but the sky was still heavily overcast and the wind had abated none of its violence, and he realized that it would be out of the question to go to the farm that night. He had best bespeak a bed at the inn at Reppington, and try to add, by a few discreet questions, to his present scanty knowledge. Until that moment he had given no thought to the course he should follow once Dorothea was found, but now he cast about in his mind for some means of speaking with her without at first disclosing his own identity. If she knew beforehand that he was the man who had ruined her brother, he was certain that he would have no opportunity to obtain the reassurance he sought regarding her present situation.

So preoccupied did he become that he allowed his horse to drop to a walking pace, but in spite of his abstraction the experience of many military campaigns could not be completely overwhelmed, and when he caught a glimpse of some bulky form which moved stealthily among the trees of a little spinney crowning the bank on the left of the road he became instantly alert. His hand closed upon the butt of the pistol in his saddle-holster, but even as he drew it forth and cocked it there was a spurt of flame from among the trees and simultaneously, it seemed, with the noise of the shot, he felt a shattering impact which almost swept him from the saddle.

Habit and training enabled him to keep his seat, and instinctively he levelled his own weapon and fired at the dim-seen figure in the spinney. As the echoes of the shot died away there was a crackling of twigs and a man tumbled head-first down the bank into the road, where he lay with outflung arms and his face upturned towards the lowering sky.

For a space Kelvin was fully occupied in quieting his frightened horse. The murderous bullet had struck him in the left shoulder, rendering his arm useless, and it was some minutes before he succeeded in regaining complete control of his mount, but at last he dismounted and stumbled towards the fallen man, still clinging with his sound hand to the black's bridle, though more now for support than from any fear that the animal might bolt. His assailant proved to be his surly acquaintance of the tavern, and he was quite dead, for by a lucky chance—certainly not by reason of careful aim—Kelvin's shot had found his heart. The decrepit grey horse must have been capable of an unsuspected turn of speed, or else, which was more likely, the would-be robber had known of a short cut which brought him to this part of the road ahead of his intended victim.

Rainham groaned and stood upright, staggering a little. Blood from the wound was already soaking through his coat, and the twilight landscape wavered curiously before his eyes as, with fingers grown suddenly clumsy, he rolled his handkerchief into a pad and thrust it inside his shirt in a vain attempt to check the bleeding. His horse was passive now, and with a supreme effort he dragged himself into the saddle, wondering dully whether or not his strength would last until he reached some place of shelter.

Of that nightmare ride through the gathering dusk and icy, buffeting wind he never afterwards retained a clear memory. Faint and sick, reeling in the saddle but held there by his indomitable will, he rode on for perhaps half a mile, his one conscious thought that somewhere ahead of him, almost within reach, was the goal he had sought for so long. He must reach the farm tonight or not at all, for he knew that to collapse here on this deserted byway, with no hope of succour, would be certain death. So, desperately, he struggled on until, with pain and a deadly, ever-increasing weakness, came the bitter certainty that he had failed within reach of success. A last vision of Dorothea's fair, calm face flashed before his eyes as he plunged into a roaring abyss of darkness, and with her name on his lips he pitched headlong from the saddle. The black horse gave a frightened whinny and bounded away, leaving its rider prone amid the muddy, half-frozen pools on the darkening road.

have been a sable or an unimpeding sort of sport, it
was—what was more likely—the world's noble head
tossed off a short cut which bravely ate to the case of
the great trunks of the splintered bark.

CHAPTER V

OUT OF THE STORM

Dorothea sat on the window-seat in the parlour at Gallows
Farm and gazed absently at the cheerless prospect without. A high wind was screaming and moaning round the
old house, and though the rain which had fallen heavily
earlier in the afternoon had now ceased, the low, wind-
driven clouds suggested that the respite was but temporary,
while the bare, tossing branches of the trees and the
sodden ground beneath them added to the desolation of
the scene.

Miss Stratton now presented a very different appearance
from the fashionably dressed lady who had aroused the
curiosity of a certain peddler the previous autumn, for
in spite of Janet's protests she had laid away her fine
attire, the silks and satins and stiff brocades, and wore
them only on the rare occasions when she visited Ardely
Place. For the rest she went clad like any country girl,
in a plain, homespun gown, the skirt shortened to the
ankle and the bodice laced in front across an under-
garment of a different colour, with a white apron tied

about her waist and her black hair uncovered and simply dressed.

But as she sat there in the gathering dusk Dorothea's thoughts were far removed from such trivial matters. In her lap lay a letter from David, a single, hastily-scrawled sheet wrapped about a much heavier package addressed to Clarissa, and it was with this, and all that it implied, that her troubled thoughts were occupied. On that fateful day when Clarissa had confessed her love for David, it was to Dorothea that they had turned for help and counsel. It was due to her efforts alone that the secret was still safe, shared only by the three of them, but a clandestine correspondence had been going on ever since, and she acquiesced almost against her will. His first letter to her had contained one for Clarissa, and though Miss Stratton had hesitated a little before giving it to her, the sight of her friend's woebegone little face, with all its natural gaiety quite banished, had prevailed against her better judgment, and now she found herself acting as reluctant go-between for her brother and his sweetheart.

Her hopes that Clarissa's feeling for David was an infatuation which would fade when she no longer saw him constantly had not been realized, neither did David's emotions show any sign of cooling, and had there been any chance that they would ever be able to marry Dorothea would have welcomed this fact. There was no doubt that his love for Clarissa was having a steadying effect upon David's character, for he had applied himself with unlooked-for diligence to the work which fell to him in his capacity of secretary, justifying his sister's faith in him and prompting Sir Edward to inform Lord Ardely, in a letter which his lordship was kind enough to show to Dorothea, that young Stratton promised well. Recalling this, Dorothea sighed, for she found something pathetic in her brother's efforts to build a new life, when he could have no hope of sharing it with Clarissa. Her ladyship's marriage, which should have taken place in March, had indeed been postponed until July owing to Lady Ardely's ill-health, but this respite, which the lovers welcomed so thankfully, would in reality avail them not at all. The summer would inevitably bring Lord Jevington to claim his bride, and Dorothea feared that the blow David must suffer in losing Clarissa might send him back to the disastrous road he had trodden until his fateful meeting with Major Rainham.

Suddenly she sat upright, startled out of her dismal reverie. The wind had dropped for a moment, and in the ensuing silence there had sounded in the distance a sharp report, followed a few seconds later by another—or was it an echo of the first? Rising to her knees on the seat, she thrust open the casement and leaned out to listen. A fresh gust of wind tugged at her hair and whistled through the branches of the trees around the farm, but there was no audible repetition of the sounds. As she knelt there one of the maids came round the corner of the house, her head bent against the wind, and Dorothea called to her:

"Polly, did you hear aught a moment since? It sounded like a pistol-shot!"

"A shot, ma'am?" the girl repeated blankly. "No, I heard naught."

Dorothea frowned and shook her head.

" 'Tis passing strange," she said. "I must have imagined it, and yet I could have sworn—oh, well, no matter! If you heard nothing I must have been mistaken."

She drew back into the room and closed the window, putting the matter from her mind. Picking up the letters, she put them away in a drawer to await a favourable opportunity to deliver that addressed to Clarissa, and then went to join Janet in the kitchen. For a while she remained there, and then, putting on a cloak, fetched a measure of corn and went out to feed the hens.

By the time she returned to the house, picking her way carefully across the muddy farmyard, it was already growing dark and rain was beginning to fall once more. The glow of firelight and candle-light shone from the diamond-paned windows of the house, heightening the contrast between the warm comfort within and the cold, wet dusk without, and Dorothea was reflecting how fortunate she was to have found so snug a haven in her misfortune when her thoughts were interrupted by the sight of Will leading a horse through the gateway which separated the yard from the lane. No unusual sight, of course, but this was no heavy farm-horse, but a spirited creature with saddle and bridle.

"Why, Will," she she exclaimed, moving towards him, "whose horse is that?"

Will smiled his wide, child-like smile and scratched his head in evident bewilderment.

"I dunno, Miss Dorothea," he replied. "I found 'un roaming i' the lane and I were just taking 'un to stable." He passed a gentle hand across the glossy black neck. " 'Tis a beauty, surely."

"Yes, Will, but it must belong to someone," Dorothea pointed out. "There may have been an accident, or——" the words were suddenly arrested, for she had placed her hand on the pommel of the saddle and found it wet and sticky to the touch, and when she withdrew her fingers they were marked with a dark red stain.

A wave of sick horror engulfed her as she stood there in the gusty twilight, with the raindrops beating upon her unprotected head, and remembered those faint sounds like distant shots. They, and now this riderless horse with the blood-stained saddle, told their own grim story; told that somewhere in the rain and the cold, windswept darkness a man lay dead or wounded, perhaps in desperate need of succour. Resolutely conquering her momentary weakness, she turned and ran into the house, leaving Will, still sorely puzzled, to lead his prize to the stable.

Her hasty, stammered story sent Thomas Ashe hotfoot in search of his stepson, while Janet, with shocked exclamations, fetched water so that Dorothea might wash the blood from her hand. Hardly had she done so before Thomas returned, this time fastening a heavy cloak about his shoulders.

"Some devilry's afoot, that's certain," he informed them shortly, and went to take a clumsy lantern from a shelf. "There's a pistol missing from the saddle-holsters, and if you heard two shots, Miss Dorothea, 'tis likely that the rider was trying to defend himself against footpads. Could you tell whence the sound came?"

"No," Dorothea replied slowly, "for I was not really

74

sure that I heard it at all, and thought no more of it until I saw Will leading in the horse. Oh, if only I had spoken of it earlier!"

"We must hope, my dear, that 'tis not yet too late to mend matters," said Thomas. "I doubt that it happened between here and the village, so we'll search the other direction first, and if we find naught before we reach the four-wents we'll prove each road in turn."

"You have a care to yourself, Thomas," his wife urged him sharply. "Those rascally footpads may still be lurking about. Best go armed yourself."

He smiled and shook his head.

"This is weapon enough for me, wife," he answered, taking a heavy cudgel from the chimney-corner. "Now don't waste your time worrying over us, but make ready to receive a wounded man—that is, if the poor soul still lives."

He picked up the lantern and went out, and they heard him calling to Will to make haste. Janet filled with water the great kettle above the fire and went off to search her linen-press for bandages, while Dorothea sat down in the inglenook and endeavoured to busy herself with a piece of sewing. At the far end of the big kitchen two maids were chattering over some household task, and she tried to listen to them and shut her ears to the moan of the wind and patter of the rain against the windows, nor think of what the searchers might find out there in the stormy darkness.

Presently Janet came back to the kitchen, and together they awaited the return of Thomas and Will. The old clock in the corner told with measured rhythm the passing minutes, while the women talked in low voices of every-day matters and their thoughts followed the men on their errand of mercy. An hour and more passed in this fashion, and then Janet broke off and lifted a warning finger. Through the sound of wind and rain they heard voices in the yard outside.

Mrs. Ashe went to open the door, Dorothea folded her sewing with hands which shook a little, and the two servants exchanged glances. Janet spoke the question which was in all their minds and her husband's voice replied:

"Aye, we found him, and alive, God be praised! (Steady, Will, lift him gently.) He's senseless, though, and I fear sorely hurt, but in the rain and darkness there was little we could do to aid him."

He and Will came slowly into the room, bearing the injured man between them, and carried him to the broad, high-backed settle before the fire. Janet bent over him to place a cushion beneath his head, and Dorothea, herself a nurse of some skill, stepped forward to give what aid she could. Then she checked, and stood quite still by the settle's end, looking down at the man who lay stricken and helpless before her, wrapped in a rain-sodden cloak which, falling open, revealed a laced coat torn and dreadfully stained. No premonition came to her, no warning that this was the man who had shattered her brother's life and reduced them both to poverty; she saw only a stranger whose still face, austerely carven and drained of all colour, might have been that of an effigy upon a tomb. Not even the warm tint of the auburn hair scattered across the pillow could dispel that frightening illusion of lifelessness, and a rush of apprehension as sharp as it was inexplicable drove the colour from her own cheeks. So long did she stand thus motionless that Thomas became aware of it, and asked:

"What ails you, my dear? Do you know the gentleman?"

Miss Stratton started, and looked up.

"No," she said hastily. "I have never seen him before. Janet, he looks—is he badly hurt?"

"You should know there's no telling that till I've seen the wound," Janet retorted. "Here, Thomas, help me with his coat."

She went briskly to work, for like most country-women of her day she was accustomed to dealing with wounds and injuries; doctors were not always available in rural districts and their services were frequently too costly for ordinary folk. Her husband helped her to remove the stranger's coat and waistcoat, and then with capable hands she cut away the blood-soaked shirt, laying bare a mangled shoulder. Dorothea averted her eyes and fought down a momentary spasm of nausea, while Janet, probing the wound with skilful fingers, frowned and shook her head.

"The ball is lodged in his shoulder," she announced, "and 'twill need a surgeon to remove it. There's little we can do now but staunch the bleeding and get the poor soul into a warm bed. Polly, run upstairs and light a fire in Sir David's room! We'd best put him there."

She proceeded deftly with her task, while Dorothea, unwontedly pale but steady now of hand and eye, gave her such aid as she required. The others Janet despatched on various errands until, when the last bandage was fastened in place, only she and Dorothea were left in the kitchen. At last Mrs. Ashe rose to her feet.

"I must see if all is in readiness upstairs," she said. "You'd best stay with him, Miss Dorothea." A gust of wind more violent than the rest rattled the windows and flung a scurry of rain against the panes, and she clicked her tongue disapprovingly. "Mercy on us, what a storm! 'Tis a blessing Will found that horse, for if the poor gentleman had lain where he was the night through they'd not have found him alive."

Left alone with the injured man, Dorothea knelt down beside the low seat on which he lay and looked searchingly at the white face, while the tempest raged round the old house like a beast baulked of its prey. A strange disquiet rent her normal serenity; she felt herself shaken by emotions new to her, called into being by the tawny haired stranger which chance or destiny had brought to her out of the storm. Beneath their ministering hands he had lain as one dead, but now as she watched he sighed and moaned, and after a moment opened his eyes— dark grey eyes, bright with pain, which rested upon her face with a look of incredulous wonder. He put out his right hand waveringly towards her, and Dorothea took the icy fingers into her own warm clasp.

"Pray be easy, sir," she said gently. "You have been injured, but you are among friends now, and all will be well."

He continued to gaze at her, a faint frown between

his brows and his eyes searching her face until she felt her colour rise beneath the intensity of his regard. He tried to speak, but before his lips could frame the words his eyes closed once more and with a sigh he sank back into a swoon. Conscious of hurried breathing and a strange, wild quickening of her heart, she remained kneeling beside him, and presently Janet found her there with his hand still clasped to her breast.

When Thomas and Will, acting under Janet's supervision, had carried the wounded man away to the room prepared for him, Dorothea sat in the kitchen inglenook and endeavoured to regain control of the thoughts and emotions so violently disturbed by the events of the evening. Polly and Nell were moving about the room, restoring it to its customary neatness, and suddenly an exclamation from one of them caught Miss Stratton's attention.

"What is it, Nell?" she asked.

"This little book, ma'am," the girl replied. " 'Twas under the settle—it must have fallen out of the gentleman's pocket."

Dorothea took the slender volume held out to her and turned it between her hands. Its binding of worn, faded leather was patched with dark stains, and when she opened it the scrawled signature of Anthony Forrest stared up at her from the fly-leaf. It was natural that she should assume this to be the name of the injured man, and so, after all, Kelvin Rainham came to Gallows Farm and the end of his quest, unwittingly sheltering beneath the identity of the dead man who had been his closest friend.

He did not regain consciousness again for many hours, and when he did he was too weak to give them any information regarding himself or his present plight. As soon as it was light Thomas sent one of the farmhands to the nearest town for a surgeon, and when he came Dorothea, whose assistance Janet had firmly declined, busied herself with household tasks and tried not to think of what must be going on in the sickroom overhead. The effort was unsuccessful, for she paused frequently to listen to Janet's familiar footsteps, and the doctor's heavier tread, moving to and fro in the room above, while her mind was filled with the memory of an austere pale face and intent and wondering grey eyes.

After what seemed a very long time someone descended the stairs, and from the window she saw the surgeon walking slowly towards the stables with Thomas, their faces very grave. Janet was still in the room above, and after only a moment's hesitation Dorothea went upstairs and tapped softly on the door of her brother's room.

Janet's voice bade her enter, and she went in. The curtains of the big fourposter were partly drawn, and Mrs. Ashe standing beside it, looking down with a troubled frown at its occupant, nor did she move as Miss Stratton came to stand beside her. One glance at the injured man showed that there was cause enough for anxiety; Dorothea thought she had never seen anyone look so utterly exhausted, and the face which she had last seen white and still was flushed now with rising fever while the tawny head moved restlessly on the pillow.

" 'Tis a bad business," said Janet in a low voice. "An uglier wound I've yet to see, and now this fever has taken him. Pray God he has the strength to survive it." She sighed and shook her head. "How I'm to find time to nurse him I don't know, for those girls can do naught unless I have them under my eye the whole time."

"I will nurse him," Dorothea said quietly. Janet looked scandalized.

"Miss Dorothea, you'll do no such thing. Bless me if I ever heard the like!"

Dorothea did not seem to hear her. She bent forward to lay a cool hand on Rainham's burning forehead, looking down at him with an expression which caused Janet, after one startled glance, to repeat her objection with greater vehemence.

"Now listen to me, Miss Dorothea! It's not fitting that you should tend the poor gentleman, and I'll not allow it. I dare say I shall manage well enough with Polly and Nell to help me."

Miss Stratton shook her head and moved away from the bed.

"Janet, you know that neither Polly nor Nell would be of any use in a sickroom. At least I know something of nursing."

"Oh, you've skill enough, Miss Dorothea, I'll grant you that, but it's not fitting, and there's an end to it. What would Sir David say if he knew you were playing nurse to a stranger we'd picked up out of the road?"

"David's opinion is of no consequence," Dorothea retorted. "I'faith, Janet, you speak as though Mr. Forrest were some vagabond gipsy—though even if he were it would be no good reason to refuse him aid."

"Better if he was a gipsy," said Janet grumpily, "for then we'd know where we stood. I warn you, my dear, there's something queer about this Mr. Forrest. His clothes are as fine as any I've seen and his pockets are well-filled, but what's he doing travelling unattended and at this time of year? People of consequence travel when they can do it in comfort."

"Oh, nonsense, Janet!" Dorothea replied, between vexation and amusement. "You are making a mystery out of nothing, for I'll warrant there is a perfectly simple explanation did we but know it. Now do not argue any more, there's a dear soul, for nurse him I will and no one is going to stop me."

She had her own way in the end, for Mrs. Ashe was influenced by the fact, which became obvious as the day wore on, that Rainham would need constant attention if he were not to perish of his wound and the ill effects of weakness and exposure. By nightfall he was in the grip of a raging fever and utterly unaware of his surroundings. Not even the presence of Dorothea could draw him back to reality, and when she bent over him he stared at her without recognition. Yet perhaps that one brief glimpse of her before the fever gripped him had sounded a warning in his mind which not even sickness could entirely banish, or perhaps the inscrutable fates had chosen to deal kindly with Kelvin Rainham at last, for when delirium clouded his mind and loosened his tongue it was not of the fortune which he had won from

Sir David Stratton that he spoke, nor even of his great and hopeless love for Stratton's sister, but of the tragedy which had begun for him seven years before in his native Somerset, in that bright summer which had witnessed the horrors of the Monmouth rebellion.

CHAPTER VI

HISTORY OF AN EXILE—SUMMER, 1685

It was high noon, and Major Kelvin Rainham was riding through the park which surrounded his father's house of Rivenoak Hall, and reflecting upon the strangeness of this homecoming after a year's absence. Behind him came half-a-dozen scarlet-coated troopers, for the red shambles of Sedgemoor was but two days old and throughout the west of England the King's men were hunting down the wretched remnants of King Monmouth's rebel army, dragging them without trial to the hastily-erected gibbets which reared ugly heads at every village and cross-roads. Major Rainham had played—was, in fact, still playing—his part in this rebel-hunt, but he brought to it none of the brutality and violence which distinguished many of his fellows; the men under his command had not been permitted to ransack and plunder the houses they searched, for though he knew that he might well be taken to task for this restraint he could not bring himself to treat as conquered enemy territory the fair countryside where he had been born and bred. In the short time which had elapsed since the battle he had witnessed scenes which had filled him with disgust of the whole sordid business, and his pale, finely-featured face between the curls of the black periwig, at all times austere and a little hard, wore now an expression even more forbidding than usual.

In spite of the distaste he felt, however, he had volunteered for his present duty, urging that as a native of the district he could discover hiding-places which a stranger might overlook. He had been urged to this course by the outrages already committed, under the pretext of searching for fugitives, by the victorious troops, and the thought that sooner or later his own home would suffer similar depradations unless he could contrive to lead the search-party himself—for his family had never taken any part in politics and he had no fear that he would find rebels sheltering at Rivenoak.

Now, on this bright July morning, as he rode at the head of his little troop through the park where he had played as a child, he wondered with faint self-mockery why he had been at such pains to protect the home where he had known little of happiness and affection. Since his parents had been at a loss to understand the reserved and sensitive nature of their younger son, all their love and dearest hopes became centred upon the elder boy, Matthew. Never, it seemed, had there been two brothers so utterly dissimilar; the elder gay, enthusiastic and immensely popular, the younger quiet and aloof, slow to make friends and, even at an early age, possessor of a mocking humour and sarcastic tongue which did little to increase his popularity. It was not perhaps surprising that he grew from a lonely child into a solitary youth, full of restless ambition and a desire to see more of the world than this quiet corner of Somerset with which the rest of his family seemed content. He determined upon a military career, and Squire Rainham, relieved to discover his unpredictable offspring possessed of such definite plans for the future, readily purchased a commission for him and bade him God-speed.

In his chosen profession Kelvin had prospered, and an unusually brilliant career was predicted for him, but still he remained as solitary as in the old days at Rivenoak

Hall. His brother-officers, devil-may-care young men for the most part, stood somewhat in awe of his unapproachable bearing and frequently blighting tongue, and since none of his acquaintances had sufficient perception to pierce his armour of calm indifference he acquired a reputation for callousness which was not deserved, and for a fanatical devotion to duty which was.

In the ten years which had elapsed since he entered the army Kelvin had seen his family only at rare intervals, and this visit to Rivenoak upon the grim business of rebel-hunting was the first for a year. In that time he had only once received news from his home, when his mother had written to inform him of Matthew's betrothal to Catherine Manville, the daughter of a neighbouring landowner. Kelvin had smiled without bitterness as he read the complacent phrases, knowing that to Mrs. Rainham it was inevitable that Matthew—gay, charming, popular Matthew—should win the hand of the county's acknowledged belle. The two families had been friends for years, and from childhood visits to the Manville home he remembered Catherine as a fat, fair child much given to tantrums when her desires were thwarted, but in her mid-teens she had suddenly and somewhat surprisingly blossomed into what even the indifferent Kelvin admitted to be a singularly pretty girl, and soon had half the young gentlemen in Somerset fighting for her favours. But it was Matthew Rainham who had carried off the prize, and that, in the opinion of Matthew's mother, was just as it should be.

The little party of soldiers breasted a slight eminence, and the old, grey manor-house lay before them, drowsing in the noonday heat in the hollow which sheltered it. Midway between them and the house could be seen the flying figure of a young boy, obviously bearing tidings of their approach, but the sight occasioned Major Rainham no uneasiness. Rumours of the violent measures adopted by the victorious troops in their search for fugitives would by now have penetrated thus far from the immediate vicinity of the battlefield, and not even the innocent would wish to be taken unawares by one of these marauding bands.

As they drew rein before the door it opened and

Squire Rainham appeared on the threshold, a tall, erect, elderly man with a strong, arrogant face. When he realized that the young officer in command of the troop was his own son his eyes narrowed, but there was no other change in his expression. He said sternly:

"Do sons now present themselves at their father's door with soldiers at their back? An unseemly custom, by my faith!"

"These are unseemly times, sir," Kelvin replied levelly. He dismounted and went up the few, shallow steps to his father's side. "I regret the necessity, but I have my orders. The house must be searched."

Looking beyond his father, he became aware of two women within the wide hall, and strode forward with jingling spurs to bow over his mother's hand.

"Madam!" His voice was formal. "I trust I see you well? Miss Manville, your servant."

Catherine Manville murmured something indistinguishable and cast a swift, upward glance at his face. She had a fair, gentle beauty which was very appealing, with large, soft brown eyes, and a perfect, oval face framed in a cloud of pale golden curls, but she was pale now and a little breathless. Conceiving that the presence of the soldiers, combined with rumours of violence wrought elsewhere, might be causing her some apprehension, he said quietly to his mother:

"Pray do not be alarmed. There is naught to fear. The house must be searched, but 'tis the merest formality and need occasion you no inconvenience."

Catherine breathed a fluttering sigh and moved to sink into a nearby chair.

"We have heard such dreadful rumours," she said softly, "and when we learned that soldiers were approaching the house I confess that I was alarmed. We did not know then that 'twas you, Major Rainham, who commanded them."

"There is no need for you to be frightened," he repeated, and turned away to issue brief instructions to his men. As they dispersed to carry out the search, and he returned to the little group about the empty hearth, it occurred to him that his mother had not yet uttered a word. She was sitting very erect in her high-backed chair, with a spot of colour burning on either cheek and her mouth set in uncompromising lines, while her eyes were fixed upon him with an expression of almost unnatural intensity.

"I ask your pardon for this, mother," he said more gently. "Pray do not think that it is in any way a pleasure to me, or that I contrived it in any unbecoming or disrespectful spirit."

The harsh lines of her face did not soften; she regarded him coldly.

"So you admit that you are here by your own contrivance," she said. "Upon my soul, you do not lack impudence."

Kelvin's lips tightened and his eyes grew hard again at the sound of the familiar, querulous voice which had echoed through his lonely childhood. He said bitterly:

"I contrived it, madam, because I knew what would follow if a stranger led soldiers here. The only hope of averting that danger was to command the search-party myself."

"You knew?" It was Catherine's voice, oddly breathless. "Is that why you came?"

"Why else, madam?" Bleakly the grey eyes met the brown. "Did you suppose that I take such pleasure in this tipstaff's work that I would seek it without good reason?"

He was about to add more, to tell them something of the vengeance already exacted by the Royal army, when he was interrupted by a commotion which arose beyond the door leading to the servants' quarters, which a moment later burst open to admit a distracted woman, with a wailing infant in her arms and another child clinging to her skirts. Two menservants were endeavouring to prevent her from entering the hall, but she eluded them and stumbled towards Major Rainham.

"Sir," she gasped, "oh, sir, help me, for the love of God! The soldiers have taken my husband, and say they'll hang him for a rebel, but he's not, sir, I swear it! He's not been from home this week past!"

She broke off, pressing her free hand against her side

86

and gasping for breath. The baby set up a fresh wail and the other child, a sturdy boy of four or five years of age, pressed closer to his mother and stared up, half-curiously, half-fearfully, at the tall, scarlet-coated officer. Mrs. Rainham was the first to speak.

"Calm yourself, Nancy," she said quietly. "If a mistake has been made no doubt it can be set right. They do not, I trust, propose to hang your husband out of hand, and he can come to no great harm for the present. Major Rainham will help you if he can, I have no doubt."

"Do, pray, sit down," Catherine broke in gently, rising and drawing forward a chair. "Have you come all the way from the village?"

The woman nodded, sinking gratefully into the chair and mechanically hushing the baby. Squire Rainham said quietly to his son:

"She is the wife of the blacksmith in the village, and she speaks truth when she says that he was not out with Monmouth. Two days since I spoke with him myself when I passed the forge."

"Praise God, your Honour, so you did!" Nancy exclaimed thankfully. "You can tell the Major my Jim's an honest man, and no rebel. Oh, sir," she added, turning to Major Rainham, "you can't take him! He's done no harm."

"If your husband is innocent he has nothing to fear," Kelvin assured her quietly. "How came my men to take him?"

"They searched the house, sir," she replied, drawing the little boy closer to her side. "They dragged his brother Diccon from his bed, and him with his arm broke by a musket-ball, poor lad! Then they took my Jim as well, and said as he were a rebel, too, and must hang for it."

"How came the man Diccon by his injury?" Kelvin asked in an expressionless voice. "Was it upon Sedgemoor Field?"

"I—I don't rightly know, sir," she faltered, "but he were hot for King Monmouth, as they call him, and went off nigh on a week ago to join him, though Jim swore that if he went he'd not come back to his house again. But then last night he came home, scarce able to walk and with his arm all shattered, and what could we do but take him in? He be only a lad, sir, scarce seventeen."

"He was old enough to bear arms against his King, and he is old enough to face the consequences," Kelvin replied coldly. "As for your husband, he had knowingly given shelter to a rebel——"

"But, sir, 'twas his brother, and sorely hurt. No man would give up his own brother."

"It was his duty to give him up, brother or no. I am sorry, my poor creature, but I can do nothing for you. Your husband was justly taken prisoner, and must remain so."

With a piteous cry of entreaty and dismay she flung herself on her knees before him, catching at his hand and sobbing an incoherent plea for her husband's life. Major Rainham drew back a pace, looking down at the distraught woman with compassion tinged with a faint distaste; the Squire and his wife exchanged glances; Catherine, who was trying to soothe the frightened little boy, said urgently:

"Oh, the poor, poor creature! And the two little children! Major Rainham, you cannot do this thing! You cannot be so harsh, so cruel!"

Kelvin glanced at her a trifle impatiently. There was no sign of relenting in his face, and his voice when he replied was level and unemotional.

" 'Tis not I, madam, but the law which is harsh and cruel. Who harbours a traitor is himself a traitor, and must pay the penalty." He turned towards the staircase as one of his men briskly descended it and came smartly to attention at the bottom. "Well?"

"We have found a man above-stairs, sir, sorely wounded," the sergeant reported woodenly, "and from the look of the injury there's small doubt how he came by it."

A sudden stillness descended upon the hall, broken only by the sobbing of the child in Catherine's arms, while Kelvin stared at the man, his stunned mind refusing to accept the implications of what he had heard. So for a few seconds he stood, while they watched him with tense expectancy. Then with an effort he roused himself, and in silence, with a terrible foreknowledge of what he would find, he crossed the hall and went up the stairs.

A trooper stood guard outside an open door, and Kelvin went forward until he stood at the foot of the bed, looking down at the white face and closed eyes of his elder brother. For a moment the room spun dizzily around him, and the sweat started on his brow as he realized the hideous position in which he had unwittingly placed himself; he set his teeth and clenched his hand upon the hilt of his sword as he fought to maintain his self-control.

Footsteps sounded behind him, and his mother came into the room, hastening to the bed to stoop above its motionless occupant. Then, as her glance sought the face of her younger son, her eyes widened in sudden apprehension.

"Kelvin!" she said, on a sharp note of anxiety. "Why do you look like that? You knew that he was here, did you not? Did you not?"

"I know it?" Major Rainham repeated in a strangled voice. "Good God, madam, should I have come here if I had?"

"But you came to save him," she insisted, her voice rising shrilly. "You said that you were aware of his danger, and came to avert it. If you did not know that he had been out with Monmouth, why are you here?"

Kelvin almost groaned aloud as the reckless words dispelled any faint doubt which might have lingered concerning the source of Matthew's injury. The suggestion of his own compliance in the affair he hardly heeded, though from the corner of his eye he saw the startled glance which the sergeant cast at him—as well he might, since Major Rainham was known throughout the regiment as a man who set duty above all else.

He looked again at Matthew, forcing himself to face squarely the terrible choice before him, while his keen brain summed up the chances of escape. If he sent his men away empty-handed—for they would not dare to question his orders—how long would it be before the alarm was raised and he himself became a fugitive? And, even with the inevitable respite, how could they hope to win free while Matthew lay senseless and wounded?

With surprise and self-contempt he realized the direction his thoughts were taking. He had always believed himself invulnerable to any form of sentiment, yet now he was contemplating the sacrifice of his military career and probably his life to a quixotic gesture which had little chance of success—and for what? For the sake of a brother who was almost a stranger to him, a father whom he had known only as a stern mentor inspiring more fear than affection, and a mother who had made not the least attempt to give him either love or understanding. It was at his mother that he looked now, as she bent over the motionless figure in the bed. Matthew had ever been her idol, her darling, around whom her whole life revolved, and Kelvin knew that she would lay down that life for him as readily as she would sacrifice his own honour and career, his very hope and ambition, in the same cause.

Yes, it was a cruel decision which faced him, yet somehow the choice must be made between, on the one side, duty, loyalty and honour—the cold, austere, exacting standards by which he had hitherto guided his life—and upon the other the lives of his brother and his father, for if he took Matthew he must take Squire Rainham also, since he had given him shelter.

With that last thought came the memory of the desperate woman who, only a few minutes earlier, had knelt before him to beg for her husband's life, and whose entreaties he had refused in the name of duty. Her frantic words—"but 'twas his brother, sir, and sorely wounded" and his own reply—"it was his duty to give him up, brother or no"—echoed in his mind with devilish mockery. She had said that no man could give up his own brother, but—could he? Could he set aside all claims of blood and kinship for duty's sake, and remember only that Matthew was a rebel, as guilty as the rest of the prisoners whom he was sending to the gallows?

So he fought his bitter, inward battle, scarcely aware, in the maelstrom of his own emotions, of the companions who watched him so anxiously. Squire Rainham had come to his wife's side, and upon the other side of the bed Catherine stood with her hands clasped at her breast and her great eyes fixed upon Kelvin with an expression of anguished expectancy. In the background the sergeant, impassive as a statue, awaited his orders, while in the doorway clustered one or two upper servants, drawn to that quiet chamber by the knowledge of what it held. Every eye was turned towards the pale, stern-faced young officer at the foot of the bed, every ear strained to catch the words which must presently fall from his lips.

Justice and duty, or the ties of kinship! Which to choose, which? Memories jostled each other in his mind; Matthew as he had seen him when they parted a year ago, laughing and debonair; the ever-growing tide of doomed prisoners, being herded under guard towards extinction; the frantic despair in Nancy's eyes when he told her that her husband must die because he had aided his brother. Duty or sentiment, which? The two opposing tides surged one against the other—and duty triumphed. Kelvin was white to the lips, and a muscle quivered beside his mouth, but his voice was steady enough when at last he spoke.

"Sergeant!"

"Sir?"

"Secure your prisoners, and convey them with the rest to Taunton gaol. Let my—let the injured man be placed upon a litter, and see to it that he is borne gently. When you have completed your search report to me below."

Catherine uttered a single, gasping sob and closed her eyes, but Mrs. Rainham, with a terrible cry in which disbelief, horror and despair strove for supremacy, dropped to her knees to fling a protecting arm across the motionless body of her elder son. For a moment the younger remained looking down at her, and then he turned on his heel and strode blindly from the room, and at sight of his face soldiers and servants alike fell back to let him pass.

With no very clear idea of what he was doing Kelvin

descended the stairs, crossed the hall where Nancy still crouched, weeping softly, and so came out again on to the steps, into the hot glare of the sunshine. Time had lost its meaning for him, and how long he remained there, staring at the familiar prospect which no longer seemed quite real, he did not know. Now that the die was cast all emotion was mercifully suspended, and he watched a small insect crawl across the broad, stone balustrade and speculated absurdly on the purpose of its laborious journey. The shadows of the trees lay dark on the smooth turf, the glossy coats of the waiting horses glistened in the sun, and the air was sweet with the scent of flowers and new-cut grass. Only the quiet sobs of the woman within the hall served as a reminder of the swiftly crushed rebellion and its aftermath of misery.

They came out to him at last, the soldiers, their faces expressionless, bearing the wounded man on a hastily-contrived litter, while beside him walked his father, his hands pinioned behind him. As he drew level with Kelvin, Squire Rainham halted and looked him full in the eyes.

" 'Who harbours a traitor is himself a traitor,' " he said grimly. "You are at least consistent, my son."

The young officer winced as though at a blow, but made no reply as he watched his prisoners taken down the steps, and the soldiers mounted their horses. From within the house came the sound of agitated voices, his mother's predominating, and he quickly gave the order which started the little calvacade on its journey across the park to join the men who had been left to search the village. He would have followed immediately, for he had no desire to face the storm of reproach and entreaty which his mother would fling at him and which it was impossible for him to gratify, but a loosened saddle-girth detained him for a moment and before he could mount she appeared on the threshold.

She seemed almost beside herself, for her face was a ghastly, greyish hue and her eyes blazing, while her dress was disordered as though she had been forcibly detained from intervening in the arrest of her husband and son. Catherine, in fact, was still clinging to her arm as though to restrain her, and behind her hovered one or two servants, their faces eloquent of dismay. For a few seconds she stood there, staring after the retreating soldiers, and then her wild gaze returned to rest upon Kelvin where he stood at the foot of the steps with his hand on the bridle of his horse. His mouth twisted and she flung out an accusing hand.

"Why do you linger?" she cried. "Have you not wrought evil enough, or do you mean to take me also? I, too, am guilty! Why do you not drag me to the gallows also?"

"Heaven forbid, madam," he replied in a low voice. "You do me less than justice if you imagine that I do this thing without a bitter struggle. I am a soldier, and it is a soldier's duty to obey, but had I known what I would find here no power on earth could have brought me to this house today."

A terrible peal of mocking, mirthless laughter broke from her lips.

"Lies, lies!" she screamed. "Always you have hated and envied your brother, and when you learned that he lay here at your mercy you came to drag him to his death. By your own words you stand convicted! The mark of Cain is upon you!" Catherine clutched her arm more tightly and tried to silence her, but she flung her off with the ease of unnatural strength. "Aye, there is blood upon your hands and upon your soul! Would that I had died ere I could give you birth, but know that if a mother's curse has power to harm I curse you now and with every breath I draw till the end of my days!"

Her voice had risen to a frenzied shriek and she flung up her hands in a gesture at once wild and menacing, but with the movement she staggered and collapsed upon the ground, her face distorted and a trace of froth about her lips. Kelvin, who all that while had stood silent and unmoving beneath the lash of her words, with only that pulse beating in his cheek to belie his outward calm, took a hasty pace forward, but as he set foot upon the lowest step the old housekeeper, who had been standing close behind her mistress and was the first to reach her when she fell, straightened her back and raised a restraining hand.

"You'd best go, Major Rainham, sir," she said in a

shaken voice. " 'Tis a seizure o' some kind, poor soul, and you can do no good by staying."

He hesitated and glanced at Catherine, who, white-faced and trembling, was leaning against the balustrade bordering the steps. She nodded.

"Yes, please go," she whispered: "I will send word to my father—she shall have every care."

Kelvin looked once more towards his mother's prostrate figure, but the women had already clustered round her, hiding her from him. He turned and swung into the saddle, touched spur to his horse and, with his mother's demented curses still ringing in his ears, rode after the melancholy cavalcade which had already disappeared over the crest of the adjacent rise.

Two days elapsed before Major Rainham's duties permitted him to return to Rivenoak and learn how his mother fared. With some misgivings he entered the house, the door of which stood wide, and paused a moment in a hall which seemed tragically quiet and empty. When he moved forward his spurred boots rang loudly upon the stone-flagged floor, and as though drawn by the sound a man emerged from an adjoining room.

It was Mr. Manville, Catherine's father, and when he recognized the newcomer an expression of anger and disgust descended upon his face.

"So you have returned!" he said unpleasantly. "I marvel, sir, that after what has passed you have the temerity to show your face in this house."

Major Rainham stiffened. Whatever he had done, Rivenoak was still his home, and he had no mind to be addressed in that fashion by one whose authority he refused to recognize. He said coldly:

"I would remind you, sir, that what happened here two days ago concerned only myself and my family. Will you have the goodness to inform me how my mother fares, since that is the reason for my presence here?"

Manville came forward until he stood on the opposite side of the table, resting his hands upon it and regarding Kelvin across its wide expanse of polished wood. There was a kind of bitter satisfaction in his face, as though he rejoiced in the fresh blow he was about to deal the man before him.

"Your mother, Major Rainham, will never recover from the seizure," he said brutally. "The shock which she suffered two days ago has turned her brain, and the physicians assure me that there is no hope of a recovery. Now, sir, I trust that you are satisfied! There have been many black crimes committed in the west in the name of duty during these latter days, but none, I think, as foul as yours."

"Father!" The cry, soft and reproachful, caused them both to turn. Catherine was halfway down the stairs, whither she had come unnoticed by either, and now as they paused she descended the remaining steps and crossed the hall towards them. Kelvin bowed in silence, noting with a stab of remorse how pale she was, her eyes reddened by weeping.

"I have just left your mother, Major Rainham," she said softly. "She is quiet now, and suffers not at all."

"I am relieved to hear it, madam," he replied. "Is it permitted that I see her?"

Catherine's glance dropped and she bit her lip.

"I—I fear it would not be wise, sir," she faltered, and cast a harassed look at her father, who shrugged and turned away. "There is a danger that any reminder of what passed two days since might provoke another attack which might well prove fatal. Her present affliction, dreadful though it is, carries with it a kind of blessing, for she recalls nothing of the events preceding her collapse. When she asks for her husband or for Matthew we make excuses for their absence and her mind soon drifts to other matters. She does not remember that they were arrested . . ." her voice became choked with tears and she turned away, pressing a handkerchief against her lips.

For a moment Major Rainham stood without speaking, looking down at the bowed, golden head and averted face. At length he said in a low voice:

"Even if I could find words to tell you how deeply it distresses me to be the cause of such grief to you, 'twould be presumption in me to suppose that aught I could say had power to comfort you."

"Presumption indeed, sir!" her father broke in angrily, swinging round to face them. "This is your home, Major Rainham, and I have no power to order you out of it, but if you possess one spark of decency or proper feeling you will refrain from forcing your presence upon those to whom you have brought such bitter pain. Your mother, unhappy lady, is in good care—better, I dare swear, than the care of a son who has forfeited all right to the name."

Kelvin's hands clenched, and for an instant there was that in his face which caused the elder man to fall back a pace in sudden apprehension. Then, without another word, he turned and went out, but as he descended the steps he heard light, swift footsteps and the rustle of a gown behind him, and Catherine's voice called his name. He paused and looked back in time to see her come running across the hall towards him, ignoring her father's exclamation of anger and surprise, until she halted on the topmost step, her eyes level with his own.

"I am discourteous, I fear," he said in a hard voice. "Pray accept my apologies, Miss Manville, and permit me to bid you good-day."

"Ah, no!" she said hurriedly, in a low, breathless voice, and put out her hand to him. "Major Rainham, I cannot let you go believing that my father speaks for us all. Feelings run high at present, but it will not always be so. What you did was hard, but there was no other way and, oh, believe me, I understood!"

So unexpected were her generous words, and so greatly was he moved by them, that he found himself unable to reply, but he took the little, outstretched hand and pressed it to his lips in silence. She stooped towards him and he heard a soft, fugitive whisper:

"Go now, but trust me. We shall meet again in happier times," and then, still not trusting himself to speak, he freed her hand, mounted, and rode away. When he glanced back from the crest of the rise she was still standing on the steps, looking after him.

CHAPTER VII

HISTORY OF AN EXILE—WINTER, 1685

Many months were to elapse, however, before Major Rainham and Catherine Manville met once more. Kelvin did not visit his home again during the time that he remained in the west country, for though Catherine's parting words had done something to ease his bitterness and pain, her father's attitude towards him had shown him very clearly the light in which his action was regarded.

Inevitably the events of that grim day had left their mark upon him. The story of what had passed at Rivenoak Hall had become widely known, and his brother-officers, while giving thanks that such a decision had not been thrust upon them, looked askance at the man whose ruthless devotion to duty had prompted him to deliver his own father and brother to the vengeance of a vindictive King. They could not tell how they would have acted in similar circumstances, but since none of them understood or greatly liked him they were ready to believe that he had chosen the path of duty without doing any great violence to his own feelings, and his reputation for callousness increased accordingly. In fact, it was said frequently in many quarters that Kelvin Rainham possessed ambition but no heart.

It was not surprising that from that time onward he became more remote and unapproachable than ever, or that the tormented spirit beneath the cloak of outward indifference should lend a new bitterness to his tongue, until even those who wished him well grew resentful of the unfailing, savage mockery with which their overtures were greeted. Always a solitary man, he now found himself almost an outcast, and sometimes wondered despondently what curse he laboured under that all affection seemed denied him.

His sole comfort in those dark days was Sally Cheriton, who at that time was living with her brother in the house which a few years later she was to transform into London's most fashionable gaming-hell. She was a woman of wide experience and deep understanding, and she had suspected from the first that the unapproachable Major Rainham was not the callous and cold-hearted martinet which common report declared him. She had been at some pains to win his friendship, and that she succeeded surprised a good many people, including the Major himself, but he never had cause to regret the day when their paths first crossed. When he returned to London from Somerset it was she alone to whom he ever spoke of that day at Rivenoak Hall, and its tragic sequel. For tragic it had been, and the blow none the less severe because it was expected. Matthew had never recovered from his wounds, and died in the overcrowded, fever-infested gaol at Taunton, but Squire Rainham survived to stand his trial at what was to become known to history as the Bloody Assize, where he was condemned to death by the monstrous Lord Jeffreys, and the sentence carried out with the grim despatch demanded by that terrible judge.

Since his surviving son never referred to the tragedy it was supposed by most people that he had put it out of his mind, and only Mrs. Cheriton guessed something of his mental suffering, though even she had but slight comprehension of the truth. Constantly before his eyes passed memories of that fateful day, foremost among them the recollection of his mother's distorted features and blazing eyes as she screamed at him the curses of which his present mental anguish was perhaps the fulfilment. Remorse, and a sense of guilt not wholly justified, went beside him day and night, and he wished passionately that he might turn back the clock to that summer noontide when he had faced the hardest decision of his life. No price, he thought, could be too high to pay for the peace of mind which he feared he would never know again.

It was upon a bitter, wintry day not long after Christmas that a letter reached him, written by Catherine Manville from the London house of her maternal uncle, Lord Edgeworth, asking him to call upon her there. He knew a slight hesitation in agreeing to this, for he suspected that the invitation was made without the approval—perhaps even without the knowledge—of her family, but because he was intensely lonely, and her generous words of understanding and forgiveness had lingered pleasantly in his memory, he at length determined to do as she asked.

When he presented himself, at the appointed hour, at the door of Lord Edgeworth's house, he was surprised to find himself admitted, not by a manservant, but by a comely young woman who from her dress and bearing he took to be a lady's maid. This supposition was confirmed when she informed him that her mistress would receive him immediately, and led him through an anteroom, along a corridor, and so, by way of a minor staircase, to the first floor. The care with which she avoided the main apartments, and her general air of secrecy, confirmed his suspicion that Catherine was acting against the wishes of her family in receiving him at all.

At length the maidservant paused and tapped upon a door. Miss Manville's voice bade them enter, and the Major was ushered into a small but elegantly appointed room. A sea-coal fire burned brightly on the hearth, and on a day-bed in front of it Catherine was reclining, dressed in the height of fashion. Her gown of rose-coloured satin was cut in the latest mode, with a deep collar of fine lace veiling her white shoulders, and her pale golden hair, dressed in a profusion of soft curls, was confined by a rose-coloured ribbon. The simple country girl had given place to a lady of fashion, but there was a deeper and more subtle change in her than the mere outward show of dress and bearing, though it was a change so elusive that he could not immediately define it. She dismissed her maid with an imperious gesture and extended her hand to Kelvin.

"You are something of a sluggard, sir," she observed as he bowed over it. "I little thought that I should be obliged to send for you."

"Until I received your note, Miss Manville," he replied, "I was not aware that you were in London. Nor, had I known it, would I have presumed to wait upon you uninvited, for it seemed improbable that I would be considered a welcome visitor."

She sat upright, drawing aside her rose-coloured skirts and motioning him to sit beside her, saying as she did so:

"You cannot seriously imagine that anything which has happened could make your presence distasteful to me, or that I would ever refuse to receive you."

"Your kindness, madam, on the occasion of our last meeting I have most gratefully remembered," he assured her. "But I recall also your father's bearing then, and now the secrecy attending this visit leads me to suppose that his opinion is shared by Lord Edgeworth."

Miss Manville laughed.

"You need not concern yourself with my aunt or uncle, sir. They are both from home, and only my maid knows of your presence in this house."

"Indeed?" He glanced at her beneath raised brows. "Is that entirely wise? It would not look well if it were discovered that you had received me alone and in secret."

"I have no fear of that," she replied. "You are right in supposing that my family cherish an unreasonable animosity towards you, but that need not concern us. Somerset is far away, and here in London we may put out of our minds all that happened there."

He shook his head.

"Distance is no obstacle to memory, Miss Manville.

I have learned that to my cost during these past months. My God, how I have learned!"

She leaned forward, her hand on his arm and her soft, brown eyes searching his face. Returning the regard, he marvelled to see her so untroubled, with no hint of past grief to mar the perfection of her countenance.

"You have suffered," she said gently at length. "The memory of that day has troubled you, has it not? Oh, it was no easy task, I know, but 'twas the only possible way and no blame can ever attach to you for what you did."

"Can it not?" Kelvin's voice was bitter. "That you have gone to such pains to keep my presence here a secret gives the lie to that."

"You imagined that I received you privately for that reason? My dear, your wits have gone a-wandering! I have told you that my uncle and aunt share my father's absurd prejudice, and while I am in their house I must appear to conform to their views, but that is all. Did you suppose that they had succeeded in turning me against you? I should be angry that you have so little faith in me."

He stared at her, frowning a little, startled by the words and the almost coquettish tone in which they were uttered, but he was destined to be startled yet further. She sank back against the piled-up cushions, and with her head a little on one side and a smile playing about her lips, regarded him roguishly.

"Faith, Kelvin, how stern you look merely because I have sought to be discreet! But you must not take me to task, my dear. These past months have not been easy for me either, though I venture to say I have played my part tolerably well—I had not been here else. 'Tis because my sustained grief was beginning to affect my health that I was permitted to come to London."

"I am grieved to hear it, madam," he replied guardedly. "I trust, however, that you will regain your health now that you are among surroundings which do not call forth painful memories."

The amusement faded from her face and her lips tightened. It occurred to him for the first time that when she was not smiling there was something a trifle hard in the perfect curves of her mouth.

"There is no need to fence with me," she said, with a hint of sharpness in her voice, "and if you fear to be overheard, let me assure you that such fears are groundless. We are quite alone."

"I should be flattered, no doubt," he replied, sardonically, "but I can conceive of nothing which I might have to say to you, Miss Manville, of so private a nature that I should fear to be overheard."

That brought her abruptly to her feet, a flush of anger mantling her cheeks. Kelvin rose also, and stood looking down at her with an ironical expression which effectively concealed his bewilderment. Remembering the gentle, grief-stricken girl who in the midst of her own sorrow had yet been generous enough to offer him a word of comfort, he felt that he was in the presence of a stranger, and was conscious of an indefinable but ever-growing uneasiness.

"So you do not fear to be overheard," she said at length. "Do you really expect me to believe that?" She flung herself down again among the cushions and looked scornfully up at him. "You fool, do you think I do not know why you came to Rivenoak that day?"

"I take leave to doubt it, madam," he replied mockingly, "but if you have any suspicion of my motive I beg that you will tell me, so that I may correct any misapprehension."

A gleam of admiration came into her eyes and her lips quivered into a smile.

"How well you play your part," she commended him. " 'Tis small wonder that no one has guessed the truth. They say that you are hard and merciless, caring for nothing but your duty, but as yet no one has perceived how greatly you have prospered by means of that same devotion to duty. Your father was a wealthy man, and Rivenoak is no mean prize."

He stared at her, while the words, with all their monstrous implications, rang hideously in his ears, and for the first time he realized the construction which might be put upon his actions. The horror he felt was visible in his face, but Catherine thought to see merely dismay

102

at her own acuteness, and hastened to reassure him.

"Do not fear that I will betray you," she said. "I do not know how you learned that Matthew had been out with Monmouth and lay wounded at Rivenoak, but I applaud your quick-wittedness in turning events to your own advantage. I have heard it said of you that you are ambitious and like to go far, and now, i'faith, I believe it!"

Kelvin put a hand to his head. His brain seemed numbed by the nightmarish unreality of this interview and he could not follow the drift of her conversation. If she believed him guilty of so infamous a crime why had she received him with such kindness? Why had she received him at all?

"You cannot believe it," he said, in answer to that unspoken thought. "It is true that Rivenoak is mine now, but as God is my witness I swear that no thought of that was in my mind when I ordered the arrests." He took a pace forward and spoke with unwonted feeling in his voice. "Do you not see that I had no choice? Matthew was as guilty as any other poor, deluded fool who followed Monmouth, and as for my father, had I not just refused mercy to that unfortunate man whose wife came pleading for his life? He had committed no worse crime than my father had done. How could I in honour send him to certain death and at the same time let my own kindred go free?"

"Honour!" she repeated scornfully. "Duty! What are they but empty words? Keep them to justify your deed in the eyes of the world, but do not come prating of them to me." He would have spoken, but she raised an imperious hand to silence him. "Wait, and hear me! You are confused, I think. I am not blaming you for what is past." She settled herself more comfortably among the cushions, while he regarded her perplexedly and his sense of uneasiness increased. He was not a fanciful man, but of a sudden this softly-lit, luxurious room had assumed the aspect of a trap. He thrust the notion aside as absurd, and gave his attention to Catherine.

"I, too, have ambition," she said musingly. "When I was little more than a child I discovered in myself a power over men, and I realized that I could use that power to climb to heights undreamed of if once I could win free of my dreary, country surroundings. That is why I agreed to marry Matthew. I had other suitors, richer than he and titled into the bargain, but it was he who promised to bring me to London when we were married." She laughed softly, a sound at once contemptuous and complacent. "It would have served my purpose very well, for usually I could make him do anything I wished, but then he must needs become entangled with that accursed rebellion. I tried to dissuade him, but you know what he was like with his wild enthusiasms. For once he would not listen to me."

She paused, but he made no attempt to reply. He was staring at her with a kind of fascination, marvelling that so fragile and lovely a creature could be guilty of such callous worldliness.

"When he was arrested," she resumed, "it seemed the end of all my fine plans. Then I perceived a better way, and persuaded my father to send me here to my uncle's house. You had not deceived me with your high-flown talk of duty, and I knew that in you I had found a man as ambitious as myself, and as ruthless. Together, you and I could cleave a path to greatness."

"You flatter me, Miss Manville." His stunned disbelief was giving way now to anger, and in his voice was the biting contempt which his associates had come to dread. "Am I to understand that you are honouring me with a proposal of marriage?"

She laughed, and cast down her eyes with an affectation of modesty which sickened him.

"Faith, my dear, is such a proposal to come from me? Why, what a brazen creature you must think me! But we understand one another very well, do we not?"

With a sudden, lithe movement she rose to her feet and stood before him, so close that the heavy, cloying perfume she wore enfolded him in a stifling wave. The firelight gleamed on her satin gown and aureole of golden curls, and beneath the veil of lace her bosom rose and fell tempestuously. She put her hands on his shoulders and looked up at the inscrutable face.

"Let us cry truce to this play-acting," she said softly. "I confess that 'twas not only ambition which caused me to promise myself to Matthew, or expediency which prompted me to seek you out. When first you left Somerset I was a child, and I had well-nigh forgotten you until you came home last year after so long an absence, and Matthew brought you to wait upon me. You were not as those others, those boorish country squires with their hunting and drinking—God, how I hated and despised them! Since then the thought of you has been like a fever in my blood—you, with your cold courtesy and damnable indifference!" She leaned closer and her arms crept about his neck. "But you were not wholly indifferent, were you, Kelvin? When you came with your soldiers that day, Rivenoak was the only possession of Matthew's that you coveted. Shall I tell you how gladly my heart welcomed you then, or shall I prove it—thus?"

With the words the clasp of her arms tightened and she reached up to press her lips passionately to his. For an instant he remained motionless, and then he grasped her wrists in a grip which wrung an involuntary cry from her, and swung her away from him with such violence that she stumbled, and collapsed once more upon the day-bed, where she crouched to stare up at him incredulously. His face was white and set, and the grey eyes regarded her dispassionately; when he spoke his voice had the searing quality of a whip-lash.

"You prove nothing, madam, save your own immodesty. I counsel you to offer your favours in quarters where they will be more warmly received, for though I must inherit Rivenoak whether I will or no, you are a legacy which I refuse either to acknowledge or accept." He picked up his hat and cloak from the chair where her maid had placed them, crossed to the door, and there turned once more to face her. His glance travelled over her with icy indifference and his brows lifted a fraction, contemptuously. He bowed. "Give you good-day, Miss Manville. We are not like to meet again."

With that he left her, and striding blindly along the corridor outside her room, stumbled more or less by chance upon the main staircase. Descending this, and ignoring the stare of a gaping lackey who chanced to be in the hall, he let himself out into the wintry twilight, while in the scented bower above-stairs Catherine wept bitters tears of rage and humiliation. At last, however, she raised her head from the disordered cushions and stared at the door through which Major Rainham had departed. An ugly expression twisted her perfect mouth and her eyes glittered vindictively.

"So I am to offer my favours elsewhere, am I?" she said aloud. "You may yet have cause to regret that advice, my friend. Yes, I fancy you will regret it very bitterly ere long."

A day or two after Major Rainham's interview with Miss Manville a new and even uglier story concerning him became known. Not content, it seemed, with sending his father and brother to the gallows, he had now added to his crimes by forcing his attentions upon the unfortunate lady to whom that brother had been betrothed, and who had consented to see him for the sake of their childhood friendship. As the story spread Miss Manville began to go about a little in Lady Edgeworth's care, and her frail, gentle beauty and sorrowful air served to arouse even stronger feeling against Rainham, though the lady herself was never heard to utter a word against him, nor indeed to permit anyone else to do so in her presence. Such forbearance, argued her sympathizers, betokened a nature almost saintly.

For his part, the Major gave no outward indication of concern at the ugly stories which were being bandied about. He faced with unvarying calm the rising tide of gossip and rumour, and if he was now always alone—well, he had ever been a solitary man! To anyone interested in his welfare—and Sally Cheriton was the only person who could be so described—the strain under which he was living was at once apparent, but casual observers saw no farther than his customary show of indifference, and found therein an additional source of disapproval.

What it cost him to maintain that air of aloofness only Kelvin knew. For months he had been haunted by nightmare visions of the fate which had befallen his family through his actions, and now to this was added the undeserved disgrace provoked by the spite of an unscrupulous woman. He found himself ostracised by company in which he had always been accepted without question; men turned their backs upon him in the street, and ladies who had smiled upon him—for his looks and his air of aloof hauteur excited feminine interest—now pointedly withdrew from a room when he entered it.

Mrs. Cheriton watched him with growing anxiety, for her affection for him had grown until it was such as she might have bestowed upon a younger brother, or upon the son she had never had. Each time they met she fancied that she saw an alteration in him; his finely-chiselled features seemed now, in their pallor and rigidity, to be carved from stone, and there were dark shadows beneath the haunted grey eyes. Even in her presence he retained his imperturbable manner, but Sally was not deceived. Sooner or later this almost frightening restraint must yield, and she asked herself often and very anxiously what would follow when the inevitable breaking-point was reached.

The reality, when it came, exceeded even her worst fears, for it was precipitated by no less a person than Colonel Lambert, Kelvin's immediate superior. The Colonel was a man of little ability, who owed his rank to wealthy and influential relatives, and he had always cherished a jealous dislike for the aloof young officer whose military talents were so widely acknowledged and appreciated. He was, moreover, an intimate friend of Lord Edgeworth, from whom he had heard the story of Rainham's alleged crimes, and in whose house he had made the acquaintance of Catherine Manville. Lambert was extraordinarily susceptible to feminine charm, and since the lady, discovering his identity, exerted herself to please, his subjugation was rapid and complete. His admiration for Miss Manville, and his dislike of the Major, were responsible for what followed.

In the presence of numerous fellow-officers, some demon prompted Colonel Lambert to make a sneering reference to Kelvin and the stories concerning him, confident in his own immunity and deceived, as others had been, by that calm indifference.

The affair blew up quite suddenly out of a clear sky. There had been some talk of horses and horse-racing, and one enthusiastic gentleman had offered to back his own favourite mount against all comers. Since he was a notoriously bad judge of horse-flesh this proposal provoked a good deal of chaffing, into which Lambert's loud voice cut with a note of evil mockery.

"Challenge whom you will, my friend. Challenge anyone and everyone—except Rainham. I counsel you to beware of Rainham. He has a peculiar talent for turning events to his own advantage, even an event as unrewarding as a hunt for rebels."

There was a murmur, and a ripple of laughter, hastily stifled. Kelvin, who had been sitting somewhat apart, alone as always and wrapped in gloomy abstraction, got to his feet so suddenly that his chair overturned with a crash. He swung round to face his tormentor, who was perched on the edge of a table, one foot a-swing and a glass of wine in his hand, and Lambert, delighted to have evoked a response from his usually imperturbable junior, essayed another witticism.

"A dangerous fellow, Rainham," he said musingly, "and yet perhaps he would deal honestly with you. You, after all, are not his brother."

The words, accompanied by a sneering laugh, were flown beyond recall, and Kelvin's rigid self-control snapped at last beneath the intolerable burden. A blind fury as violent as it was alien to his nature swept over him, he saw Lambert's heavy face as through a blood-red mist, and without conscious thought struck with all the force he could command at the grinning mouth. The face disappeared as the Colonel sprawled in an ungainly heap on the floor, and Kelvin, still in the grip of that insane rage, dragged his sword from its scabbard and wildly bade him rise and back his allegation with cold steel. In an instant all was confusion, and while some of the company were assisting Lambert to his feet, half-a-dozen of their companions flung themselves upon Rainham, wrenching his sword from his hand and restraining him, not without difficulty, from a further attack upon his superior. He came to his senses to find himself under arrest, with the knowledge that those brief moments of madness had cost him his career.

It was his first and almost his only surrender to emotion, for throughout the humiliation of court-martial and degradation from his military rank he maintained an unmoved countenance, but on the evening of the day which had witnessed his final, public disgrace, turning instinctively to his one remaining friend, he sought out Sally Cheriton at her brother's house. Only she, the shrewd, good-hearted, worldly-wise adventuress, was a witness of the passion of grief and despair to which he surrendered then, and when it was over she perceived in him a new bitterness, and a cynicism which boded ill for his future.

He set about the ordering of that future with characteristic decision and despatch, for his chief desire now was to leave England and put behind him the ruins of his life and ambitions. His military training assured him of a means of livelihood as a mercenary soldier, but first his affairs in England must be set in order.

Rivenoak Hall and all its lands he sold, with the exception of a single, modest house for his mother's use, where she could live in the care of her old housekeeper and one or two trusted servants. She was destined to linger, a hopeless invalid, for two more weary years, and the bulk of the fortune which he had realized from the sale of his inheritance went to support her, and to secure for her every possible comfort.

These arrangements could not be made in a day, and it was some months before he was free to quit England. At last, however, on a grey and cheerless day, he stood upon the deck of a ship bound for France and gazed through a veil of rain at the white chalk cliffs as they faded slowly into the distance. It was the last glimpse which he was to have of his native land for seven long years.

CHAPTER VIII

THE AWAKENING

The pale, serene light of a full moon washed in a silvery flood over Gallows Farm, filling the hill-girt hollow from end to end. No breath of wind stirred the frosty air, the branches of the trees hung black and motionless against the sky, and the whole landscape had the frozen immobility of an engraving. Dorothea stood at an upper window of the farmhouse and looked out over the now familiar scene, but its cold beauty made no impression upon a mind preoccupied with graver matters. It was long past midnight and the house was very quiet, for the rest of the household had retired hours ago and only she kept watch in the room where the sick man still tossed and moaned in a high fever.

For three days Kelvin Rainham had hovered between life and death, and Dorothea had fought with every means in her power to save him. She had slept little during that time, and her face was drawn with fatigue, but she hardly heeded her own weariness while every effort of mind and will was concentrated upon saving the life of the man she knew as Anthony Forrest. Mrs.

Ashe told her husband that if the gentleman did recover it would be entirely due to Miss Dorothea; if he did not—Janet sighed and shook her head. Her shrewd, loving eyes had perceived from the first that the younger woman's concern for the sick man went far deeper than the pity which his condition warranted.

Dorothea herself was well aware of this, for hers was not a nature versed in self-deception, and the clarity of vision which Michael Ashton had remarked in her was a two-edged weapon, piercing straight to the heart of things in her own case as in others. It was useless to pretend indifference when she was conscious of an intensity of feeling such as she had never known; her natural honesty compelled her to admit—to herself at least—that when she knelt beside the wounded man in the kitchen of Gallows Farm she had known with a sudden sense of revelation that this was a turning-point in her life. She had been wooed by many men without once experiencing the slightest response, yet now, even before they had exchanged a single word, she had given her heart to this grey-eyed stranger who had come so mysteriously out of the night and the storm.

She pondered the strangeness of it now, as she stood gazing out at the moonlit landscape, and speculating, as she had done more than once during the past few days, concerning the expression with which he had regarded her during those brief, significant moments. There had been wonder in his eyes, and gladness, and a kind of amazed recognition which she found it impossible to explain, for how could he recognize her when they had never met before? The question seemed unanswerable, and in her heart was a secret, unacknowledged dread that it never would be answered.

The mystery of the stranger's plight had been only partly explained by the discovery, on the morning following the storm, of the body of the man who had attacked him. The fellow had an unsavoury reputation in the neighbourhood, and when he had been traced to the tavern where the solitary traveller had dined it was not difficult for the local justices to reconstruct what had occurred. One of them visited the farm to question the injured man, and, and, finding this impossible, requested Thomas Ashe to inform him as soon as Mr. Forrest was well enough to receive him. Meanwhile, inquiries were set afoot in the hope of discovering his friends or family, but these not unnaturally proved fruitless. There was no one, it seemed, to be concerned for the man who lay so desperately ill at Gallows Farm.

For three days the fever had its way with him, and between long periods of unconsciousness he lived again those anguished days now seven years past, and spoke wildly of the terrible decision which had faced him then, and of the woman who had wrought his downfall. Dorothea listened to his delirious ravings and wondered; who was he? Whence had he come, and what was the trouble which weighed so heavily upon his mind that in sickness and delirium he spoke of nothing else? And—most insistent question of all—who was Catherine? There had been little sense in the disjointed phrases which had fallen from his lips, only the hint of some momentous decision, of an inward conflict between duty and inclination, but that name had recurred constantly. She might have supposed it the name of wife or sweetheart but for the tone in which it was uttered, for his voice when he spoke of the unknown Catherine was fraught with reproach and a bitter contempt.

With a sigh Dorothea dropped the curtain into place again, shutting out the cold, black and silver world without, and turned once more to face the room. She knew that the crisis of his illness was at hand, but she had refused Janet's offer to stay with her, for there was little that she or anyone could do. This vigil she must keep alone, no matter how it ended.

She left the window and moved softly to the bedside, hoping against hope that she would see some improvement in his condition. The room was dimly lit by fire and candle-light, the bed-curtains arranged to shield the sufferer's eyes from even that faint illumination, and, in the stuffy darkness between, a weak, tormented voice was murmuring fitfully. She bent over him and heard a few disjointed words.

"The way is too hard . . but there is no turning

back . . . ah, God, for a second chance . . . a second chance!"

He repeated the last words several times in a tone of yearning agony that wrung her heart, and then unexpectedly his eyes opened and he looked up at her. For a few seconds the bright, feverish gaze held hers, and then he spoke again.

"Catherine!" he said bitterly, "you can harm me no more. Leave me in peace."

"Catherine is not here," Dorothea replied soothingly, putting back the tawny hair from his brow. "No one seeks to harm you now."

She had no expectation that the words would mean anything to him, and merely hoped that the sound of her voice might calm him a little, but to her surprise he seemed to comprehend her meaning. His right hand came up to close feebly about her wrist and he said uncertainly:

"Catherine?"

"No, not Catherine," she repeated gently, and, acting upon a sudden inspiration, moved the curtain a little so that the light fell directly upon her face. "Catherine is not here. 'Tis Dorothea."

He continued to stare at her, and slowly into his eyes crept a faint reflection of the wondering recognition which she remembered so vividly. She drew forward a chair which stood nearby and sat down, taking the beautiful, wasted hand between her own. His fingers closed weakly about hers, and as though her presence and her touch brought him comfort he lay quiet, gazing at her. The silence of the sleeping house enfolded them, while Dorothea's world narrowed to one shadowy room, and all eternity to the few short hours which must decide this soundless struggle between life and death.

"Dorothea," said the failing voice at length, charged now with such wistful tenderness that her eyes filled with sudden tears. After that he did not speak again, but presently he sighed as one who is very weary, and the grey eyes closed once more. Afraid to move lest she disturb him, she sat motionless, with his hand in hers.

Slowly the night wore on. Once she tried to withdraw

her hand, but he moved restlessly and she immediately desisted. She grew stiff and cramped, and a deadly weariness took possession of her, until the dim room wavered before eyes grown heavy with sleep. Several times she roused herself, but each time the effort was greater and at last her head sank forward, low and lower, until her cheek rested upon their clasped hands, and she slept. The silence was broken only by the scratch and scurry of a mouse in the wainscote; the shadows seemed to press closer as fire and candles burned low, and a finger of moonlight, finding its way between the curtains, crept slowly across the floor. At intervals, somewhere in the quiet house, a clock chimed softly.

The sun had not yet risen when Janet Ashe emerged from her bedchamber and, candle in hand, made her way quietly towards the sick-room. She opened the door upon darkness and silence, for the candles had burned out and the fire sunk to a heap of dully glowing embers, and a sudden fear took possession of her. She advanced into the room and her own light revealed Dorothea asleep in the chair beside the bed, her head pillowed on her hand which still clasped that of the injured man; and he——? Janet moved closer, lifting her candle, and saw that he was sunk in a deep slumber and free at last from the grip of the fever. She set a hand on the girl's shoulder, shaking her gently back to wakefulness.

"A fine nurse you are, Miss Dorothea," she whispered, with a sharpness belied only by the kindliness in her eyes. "Here's the fire all but out, the candles burnt to the socket, and you so sound asleep you never stirred when I came in. I knew 'twould come to this in the end."

"Oh, Janet!" Dorothea's voice was stricken, and the glance which she cast towards Rainham so charged with apprehension that Mrs. Ashe added hastily:

"He's sleeping quietly, God be praised, and the fever has left him at last! He'll start to mend now, you may depend." She broke off as Dorothea's head went down once more upon her hands, and though when she resumed her voice was still brusque, the touch which she bestowed

114

upon the black hair was very gentle. "Come now, Miss Dorothea, that's no call to weep. Go to your bed, my dear, the worst is over."

Janet's prediction proved to be correct, and when Rainham awoke some hours later it was, for the first time since he was brought to the farm, to a complete realization of his surroundings. He opened his eyes and lay looking up at the tester of the bed, conscious only of pain, and a weakness which made the smallest movement an effort.

At last, however, he summoned the strength to look about him, and found that he was in a room which he had never seen before. Beyond the half-drawn curtains of the big fourposter in which he lay was a spacious, low-pitched chamber with massive beams in walls and ceiling, and a broad, latticed window through which shone a pale gleam of wintry sunshine. Opposite the window, in a cavernous fireplace, a bright fire was making small, cheerful crackling noises, and faintly from beyond the tight-shut windows he could hear cattle lowing.

His puzzled glance roved over the unfamiliar scene, and he tried to think where he was and how he came to be there. His mind was still confused by the dreams which had troubled him in his delirium; he thought of Matthew, dead these seven years; of beautiful, coldhearted Catherine and his own dishonour; but through these tragic memories moved a figure which had no part in them, a girl with a sweet, calm face and clear blue eyes. Dorothea! His weary mind clung to the thought of her as to a guiding star. There was a curious vividness about his dream of her; he seemed to hear her voice, feel the cool touch of her hands. . . .

The sound of the latch lifting softly recalled him to the present. He could not see the door from where he lay, but knew a moment's mad conviction that it was Dorothea herself who had entered. Then footsteps approached the bed, a stout, grey-haired woman came into view, and he realized that his dream was but a dream after all.

The newcomer regarded him with evident satisfaction. "So you're awake at last, Mr. Forrest," she remarked.

"A fine fright you've given us these three days past, I must say, but praise be, 'tis over now." She nodded at him in motherly fashion, and turned to speak over her shoulder to an unseen companion. "Nell, go down to the kitchen and fetch a bowl of broth, as I bade you. Quick now, and no loitering!"

"Madam," said Kelvin as she came back to the bedside, and then paused, startled to discover that he could achieve no more than a feeble whisper. Mrs. Ashe smiled and shook her head.

"You're too weak yet to be talking, sir," she said. "You've no call to worry, for you're in good hands here, and there will be time enough later on for questions, but if you're wondering how I happen to know your name— why, 'twas in the little book you carried in your pocket."

He had been about to correct her concerning his name, but suddenly her mistake seemed to be of no importance. Later, when he felt equal to lengthy explanations, he could tell her the truth, but for the present a great lassitude had taken possession of him, and he was content to remain "Anthony Forrest."

Janet rearranged his pillows with capable hands, and presently, after he had swallowed some of the broth she had sent for, he fell asleep again. When he woke his mind was clearer and he would have liked to learn something of his benefactors, but the benevolent tyrant whom he had seen upon his first awakening, and who appeared to have the ordering of his existence, would permit him to ask no questions, bidding him wait until he was stronger. Having no choice, he obeyed, and between sleeping and waking lost all count of time, for sometimes when he woke the room was bright with day, and sometimes the curtains were drawn and the candles burning.

It was Mrs. Ashe who tended him during those first days of his recovery, for Dorothea, who had not spared herself until that recovery was reasonably assured, now yielded to Janet's commands and sought rest herself. She was quite worn out, and now, moreover, was conscious of a slight reluctance to encounter Mr. Forrest, and a shyness which she had not known while he was so desperately ill.

A slight sound which he could not immediately define roused Rainham from a deep slumber, and, turning his head to locate its source, he beheld a woman standing before the fire with her back towards him, while she lit the candles on the small table nearby. He blinked and looked again, for this was not his grey-haired nurse, nor even the plump maidservant whom he had occasionally seen, but a slender, graceful figure with heavy, raven hair. Kelvin's heart began to beat faster, his sound hand clenched suddenly upon the coverlet, and he told himself that he was either mad or dreaming. Then, while he stared, she turned, and through a golden haze of candle-light he saw the face which for months had been at the heart of his dearest dreams.

Startled and confused at finding him awake, she stood quite still, silently regarding him. The room was shadowy with approaching darkness save in that one spot where fire and candle-light shone around Dorothea, and to the sick man her motionless figure appeared unreal, framed in an aureole of light. The conviction came upon him that he was once more a prey to tantalising visions, and abruptly he turned his head away while a bitter murmur broke from his lips:

"Must I be dreaming yet? My God, is there to be no end to it?"

Came a light footfall, and then a cool touch upon his tight-clenched hand and a voice which said softly.

"Pray forgive me, Mr. Forrest. I fear I startled you."

Both voice and touch seemed real enough; was it possible that after all he was in his right senses? Slowly Kelvin's head turned once more, and he knew at last that this was no dream but a miraculous truth. She was here beside him, and looking at him with that in her eyes which he had, indeed, dreamed of seeing there, but had never thought to see in reality. His hand moved beneath hers, and closed about it, but his eyes never left her face.

"So it was no vision," he whispered. "You are Dorothea."

"Indeed, sir, that is my name, though I did not suppose you would remember . . ." the words faded away, and so for a space they were silent, looking into each other's eyes and knowing, with a supreme certainty which swept aside all barriers, that they were destined to love, and to be loved in return.

It was the man who first broke free from the spell of that enchanted moment, for a warning voice seemed to ring suddenly in his ears, reminding him that he must betray no previous knowledge of her if he wished to keep his real identity a secret. Slowly, reluctantly, his clasp upon her hand relaxed and he said, in a voice into which he tried to infuse a proper formality:

"Madam, I must make you my apologies. My mind is still confused, and I do not know where I am or how I came here, for the good soul whom I have seen ere this will tell me nothing, nor permit me to question her."

His words and manner helped her to recover something of her normal composure, and to dissemble the strange, wild gladness which was thrilling through her whole being. She shook her head.

"Sir, you have been very ill. Indeed, there was a time when we feared——" she broke off and made a little movement with her hands. "But happily that danger is past. You are at Gallows Farm, near Reppington in Kent, whither you were brought after being attacked by footpads. We found your horse wandering riderless and with blood on the saddle, one stormy night nearly a week since."

Her words supplied the clue his memory had been seeking, and he recalled the shot from among the trees, the dead man lying in the road, and his own struggle to reach the end of his quest. Remembering what the elder woman had said concerning his name, he realized that the shot which had nearly cost him his life had served him well after all—that, and his possession of the book bearing Anthony Forrest's signature. He realized, too, that if Dorothea discovered the truth while illness still held him prisoner at Gallows Farm, the situation would become intolerable, and that therefore he must continue to bear his involuntarily assumed name. It was a respite which he welcomed with heartfelt gratitude.

"May I inquire," he said at length, "the name of the good Samaritans who have given me sanctuary?"

"The farm belongs to Thomas Ashe," she replied, "and 'tis his wife, Janet, who has been nursing you."

"And yourself, madam?" he prompted, as she paused. "May I not know your full name?"

"I am Dorothea Stratton," she said quietly. "I, too, have found sanctuary at Gallows Farm." Her eyes grew thoughtful for a moment, and then he watched with delight as a smile, of which the portrait had held the merest promise, dawned about the lovely lines of her mouth. "Janet would berate me for permitting you to tax your strength by talking. She bade me tell her if you awoke, and I had best do so."

She went out of the room, leaving the sick man in a state of mind composed almost equally of pleasure and pain. To have found Dorothea, to see at last the shadowy figure of his beloved assume substance and reality, and stand before him a living, breathing woman, was a joy tempered by the knowledge that had she the least suspicion of his true identity the kindness in her voice and eyes would be banished for ever. Yet this knowledge he was able to thrust into the farthest recess of his mind and remember only that for the present at least he could see her and speak with her on equal terms. That he was thus preparing for himself a future hell he knew, but it seemed a small price to pay for his present happiness.

It was not until the following day that he saw Dorothea again, and then she came to his room to suggest that he might wish to send a message to his family and friends, who must surely be alarmed at his prolonged absence. Since he was unable to write himself, she offered to do so at his dictation, but Kelvin shook his head.

"I thank you for the thought, Miss Stratton, but I have no living relatives, and only one friend who is likely to feel concern that I do not return. I am a somewhat solitary creature, you see."

"You have friends here at Gallows Farm, sir," Dorothea replied, not looking at him, "if—if you so wish it."

"Can you think that I should wish otherwise?" His glance lingered lovingly on her averted face. "I can find no words to express my gratitude for the generosity and kindness I have met with from everyone here, and most of all from you. Mrs. Ashe has told me that it was your skill and care which saved my life; that you wore yourself out in nursing a stranger who had no claim upon you. I had forgotten—if, indeed, I ever knew—that such women as you exist."

Dorothea's eyes met his for a moment in a level, questioning glance, and then she looked away again. He has suffered, she thought, at the hands of some woman, and remembering the pain and horror of his delirious ravings, the question passed once more through her mind—who is Catherine? What has she done to hurt him so bitterly?

"Janet seeks to give me credit which she should share, sir," she said quietly, "but what little skill I have I used so very gladly. I like to believe that were my brother in similar straits he would find someone to do as much for him."

"Your brother?" The words gave him a stab of uneasiness, for he had wondered a little at the absence of Sir David Stratton. "He is at the farm?"

Dorothea shook her head.

"No, he is secretary to Sir Edward Amberstone, and has been living at his home in Hampshire since last autumn. He is not likely to return here for some time, I fear."

There was a regret in her voice which her companion could not share. After a little he said:

"Miss Stratton, is Gallows Farm your home?"

"It is now, Mr. Forrest," she said quietly, and was silent. Kelvin stifled a sigh.

"Forgive me," he said. "The question was impertinent."

"No," she looked at him, smiling somewhat ruefully. "There is no reason why you should not know the truth. Indeed, if you chanced to be in London last summer you may have heard the tale already, a tale of weakness and folly, which is not, I believe, so very singular. My brother, sir, is young and spoiled, and was extremely wealthy. Gaming was his ruling passion, he fell into evil company, and"—she shrugged—"the rest you may guess. In five nights of play he lost all he possessed to a man shrewd enough to perceive his weaknesses and callous enough to exploit them to the full."

As though the recollection was too disturbing to permit of her remaining still, she began to move restlessly about the room, and Kelvin's glance followed her with a look of undisguised distress. In spite of the pain it caused him, however, he felt impelled to pursue the matter further.

"You speak as though with knowledge of the man. Can it be that 'twas to one of his friends that your brother lost so much?"

She shook her head.

"No, it was a stranger whom David met in a gaming-hell he frequented. You will say, no doubt, that a man foolish enough to play so deep with a chance acquaintance deserves to be fleeced, though one who was present and whose judgment I have every reason to trust assures me that the game was above suspicion. Oh, but there are ways and ways of cheating! This Major Rainham, it seems, has a gift for bitter mockery, and he taunted and sneered at my poor David until he did not know what he was doing. A golden tongue, i'faith, that can mock its owner into possession of a fortune! And now David must eat his heart out in a menial employment, while Rainham dwells in his house and squanders his substance. The desire for vengeance is perhaps an unworthy one, but I confess that I would give much to make him regret the wrong he has done the Strattons."

She had spoken with deep feeling, and when she paused there was silence for a space. After a little she glanced at her companion, and was dismayed by what she saw in his white face.

"Mr. Forrest!" she exclaimed anxiously, and coming to the bedside caught his hand impulsively in her own. "I should not have spoken of it! Such melancholy subjects have no place in a sick-room, and this hateful tale has disturbed you. Oh, forgive me!"

"How you must hate him," he said in a stifled voice. "He has deprived you of so much. Could you ever forgive him for what he has made you suffer?"

She regarded him with troubled eyes, half afraid, from his expression and the convulsive grip of his hand upon hers, that he was suffering a recurrence of the fever.

"It is not easy to forgive a man who has robbed one of home and fortune to satisfy his own greed," she said. "I am happy enough here at the farm, but David is different and now he has an added reason——" she broke off, as though regretting that she had said so much, and studied him anxiously for a few seconds. "I should not have told you the story. Heaven knows 'tis not a pleasant one!"

"You could not forgive him!" Kelvin released her hand and sank back against the pillows. "To forgive the one who has ruined your life is well-nigh impossible. I know that only too well."

He turned his head to look from the window at the bare branches tossing in the wind, his face set in lines of such bitter hopelessness that she felt a sudden rush of tenderness and pity. She put out her hand towards him, but once again the question "who is Catherine?" rang in her ears, this time with a note of doubt and warning, and her hand dropped once more to her side. For a little longer she studied the stern, hard profile, and then with a tiny sigh she turned and went softly from the room.

When she had gone Kelvin lay for a long while without moving, a prey to very bitter thoughts. At last he sighed, and shifted a little in an effort to ease the pain of his injured shoulder.

"Make him regret the wrong he has done the Strattons," he said aloud. "Oh, my love, he regretted it long ago!"

CHAPTER IX

THE IMPOSTER

Kelvin's recovery was slow, for the murderous bullet had wrought havoc which refused to heal, and the pain of it was ever-present and often agonizing, yet in spite of physical suffering those weeks at Gallows Farm were the happiest he had ever known. Dorothea was with him constantly, at first with hands gentle and deft to ease his pain, and later, as time passed and he grew stronger, to beguile the time by reading to him or playing chess, for both were skilled players and Dorothea had brought a set of chessmen with her to the farm. Sometimes she would bring her sewing and, sitting in the chair before the fire, talk of the old days at Hope Stratton before her father's death, or fall into companionable silence with her dark head bent over her work, but glancing up now and then to meet his eyes with a smile that set his heart racing.

Occasionally she spoke of her present circumstances, and mention was made of the Lady Clarissa Spencer-wood. On several occasions Kelvin heard a merry, girlish voice in the house below, and knew that her ladyship was making one of her periodic visits, though not until he was strong enough to leave his bed and sit for awhile in the cushioned chair beside the window did he catch a glimpse of this light-hearted lady. By that time the days had lengthened, the first green of spring-time was upon the trees, and the high-pitched bleating of lambs penetrated now and then to his room, and one bright afternoon when Kelvin was seated thus he saw Dorothea and another girl walking in the garden below. They were engrossed in conversation, apparently concerning the letter which Miss Stratton held in her hand, but as they passed beneath his window Dorothea looked up and smiled. Her companion also raised her head, and he saw a vivid, heart-shaped face and large brown eyes, wearing now an expression of the liveliest curiosity. He bowed as well as he could from a sitting position and she dimpled responsively. Lady Clarissa, it was clear, affected none of the mannerisms of a lady of fashion.

That evening he and Dorothea sat facing each other across the chess-board, but it soon became apparent that Miss Stratton's mind was not upon the game. She made her moves quite at random and eventually fell into a reverie, her hands lying idle in her lap and her eyes fixed upon the fire before which they sat. For a while Kelvin remained silent, content to watch the play of light and shadow upon her face, storing up yet another memory to be a torment and a consolation in the empty future. At last she sighed, and her gaze wandered once more to her companion. For an instant she regarded him blankly, and then a look of consternation came over her face and she glanced quickly at the neglected chess-board.

"Oh!" she said guiltily. "Pray forgive me! I fear I am poor company tonight."

He smiled and shook his head.

"The game is of no importance," he assured her, and paused, looking searchingly at her face. "Something is troubling you, is it not?"

"Yes," Dorothea's clear gaze lifted once more to meet his, "but I am sorry that you should have perceived it. I have no wish to burden you with my troubles."

"To share a trouble is surely to lessen the burden,"

he said gently. "May I not have an opportunity to help you, who have done so much for me?"

"If any help were possible———" she broke off, running a finger along the edge of the chess-board and seeming to deliberate within herself. At length she said abruptly: " 'Twas Lady Clarissa whom you saw with me in the garden today. She is to be married shortly."

"Married?" Kelvin was half amused, half incredulous. "But surely she is only a child?"

Dorothea smiled ruefully.

"Clarissa is sixteen, though I own she looks younger. She was betrothed as a child and her marriage should have taken place this spring, but was postponed owing to her mother's ill-health."

She paused again, seeming to find some difficulty in continuing; after a little Kelvin said quietly:

"May I hazard the guess that Lady Clarissa is not entirely happy in her betrothal?"

Dorothea nodded.

"You are quite right, though she was, if not happy, at least resigned, until she and my brother met. Now they are desperately in love with one another." She looked up at him a trifle anxiously. "You understand, of course, that only we three were aware of this, and that no one else must ever suspect the truth?" He nodded without speaking, and as though reassured she continued with less constraint in her voice. "There is no hope that they can ever marry. David is entirely dependent upon his post with Sir Edward Amberstone, and Sir Edward is the uncle of the man to whom Clarissa is betrothed. He is determined upon the marriage, and if David did anything to prevent it he would never forgive him. Clarissa is breaking her heart over it, and David———" she moved her hands helplessly. "His letters are full of wild threats and promises. He vows that he will marry her out of hand, and I fear that he is capable of even that folly. Clarissa, too, for all her sweetness, is wilful and headstrong, and she would not refuse him. The fact that they would be penniless would weigh with neither until it was too late."

She paused and looked at Kelvin, who sat with his

frowning gaze bent upon the chessman which he was twirling between the fingers of his sound hand. Feeling her gaze upon him, he said quietly:

"I think you are unduly fearful, Miss Stratton. Your brother may threaten, but if he truly loves Lady Clarissa he will scarcely marry her if he cannot support her."

Dorothea sighed.

"I wish I could believe that. Unfortunately, David encountered Lord Jevington, whom she is to marry, when we were in London, and he declares that his life is notoriously evil, in spite of his youth. I do not know how much of that is truth, and how much unreasoning jealousy, but 'tis not like David to make such an accusation without some justification."

"But if it is so," suggested Kelvin, "is it not possible that he is right, and that Lady Clarissa would be safer and happier with him, even though they would be poor?"

Dorothea shook her head.

"How can you say so? She has never known poverty."

The grey eyes lifted suddenly to meet hers.

"Forgive me, Miss Stratton, but I believe that until very recently you had no such knowledge either."

"Oh, but I have been very fortunate, sir. I have found a home here, but David and Clarissa would have no such haven. Oh, if only they could have met a year ago! She has brought out the best in him as I never succeeded in doing; his love for her might have been his salvation, but if he loses her I fear 'twill prove his ultimate undoing." Her voice broke, and she put one hand over her eyes. "If only I knew what to do for the best!"

Kelvin leaned forward and laid his hand over hers where it rested upon the chess-board.

"My dear," he said gently, "must it always be upon your shoulders that the burden falls? Your brother is not a child. Leave him to work out his own salvation as best he may." Her hand fell away, and startled blue eyes were raised to his. He smiled and shook his head. "You cannot keep him tied to your apron-strings for ever."

Dorothea withdrew her hand from his, stood up, and moved away from the table, restraining him from rising also by a light pressure upon his shoulder as she passed his chair. She walked to the window and back again, while he wondered whether his words had mortally offended her. At length she said:

"I had never before regarded it in that light. David is wild and thoughtless and I have tried to be wise for both of us, but perhaps you are right." She sighed, and came back to her chair; across the table her eyes met his candidly, with a glimmer of rueful humour. "In fact, sir, you recommend me to mind my own business?"

"I trust I was not guilty of such discourtesy," he replied, smiling, "but I have observed that intervention in such matters, no matter how selfless the motive which prompts it, is rarely welcomed." He studied her for a moment in silence, and then added more seriously: "Do not, I beg of you, disturb yourself too greatly over your brother's unconsidered words. 'Tis unlikely, I think, that he will carry out his threats."

"I hope not, indeed," Dorothea replied, "for such madness, I am sure, could not end well. Of course, if he were still master of Hope Stratton he might carry her off and brave Lord Ardely's anger, which probably would not be of long duration. As it is——" she sighed, and pain and bitterness deepened in her voice. "I ask myself what malignant fate sent Major Rainham across my brother's path. Were there no others? Could he not have chosen his victim elsewhere? I wonder sometimes what manner of man he is, cold-bloodedly to fill his pockets careless of the grief he was bringing upon others. David tried to kill himself that morning, but would Rainham have cared if he had? No, for he had possessed himself of lands and gold and what matter if the cost were a man's life? I think he must be a man without pity and without honour."

Scarcely aware of what he was doing, Kelvin had picked up the chessman again and now sat with his fingers clenched about it and his head bent, while every word she uttered dealt him a fresh blow. When she paused he heard himself say, in a voice he hardly recognized as his own:

"It may be that the riches he won from your brother

have proved a curse to him rather than the blessing he thought them at the time."

He looked up at her as he spoke, and saw her face harden into an expression of such implacable bitterness that he felt a stab of pain sharper than all the rest. He felt, too, the intolerable falseness of his present situation, and yet knew, even while he despised his own cowardice, that he could not yet find the strength to tell her the truth.

"If there is any justice in the world," said Dorothea at length, in a clear, cold voice which struck utter hopelessness into his heart, "the fortune which Kelvin Rainham won from my brother will prove his own ultimate damnation. I hope with all my heart that it may be so."

By the time that Clarissa paid her next visit to the farm Major Rainham's health had improved sufficiently for him to leave the room to which illness had confined him for so long. His left arm, supported in a sling, was still useless, and any but the slightest exertion tried his strength to the uttermost, but he knew that the time was approaching when he would no longer have any excuse for lingering at the farm. One day he referred tentatively to his departure, but Mrs. Ashe told him sharply that there was to be no such nonsense thought of yet awhile. She would not permit his recklessness to undo the results of weeks of careful nursing; Mr. Forrest would remain at Gallows Farm until his wound was completely healed. Dorothea said nothing, but her eyes told him more clearly than any words that she wished him to stay, and he did not know whether gladness or shame predominated in his heart as he met that clear and loving gaze.

He reflected sometimes, almost with wonder, upon the manner in which he had been accepted by the inhabitants of Gallows Farm, and at his own contentment at being there. It was not merely Dorothea's presence which inspired that inner happiness, for in his feelings for her pleasure and pain were so inextricably tangled that it was a constant torment. Yet content he was, in a way that he had never before known; always there had dwelt within him a demon of restlessness, driving him on in a search for some indefinable happiness, which he had found at last at this quiet farm among the Kentish orchards. To live out his life there, with Dorothea by his side; to assume his own identity once more, and, sweeping away for ever the shadowy figure of the Anthony Forrest who had never existed, make her the wife of Kelvin Rainham, was the dream which hovered ever before his dazzled eyes, the tantalizing vision of a Paradise which the beggar on horseback might never attain.

Yet, with an irony which served only to intensify his pain, the dream might not, but for the one insuperable barrier, have been impossible of fulfilment. As his health improved Kelvin spent much time in conversation with Thomas Ashe, and, each recognizing in the other qualities to be admired, there grew up between them a friendship such as the younger man had so rarely known. From these talks Kelvin learned that the future of Gallows Farm was causing its owner some uneasiness, for Thomas, the last of his family, was growing old, and had no one to succeed him. He would gladly have left it to his stepson, but Will was unfitted by nature to become the master of so large a property, and though Ashe liked the Strattons well enough he knew that Sir David would never consent to become a farmer, and his sister could not manage the place alone. Of course, said Thomas, if Miss Dorothea were to marry—he glanced under his brows at Kelvin, and so was silent, puffing at his long clay pipe.

Yes, it would have been so simple, had he been still the wandering soldier-of-fortune, but the cards which had made him a rich man had robbed him of every chance of happiness. The acquisition of that fortune had raised a barrier between himself and Dorothea as surely as its loss stood between Sir David Stratton and the lady of his choice. It was an impasse from which he could see no road of escape for either couple.

It was on a grey, gusty afternoon in early April, an afternoon of sudden showers and fugitive gleams of sunshine, that Lady Clarissa came again to Gallows Farm.

Dorothea went out to greet her and presently brought her into the parlour, where she and Kelvin had been sitting until her ladyship's arrival. He got up as they entered, and stood, very tall and erect in the low-pitched room, while Dorothea performed the necessary introduction.

Clarissa acknowledged his bow in an unwontedly subdued manner, a trifle disconcerted at finding herself face to face at last with the stranger who had been an unseen presence at the farm for so many weeks, and who occupied so prominent a place in her friend's thoughts. Also, country-bred as she was, she was a trifle daunted by the formality of his manner and the faintly mocking expression in the fine, stern face. Perceiving her shyness, and amused by it, he looked down at her with that smile, too rarely seen, which so transformed his face; Clarissa, reassured, smiled confidingly back at him, and so set the seal upon a friendship which was never afterwards in doubt. Her ladyship suffered no recurrence of her early diffidence, while for his part Major Rainham had no difficulty in understanding why Sir David Stratton had fallen in love with this fascinating child. It showed, he thought, unexpected good taste on Stratton's part.

"I like Mr. Forrest," Clarissa announced when next she and Dorothea were alone, "but I think that when he is not smiling he looks as though he was once very unhappy."

Dorothea said nothing, but remembering the agony and torment of those hours of delirium, she knew that Clarissa's instinct was not at fault. Some dark shadow lay across his life, and she had no means of knowing what it was, but the thought of it was a brooding fear which went beside her day and night.

"There's no doubt, however, that he is happy here," pursued Clarissa. "Oh, Dorothea, 'tis so romantic! First you saved his life, and then—now pray do not try to pretend you do not know what I mean! I have seen how he looks at you, and you do the same when you think no one is watching."

"You see a deal too much, my child," Miss Stratton

told her severely, though with twinkling eyes, "and imagine a great deal more."

"I have imagined none of it," said Clarissa indignantly. "Do you think I do not understand?" The big, brown eyes clouded suddenly, the expressive lips quivered. "Oh, Dorothea, for your sake I hope that your love may be happier than mine!"

Major Rainham was sitting on a fallen log halfway up the slope of the apple-orchard. Above his head, drifts of blossom which ranged in colour from the deep crimson of unopened buds to the delicate pink of full-blown flowers almost obscured the cloudless April sky, and the young grass beneath his feet was scattered with daisies. A short way off, two lambs, orphaned at birth and reared by hand by Dorothea, were playing together after the ridiculous fashion of their kind.

He had been sitting there for a long time, his troubled gaze taking no account of the pleasant prospect around him, but dropping now and again to the book in his hand, a stained, leather-bound volume which, open at the fly-leaf, disclosed the scrawled signature of the friend who had destroyed his honour and saved his life, and who now lent him his name to cloak his true identity in a house where his own name was a thing accursed. Kelvin was not sure whether he was glad or sorry for that unwitting deception. It had granted him the inestimable privilege of acquaintance with Dorothea, but it had also imposed upon him a duty from which he shrank more and more as the need for it increased.

She must be told the truth. Somehow he must find the courage to confess his sin, and the strength of will not to plead for forgiveness. She would be angry, of course, angry and disgusted at the deception practised upon her by the man who had already brought poverty and humiliation upon her family, and he must fan that anger into a blaze which would consume any tender feelings she entertained for him. It should not, he thought wretchedly, be beyond the power of the tongue which had already mocked the brother out of possession of a fortune, to mock the sister out of love.

He fetched a sigh as he looked down the hillside towards the farmhouse, barely discernible through the clouds of blossom. Even had it not enshrined all that was dearest to him, he would have been loth to leave it, for in doing so he must leave so much that he had come to prize. The friendship of Thomas Ashe, with his downright honesty and common sense and deep, unspoken love of the rich land he farmed, a love which Kelvin, to his own surprise, was beginning to share. The motherly kindness which Janet's sharp tongue concealed, the gaiety of Clarissa, the easy comradeship of her brother Andrew— all were part of the strange enchantment of Gallows Farm, an enchantment which had at its heart Dorothea, serene and lovely and for ever unattainable.

He closed the book and sat looking down at its faded cover, a certain grimness about his mouth. He must delay no longer, for he was now strong enough to make the journey to London, and every day he lingered, lacking the excuse of sickness, deepened the morass of treachery and dishonour in which he was sinking. At the first favourable opportunity he would confess the truth, accept his dismissal, and go.

The resolve taken, he thrust the book into his pocket and looked once more towards the house. Then he sat very still, a cold dread tightening about his heart, for the opportunity was no longer in some indefinite future, but here and now. Up the flowery hillside, through sunlight and shadow beneath the blossoming branches, Dorothea was coming towards him. Her head was bare, she wore a simple gown of a blue that matched her eyes, and she was laughing as she came, for the two lambs, recognizing their benefactress, were leaping towards her with joyful bleats, to thrust themselves against her skirts like fawning puppies.

She reached at last the man who stood watching her beside the log from which he had risen, but something in his face checked the laughing greeting upon her lips. Kelvin knew what he must say—"Miss Stratton, it is time you knew the truth about me. My name is not Anthony Forrest. I am Kelvin Rainham, the man who wrought your brother's ruin." The words, abrupt and brutal, were in his mind, but his lips refused to utter them. So for a space they faced each other in silence beneath the apple trees, while a breath of wind stirred among the boughs, a handful of petals fluttered like tinted snowflakes about them, and the lambs continued to utter their plaintive, high-pitched plea.

"Dorothea," he said at last, and in his voice was passion and tenderness and desperate longing, overlaid by a note of unutterable pain. Almost of its own volition his hand went out towards her, and wordlessly, in answer to that desolate cry, she went into his arms and surrendered her lips to his.

"Anthony," she whispered tenderly, "beloved!" and, her cheek against his, did not see the sudden agony in his eyes at the sound of the murmured name. Even through the ecstasy of that moment he was aware of the searing knowledge that it was not to Kelvin Rainham that she came in such sweet surrender; dishonestly had he won her love, and betrayed her into a confession of it which must be her abiding shame when she learned the truth. Years before, his name had been stained beyond repair, and later, for friendship's sake, he had publicly branded himself a cheat, but it was now, on this sunlit morning among the apple-blossoms, that, secretly as a traitor should, he tasted for the first time the bitterness of deserved dishonour.

CHAPTER X

CONFLICT

The fire which burned in the mighty fireplace of the parlour at Gallows Farm was blazing merrily, its cheerful light dispelling the gloom which a grey and cloudy evening had induced in the low-roofed chamber. On a small table before it, chessmen were scattered about their chequered board, but the game had been abandoned and the players now sat side by side on the settle to the right of the hearth, Dorothea encircled by Kelvin's arm, her head against his shoulder and her hand in his.

Two days had passed since the open avowal of their love, days in which she had waited with serene confidence for him to tell her of the trouble which oppressed him. That he was troubled a less perceptive eye than Dorothea's could easily discover, and she could only suppose that something in his past life raised a barrier between them. Even now she knew so little about him, who he was or whence he came, and in the circumstances it was not surprising that she should remember the secret hinted at in his fevered ravings, and the woman's name so angrily, contemptuously spoken. Who was

Catherine, and what claim had she upon him? The thought had become a torment to her, and though she had not meant to force an explanation from him, she felt that she could endure her doubts and fears no longer.

She sighed, and stirred a little in his arms, and with her troubled gaze still upon the leaping flames said softly:

"Anthony, who is Catherine?"

There was an instant's pause, and then he answered her question with another.

"What do you know of Catherine, Dorothea?"

"You spoke her name often in your fever. Once you fancied that I was she, and bade me leave you in peace, for I could harm you no more." She drew away from him a little and met his gaze squarely. "Will you not tell me, Anthony? Have I not the right to know?"

He looked at her, the shadow deepening in his eyes.

"Yes, you have the right. Catherine was my brother's affianced wife, a woman with the face of an angel and the soul of—but no, Catherine possessed neither heart nor soul! Beneath her beauty was only greed and vanity and a calculating ruthlessness."

He told her then the story in which Catherine had played so prominent a part, and which never before had he confided to another, for even Mrs. Cheriton had garnered the tale from various sources, and almost forced Rainham to fill in the gaps with bald facts baldly told. But to Dorothea he spoke freely, finding an immeasurable relief in voicing at last the agony of remorse which had haunted him for seven years, and the bitter, unspoken anger against the injustice of which he had been a victim.

Sitting with her hand still in his, Dorothea listened appalled to the story of the ruin wrought by a woman's vanity and spite. She made no comment as the tale progressed, but watched his face with tender, pitying eyes, and because she loved him she saw even more than he intended, and realized how great had been his suffering. A proud, lonely man, of deep passions sternly repressed, had shaped an austere and empty life to a high ideal of duty and of honour, sacrificing to it all gentler emotions, and upon that stainless name had been cast the mire of public disgrace and infamy—it was small wonder, she thought, that the sensitive nature had grown warped and bitter.

"No sooner was the deed done beyond recall," he concluded in a low, strained voice, "than I began to regret it. Regret grew into remorse, until I would have given anything I possessed, even to life itself, to undo the harm I had done. I knew then that I had been faced with the most momentous decision of my life, and that I had failed the test."

"Could you have saved them, Anthony?" Dorothea asked quietly, and Kelvin's sombre gaze transferred itself to her face in faint surprise. "Had you not arrested them," she repeated, "would it have been possible to arrange their escape, to place them beyond all danger?"

"No," he replied slowly, somewhat bewildered, "Matthew was in no state to attempt escape, and my parents would never have left him. Moreover, the men under my command knew him for a rebel, and would have given the alarm at the first opportunity."

"Then wherein lay the choice? Surely, only if it had lain between ordering their arrest and giving them complete freedom would you have been justified in neglecting your duty. Someone else would have been sent to take them, and might well have used them, and the women also, with unnecessary violence. Oh, my dear, do you not see that even had you spared them the end would have been the same?"

She paused to regard him searchingly, but he made no reply; after a little she continued earnestly:

"To save their lives no price could have been too great to pay, but you could not have saved them. You would have betrayed your trust and flung your life away in a futile, heroic gesture which accomplished nothing."

"Better that, could I have found the courage to do it, than to step into their shoes and inherit Rivenoak. That is the doubt which most torments me—how much was my decision influenced by thought of self?"

Dorothea shook her head.

"Did you then gain so much? You knew, when you chose to follow the path of duty, how such an act must be regarded by the world. Was it so much easier to face that than to make the useless, flamboyant gesture, and go with them to the gallows?"

There was a pause. The fire crackled, a sudden scurry of raindrops pattered against the window, and Dorothea's low-voiced question hung upon the silence. But in Kelvin's mind an answer to it was taking shape, as he realized with dawning wonder that what she said was true. Death would have been preferable to the hell he had endured, the hell of secret remorse and public disgrace, and voluntarily to brand himself a traitor rather than send his father and brother to certain execution would, in the eyes of the world, have been a splendid folly to excite indulgence and admiration.

"Dorothea," he said uncertainly, and bore her hand to his lips, "my lady of comfort! For the first time since that accursed day I know some measure of consolation."

She smiled, and touched the bowed auburn head with her free hand.

"Perhaps it is the first time that the whole story has been told," she said gently. "When only half the truth is known there can be neither understanding nor comfort." Then her eyes clouded suddenly and she shivered. "But I pray Heaven that no such decision may ever be asked of me! I think my heart would break if ever I had to choose between David and you."

"If ever I had to choose!" The words pierced him like a sword, for he knew that such a choice would face her as soon as he revealed his true identity unless, indeed, her anger and humiliation were great enough to turn her completely against him. Almost he hoped that it might be so, if in that way he could make reparation for the wrong he had done, but it was not in his power, he reflected bitterly, to spare her the pain which such a disclosure must provoke, for Dorothea's was not a nature to love lightly. All that he could do was to tell her as gently as may be, and trust that time, and the scorn with which she must inevitably regard him, would heal the wound he dealt; tell her now, before his resolution had time to waver again.

"Dorothea," he began huskily, and then realized that

she was not attending to him. Recalled from his pre-occupation, he became aware of a sound which for some minutes had been threading the silence, the sound of approaching hoofbeats. He paused, for the rider might possibly be Clarissa, and he had no desire that their privacy should be invaded while he was in the midst of his confession.

The hoofbeats grew suddenly louder as the rider rounded the last bend; they rang upon the cobbles before the farmhouse door, and Thomas's voice spoke in surprised greeting; a masculine voice answered him, and Dorothea pulled her hand from Kelvin's and started to her feet.

"David!" she exclaimed, and stood a moment, with clasped hands and parted lips, listening to the familiar, well-loved tones. Then, adding joyfully: "'Tis my brother!" she ran towards the door.

"Dorothea!" There was urgency in Kelvin's voice and something more, a note almost of fear, but the cry fell upon deaf ears. She had already left the room; he heard her light footsteps receding across the stone-flagged hall, and her voice calling her brother's name, and with sheer horror sweeping over him buried his face in his hands.

He was on his feet, however, erect and white-faced in the firelight, when Sir David Stratton entered the room. He came in laughing, with his arm about his sister's waist, but the laughter died on his lips as he caught sight of Rainham. An instant he stood at gaze, and then with a crashing oath sprang forward and seized him by the throat.

Dorothea cried out, but before either she or Thomas, who had followed them into the house, could intervene, the brief struggle was over. David's first attack sent Kelvin staggering back against a great carved press, taking the whole force of the impact on his injured shoulder, but next moment, in spite of the intense pain of the blow, he succeeded in breaking Stratton's hold and thrusting him away. The younger man stumbled and clutched at the settle to save himself, while Kelvin, who had felt his wound reopen with a sickening wrench of agony, remained leaning against the press, grey-faced and with sweat standing on his brow. Dorothea ran to him and caught his sound arm in both hands.

"David, are you mad?" she cried angrily. "Anthony—"

"Stand away from him, Dorothea, you have been deceived," her brother panted, and then rounded in furious mockery upon Kelvin. "My God, Rainham, was it not enough to take our home and fortune, that you must have also a Stratton for your bride? Or do I flatter you in supposing your intentions honourable?"

"Rainham?" Dorothea whispered, and her hands fell away from him, while Thomas—and Janet, who had come from the kitchen at the sound of David's voice— stood silent and dismayed in the background.

"Aye, Rainham!" Stratton gibed savagely. "Major Kelvin Rainham, now of Hope Stratton, late of devil knows where! The gallant Major, who waits until my back is turned before he comes crawling under a false name to dishonour my sister!" He took a pace forward, and the mockery died out of his voice, leaving only anger. "Get out of my sight, you damned, cheating cur, and when you are sound again we'll settle this matter in the only possible way!"

Kelvin had neither moved nor spoken throughout David's furious tirade, for sheer physical pain possessed him to the exclusion of all else. He had instinctively thrust his left arm behind him when he felt a slow trickle of blood creeping down it, but only the support of the press had prevented him from slipping to the floor. Now, however, he was becoming aware of his surroundings again. David's insults he had scarcely heard, but Dorothea's pale face, stunned and horrified, seemed to float before his eyes, and the little, gasping cry with which she had greeted her brother's disclosure would sound in his ears, he thought, to his dying day. He saw Janet come forward and put her arms about the girl, and with an effort he stood upright and moved towards the door. There was nothing more to do or to say. The brief, bitter-sweet idyll was over.

Pride kept his head erect and his step firm as he went out of the room, and because of this, his dark-coloured coat and the dim light, none of his companions suspected the extent of his injury. In the hall, where for a moment he paused dazedly, Thomas came, grim-faced, to join him.

"You'd best be off, Major Rainham," he said gruffly. "Go to the inn at Reppington, and I'll have your gear sent to you there. Sir David's ripe for murder, and I can't say I blame him." He became aware of the other's pallor and gripped him by the arm, his voice changing. "Why, man, what ails you? Are you hurt?"

"My shoulder—I struck it," Kelvin replied with difficulty, "but 'tis no matter. For God's sake, Tom, let me go! Contempt and anger I can bear, but not pity."

Reluctantly Ashe released his grip, and Kelvin crossed the hall with uncertain steps and went out. Thomas watched him with troubled eyes, and then, sighing and shaking his head, he turned away.

Kelvin crossed the yard over ground which rocked curiously beneath his feet, and stumbled rather than walked into the pungent gloom of the stables. Will, busy with Sir David's horse, stared at him blankly.

"Will you saddle my horse for me, Will?" Kelvin clutched at the wall to steady himself and tried to focus his gaze upon the other's bewildered face, which seemed to grow and dwindle in the midst of a swirling mist. After a moment he felt Will's great hand beneath his elbow and heard his puzzled voice inquire:

"What's amiss, sir? Be 'ee ill?"

"I am well enough. The horse, Will, quickly!" Kelvin spoke impatiently, and with another dubious look at him Will went to do his bidding, leaving Major Rainham to cling to the wall and pray that his strength would not desert him before he succeeded in leaving the farm. After what seemed a very long time Will brought his mount and assisted him into the saddle, repeating his anxious, bewildered question. Kelvin, his left arm hanging useless by his side, gathered the reins into his right hand and with no word of answer or farewell rode out of the yard, while Will gaped after him in consternation. Where the Major had stood to await his horse the ground was flecked here and there with blood.

In the parlour Sir David Stratton took up his stand before the fire and gave vent to his feelings in a stream of profanity until Janet sharply bade him desist.

"Have some respect for your sister, Sir David," she told him bluntly, and then, bending over the chair in which she had placed Dorothea, added gently: "There, there, my lamb! What you need is a cordial to restore you, and I have just such a one in the still-room. Bide quietly there while I fetch it."

She went briskly away, leaving brother and sister alone. Dorothea sat very still in the high-backed chair, her hands inert against its dark, carved wood, her eyes closed and her face a pale mask of utter desolation. Her brother's brutal revelation of Rainham's identity had struck her with stunning force, but now the merciful numbness was passing and she felt the first stirrings of the agony which was presently to engulf her.

Her brother, silenced by Janet's uncompromising words, regarded her morosely. His unexpected return had been prompted by a letter from his friend Andrew Spencerwood, which had hinted, discreetly enough, that it might perhaps be prudent for David to make the acquaintance of the gentleman now staying at Gallows Farm. Mr. Forrest, Andrew suggested, was a somewhat mysterious individual; he appeared to have neither family nor friends, and though looks and bearing betokened the gentleman, and he was apparently blessed with an abundance of the world's goods, he practised concerning his personal affairs a reticence amounting almost to secrecy. From his own observation, and more particularly from remarks which his sister had let fall, Mr. Spencerwood feared that Miss Stratton's affections were already engaged; Sir David, studying now her white, unheeding face, from which all its habitual tranquillity had vanished, deemed the fear more than justified.

"God's death!" he said violently at last, to break that lengthy silence, "is the rogue insatiable? The Stratton lands, the Stratton fortune, and now the Stratton honour! I trust, however, that I come in time to frustrate that last, base design?"

"David!" Dorothea's eyes remained closed, and the

141

words broke from her in a strangled whisper. "Dear Heaven, have you no pity? Can you indeed believe that of me?"

A sudden spasm of pain crossed his face, for beneath his outward selfishness he loved her dearly, and he remembered, too, the comfort she had given him in the hour of his trouble. Now it was she who stood in need of comfort. He went to her and drew her up out of the chair and into his arms.

"My dear, I would as soon believe ill of a saint in Heaven, and though I am angry God knows it is not with you." He set a hand beneath her chin and turned her face towards him, studying it with troubled eyes. "Had I paused to consider I would not have blurted out his name in that fashion, but when I recognized him it drove every other thought out of my head."

"You cannot be blamed, David," she replied, and because she had always sought to spare him she strove now to dissemble the extent of her suffering. "I am well enough now. 'Twas the shock of it which so distressed me. To learn that he is Kelvin Rainham . . ." she freed herself from his clasp and went towards the fire, repeating the last words beneath her breath. Even now her mind could not quite accept the truth. Anthony Forrest, whom she loved, and Kelvin Rainham, whom she hated, one and the same—no, that was not quite true, for Anthony Forrest did not exist. She was conscious of David's eyes upon her, and because she felt the need to be doing something she began to lay the chessmen away in their box, until the thought of the man who of late had so often handled them stabbed her heart with fresh realisation of her loss. One could love and hate simultaneously, it seemed.

David came and sat on the settle close to the fire and regarded his sister dubiously. He was no longer so certain that Andrew Spencerwood's suspicion was justified; Dorothea seemed to have recovered her normal serenity, and as for the emotion she had betrayed earlier, well, it was no small thing to discover that the man whom she had nursed through a serious illness was the scoundrel responsible for her family's fallen fortunes. Once more he blamed himself for the manner in which he had made the disclosure, and for the ugly violence of the scene she had witnessed.

Janet came back with the cordial and stood over Dorothea while she drank it, though, as she told Thomas afterwards, no draught ever distilled had the power to heal a broken heart. She was not deceived by Miss Stratton's outward calm; it was, she knew, a cloak instinctively assumed to conceal a mortal hurt.

Her glance fell upon Sir David, lounging with one foot on the settle and his arm resting on his bent knee, and she eyed him with disfavour. What was amiss, she asked, that he must needs come home so suddenly and with no word of warning, and set the whole household in an uproar?

He told her, and added indignantly that had he known that the wounded stranger they had made so much of was his own worst enemy, foisting himself upon them under an assumed name, he would have returned long ago. Mrs. Ashe was not impressed.

"Your worst enemy is yourself, Sir David," she told him roundly, "and as for Major Rainham, poor soul, he was in no case to be foisting himself on anybody when we brought him here. We found a book with the name 'Anthony Forrest' in it in his pocket, and it never occurred to any of us to ask him whether it was his name or not."

David scowled, and brushed some dried mud from his coat.

"Oh, I can see that you are both vastly taken with the rogue, but I suppose I should have expected that. 'Tis of a piece with his reputation. Ashton tells me that when Rainham was in London last year half the fine ladies in town were his for the asking." He glanced sidelong at Dorothea as he spoke to mark the effect of his words. "He's a cold-blooded devil, though, and 'tis said there was only one woman he ever wanted, and that he sent his own brother to the gallows to reach her. But I must tell you the whole story! 'Tis a pretty tale, and ends with our fine Major being cashiered."

Dorothea rose suddenly to her feet, and there was

a suppressed violence in the movement, but when she spoke her voice was quiet and untroubled and only Janet remarked the little quiver of pain running through it.

"Forgive me, David, but I do not wish to hear any more of the matter. It has been a great shock to me, and I fear I need time to accustom myself to the thought that for all these weeks we have extended hospitality to Major Rainham." She turned to Mrs. Ashe, and the elder woman flinched from the stark agony in her eyes. "Janet, your cordial is making me feel absurdly sleepy. I think I had better go to bed."

Mrs. Ashe, who knew that that particular draught had no such effect, patted her hand and said that it was the best thing to do, but David was inclined to be put out.

"But, Dorothea," he protested, in tones distinctly aggrieved, "you cannot go to bed yet. There are matters I wish to discuss with you. Private matters," he added, lest she should be in any doubt of his meaning.

"David, I will discuss anything you like tomorrow," Dorothea was perilously near the end of her endurance, and in spite of her resolution there was a ragged edge of hysteria to her voice, "but for Heaven's sake leave me alone tonight!"

She went quickly out of the room, but when Mrs. Ashe would have followed her David, his suspicions reviving, gripped her by the arm.

"Janet," he said urgently, "she has not really grown fond of that fellow, has she?"

Janet's lips tightened. She could never bring herself to regard Sir David as anything more than a remarkably troublesome boy, and at that moment he was decidedly out of favour with her, for she had become attached to the quiet stranger who had lain ill in her house for so many weeks.

"That's not for for me to say, Sir David," she replied shortly. "You should know your own sister better than I do."

The answer did not please him. He suspected her of prevarication, and swung petulantly away to the fireside again.

"I know one thing, at least," he said over his shoulder.

"She'll not let sentiment blind her to that trickster's true worth now that she knows him for what he is. She has enough of the Stratton pride, thank Heaven, to prevent her from making a fool of herself."

Janet looked at him, opened her mouth to make some comment, and then thought better of it and turned away. The sound of the door being closed with a hint of violence informed David that he was alone, and he swore beneath his breath. This homecoming was not at all as he had pictured it.

Janet found Dorothea in her bedchamber, standing dry-eyed and silent beside the window. She went to her and put her arms around her, but there was no response; the girl stood motionless, and in her still, white face only her eyes seemed alive.

Mrs. Ashe was frightened, for this dumb agony was something she could not comprehend. Comfort or advice she would gladly have given, but Dorothea asked for neither, and not even Janet's deep affection could make any impression on her frozen calm. She yielded passively to her ministrations, allowed herself to be undressed and tucked into bed, and obediently swallowed the hot posset which Janet presently brought her, but her actions were mechanical and her spirit seemed to have passed into some dark realm where no one could follow. Only once did she speak, and then she said in a quiet, lifeless voice which brought tears to the elder woman's eyes:

"Why did he not tell me himself? Surely he would have told me, had David not come back so soon."

"There, there, my pet, of course he would," Janet said reassuringly, but Dorothea did not seem to hear. Mrs. Ashe sighed and shook her head, and, drawing the curtains close about the bed, went quietly away, hoping that in a little while the shock would pass and reaction bring the blessed relief of tears.

Alone in a little world of pain, Dorothea lay staring into the darkness while the tide of anguish which will-power had hitherto held in check swept over her at last. She gave no credence to David's insinuation that Rainham had deliberately sought her out; she believed that fate had played a cruel trick upon them both in sending him

145

into her life wounded and stricken, with evidence about him which suggested that he was other than he was. She did not even blame him, since she perceived the reason for it, for continuing the deception—until these past two days. Then, surely, he could have told her. Had he ever intended to do so? It was a question to which she would never know the answer.

Through the leaden-paced hours of that dreadful night she lay awake, while upon the darkness pictures formed and vanished and formed again, memories of the past weeks which acquired new significance in the light of her present knowledge; incidents which had puzzled her at the time and had been forgotten, but which now became hideously clear. Kelvin Rainham, the callous opportunist, the bitter-tongued gambler who had ruined her brother for his own profit; Kelvin Rainham, disillusioned and lonely, haunted by the tragic past, whom she loved as she had loved no man before and—she knew it instinctively—would never love again. Two images that seemed irreconcilable; two men, so utterly dissimilar, who yet were one and the same.

With the first grey glimmerings of dawn sheer exhaustion caused her to fall into a dream-haunted slumber, from which she awoke some hours later heavy-eyed and unrefreshed. The thick curtains surrounding the bed shut her into stuffy darkness, but when she stretched out a listless hand and twitched them apart she was dazzled by a blaze of morning sunshine.

She rose and dressed with the same mechanical movements which had occasioned Janet such deep concern, for life must go on somehow though hearts break and love itself prove vain. As she did up her hair before the mirror she marvelled, with a curious detachment, that her vigil of grief had left so little mark upon her face. A stranger, she thought, should have looked back at her from the glass.

She went downstairs, and in the hall encountered David, booted and spurred and carrying his hat and gloves. He kissed her affectionately and asked her how she did, but seemed in some haste to be off. Dorothea was not surprised to learn that he was bound for Ardely Place.

"Both Sir Edward and his lady entrusted me with letters," he explained with a grin, "and 'tis no more than my duty to deliver them as soon as may be. Egad, 'tis not often that duty goes hand-in-hand with pleasure!"

"David, promise me that you will do nothing foolish!" With an effort, Dorothea shook off some of her own listlessness in order to utter the warning. "Remember, Clarissa will not be expecting to see you and she may be startled into some show of feeling. For Heaven's sake try to be discreet."

"I will, I swear it!" he assured her easily, and added, as though he felt that something more was expected of him: "Why not ride with me? 'Tis a fine morning, and might put some colour back into your cheeks."

She thanked him, but declined, and he did not urge her to change her mind. She walked with him to the stables, and as they went he said abruptly:

"You need have no fear of importunities from that scoundrel Rainham. His belongings were packed off to him at the inn last night, and I've no doubt that before long he will be on his way to London. Faith, 'twas a scurvy trick he played upon you! I would give much to know how he learned where to find you, for I'll swear Michael never betrayed us."

"He could not have known," Dorothea replied wearily. " 'Twas chance, no more."

"Chance!" David repeated scornfully. "Believe me, my dear, 'twas no chance that brought Kelvin Rainham to this outlandish corner of Kent in the depths of winter. Do you not yet realize the colossal vanity of the man? A fine triumph it would have been for him could he have tricked you into wedding him, and so returned to London with Dorothea Stratton on his arm! You should be grateful to Andrew Spencerwood. It was his letter which brought me home in such haste."

They had reached the stables by now, and Will led out Sir David's horse. He mounted, but paused a moment longer to look down at his sister.

"Shall I ask Clarissa to visit you as soon as may be? You will wish to see her, no doubt." A happy thought occurred to him, and he perceived a way to arrange a *tête-à-tête* with his lady. "I have it! I will ask her to ride back with me, for you need some diversion to distract your mind from what happened yesterday."

He rode off, well pleased with himself, and Dorothea went back to the house. She made a pretence of eating the food which Janet hastened to set before her, but escaped as soon as she could from the elder woman's presence, and, finding the house too full of poignant memories, went out again into the bright, glad, mocking sunshine. She wandered aimlessly about without taking much heed of the path she followed, and presently found herself climbing the slope of the apple orchard. She paused beside the moss-grown log and looked about her like one awakening from sleep, seeing with a sudden, agonizing clarity the scene which was as beautiful now as it had been two days before. Her two pet lambs still frisked across the flower-dappled grass between the gnarled tree-trunks, the rosy drifts of blossom were still piled against the blue April sky. Dorothea put out her hand to touch one of the fragile blooms; brief as was its life, her happiness had been even more transient. Even before the apple-blossom had withered from the trees he would have ridden out of her life for ever.

She caught her breath on a choking sob, and realized that the tears were running down her cheeks and carrying away, it seemed, the aching desolation which had gripped her heart for so many hours. A thought which had hovered beyond the confines of her mind through the night's anguished vigil took shape at last, and with sudden self-knowledge she understood that yesterday's disclosure had altered nothing. She had cherished a bitter hatred for a stranger named Kelvin Rainham, and she loved a man who called himself Anthony Forrest, but now that she knew that the twain were one, love had proved stronger than hatred.

She dashed the tears from her eyes and, turning, ran down the hillside, through the shafts of sunlight and the dancing shadows, towards the farmhouse. On the threshold she came face to face with Polly, and paused to catch her by the arm.

"Bid Will saddle the black mare, Polly," she said hurriedly, "and hasten, girl, hasten!"

Without waiting to see if her command was obeyed she ran on to her bedchamber, and with trembling haste changed into her riding-habit. It was now almost noon, and her one fear was that Rainham might have left the inn before she could reach it. By the time she went downstairs again Will had the mare at the door, but as he lifted her into the saddle Mrs. Ashe came out of the house.

"Miss Dorothea," she exclaimed, "if you're thinking of riding after Sir David you know you can't go that far alone. Bide a minute, and let Will go with you."

Dorothea shook her head.

"I cannot wait, Janet," she replied, "but do not worry. I am going no farther than the village," and without giving Mrs. Ashe time to answer her, she wheeled her mount and rode quickly out of the gate. Janet watched until the first bend of the lane hid her from view, and then she turned and went back into the house, smiling to herself.

"No farther than the village," she repeated. "Now Heaven be praised for that!"

The "Brindled Hound" at Reppington was kept by one Jonas Potter, whose wife, Kate, was Janet's sister and therefore familiar with recent events at Gallows Farm. Within the past twenty-four hours, however, matters had moved with a rapidity which left her somewhat out of her depth. She had seen Sir David ride through the village the day before, and suspected that "Mr. Forrest's" abrupt departure from the farm arose out of his return, though she had been sorely puzzled when the man who carried the gentleman's belongings to the inn announced that they were the property of Major Rainham. It was therefore with strong relief, not unmixed with curiosity, that she saw Miss Stratton draw rein at the door, and at once hurried out to greet her.

"You'll have come seeking news of Mr. Forrest, ma'am, I dare say," she said at once, "and right glad I am to see you. I'd have sent a message up to the farm, only the gentleman said I was on no account to do such a thing."

"Then he is still here?" Dorothea's voice was a trifle breathless. "I feared that he might have set out for London."

"He'll not be leaving yet awhile, I'll warrant," Mrs. Potter assured her somewhat grimly. "Lord, what a fright I had when he came stumbling in here yesterday, with no hat or cloak and his face as white as death and the blood running down his arm—why, Miss Stratton, ma'am, what ails you?"

She caught at the girl's arm to steady her, for Dorothea's own face had paled and she had put out a hand rather suddenly to clutch at the door-post, but she brushed Mrs. Potter's solicitude aside.

"It is nothing—I had not realized—it was all over so quickly," she said incoherently. "Kate, where is he?"

"In the parlour yonder, though he should be in his bed. He had some crazy notion of leaving, but he's in no case to mount his horse, much less make a journey." She broke off, realizing that she was addressing the empty air. Miss Stratton had already gone.

Dorothea hesitated a moment at the parlour door, and then tapped softly upon it. His voice bade her enter and she went in, but he, thinking no doubt that it was one of the inn-servants, did not turn his head. He sat slumped in a big chair before the fire, his injured shoulder turned from her and his other hand lying listlessly along the arm of the chair. He was apparently lost in melancholy thought, and tears stung her eyes anew as she looked at him, for the mask of stern self-control had fallen away and in his face was naked agony and a profound hopelessness. She was obliged to speak before he took heed of her presence, and somehow it was his own name, and not that by which she had hitherto known him, which came most readily to her lips.

"Kelvin," she said softly.

She saw the slouching figure stiffen, the fine hand tighten suddenly on the arm of the chair, and then slowly, almost fearfully, he turned his head and saw her standing there. He sprang to his feet, but the shock and the sudden movement together were too great to be borne. The room spun giddily around him, he knew that he was about to fall—and then in that moment her arms were about him, cherishing arms that guided him back to the chair and pillowed his aching head upon her breast.

"Dear love, forgive me," she murmured. "I should not have come so suddenly upon you. Ah, how could you go like that, concealing your hurt? You could not think that we would deny you aid?"

The reeling world had steadied itself again. He drew away from her and spoke with a hint of bitterness.

"Was I to remain on sufferance, trading upon a chance injury? Dorothea, was it pity that brought you here today?"

She did not reply at once, but paused to cast aside the broad, plumed hat which had shaded her face. Then she knelt beside his chair and looked up at him.

"Until I reached the inn I knew nothing of your injury," she said quietly. "Look into my eyes, Kelvin. Is it pity that you see there?"

For the first time that day he ventured to look full into her eyes, and saw shining there such depths of love and tenderness that wonder filled his heart, and with it a sudden humility. Almost timidly he put out his hand to touch her black hair.

"My beloved," he said, "can you indeed forgive me?"

"I love you," she replied simply. "You, my dear, not the name you bear, whether it be Anthony Forrest or Kelvin Rainham. Yesterday, in the first shock of discovery, I did not realize it, but now I see the truth clearly at last. That is what brought me here."

So the obstacle between them, which had seemed insurmountable, proved in the end intangible as the shadow it had cast across their love. The dream might come true, the beggar attain his Paradise. Kelvin's voice was not quite steady as, with his hand lingering still upon her hair, he said quietly:

"Dorothea, will you be my wife?"

The clear gaze held his without faltering, and there was neither hesitation nor shyness in her face. All her doubts had been resolved in her night of agony, and since that moment of revelation in the apple orchard she had known with a glad certainty that her destiny lay here, with the man she had thought to be her bitterest enemy.

"Yes, Kelvin," she replied softly, "I will."

For a space they remained thus, gazing at each other, and then he clasped her to him with his sound arm and for the first time kissed her with no sense of guilt or dishonour. Her lips were warm and yielding, but after a little she freed herself from his hold and, searching his face with loving, anxious eyes, demanded to be told the extent of his injury.

" 'Tis nothing," he assured her, smiling. "It was no bodily wound I suffered, dear heart, and my true hurt you have already healed."

She smiled also, but shook her head.

"No bodily wound, when you reached the inn scarce able to stand and with your sleeve soaked with blood? Fie, sir, have I not nursed you these many weeks? Tell me what hurt you sustained."

"Little enough," he replied lightly. "I struck my shoulder against the press and the wound reopened, but 'tis no cause for concern. Mrs. Potter tended it, and she is as skilled, almost, as her sister."

"Yet you would have disregarded her advice and ridden away this morning could you have found strength to do so. Oh, Kelvin, did you really intend that? To go with no word to me?"

He looked away from her, and some of the old bitterness darkened his eyes.

"I thought I had no choice," he said. "What could I say, when I had been unmasked in such a fashion? 'Forgive me, for I meant to tell you'?" He shook his head. "What right had I to hope for forgiveness, when I had so tricked and deceived you? God knows I meant to tell you; I tried so many times, but lacked the courage—and my accursed cowardice was the cause of the pain you suffered yesterday!"

Dorothea put up her hand to touch with gentle fingers his brow where a frown yet lingered. She said gently:

"I think I did not suffer alone, and a love tempered

in the fires of pain grows but the stronger. I regret nothing, and as for deceiving me, did I not deceive myself when I assumed the name in the book to be your own?"

"It was natural that you should do so. Anthony Forrest was my closest friend. We were comrades-in-arms, and he saved my life at cost of his own. I carry the book always in memory of him." He did not think it necessary to say more. That incident, as he had told Sally Cheriton, was forgotten long ago.

"So that was why," she murmured. " 'Twas all part, was it not, of the strange chance which brought you here, to the one spot in all England where we might meet?"

He shook his head.

"Chance did not bring me here, Dorothea," he replied. "I came seeking you."

"Seeking me?" she repeated incredulously. "But, Kelvin, why?"

"Because I love you, and because I knew to what straits you were reduced by reason of my luck and your brother's folly. Oh, believe me, I had no hope then of winning your love. There was too much, I thought, between us. I sought only reassurance of your safety, and some means of restoring to you that which I had unwittingly stolen."

Dorothea put a hand to her head.

"My dearest, this is madness! You had never even seen me until that night when you were brought wounded to Gallows Farm."

"Had I not?" he replied. "Have you forgotten the portrait which hangs in the West Room at Hope Stratton?" He saw the dawning wonder and comprehension in her eyes, and smiled. "I knew and loved you long before we met. That was why I knew your name that day after the fever had left me."

So now at last she knew the true meaning of the expression in his eyes when on that night of storm they rested upon her, as she had supposed, for the first time. For a little that thought alone absorbed her mind, and then she perceived another curious fact.

"But how did you know where to find me? No one

but Michael Ashton knew that we had come to Gallows Farm."

He laughed quietly.

"Servants will talk, my heart, and no secret is safe from them. I learned that you had made your home at a Kentish farm, and I knew that if I searched long enough I should hear talk among the rustics of the lady of fashion and her brother who had come to dwell among them. It fell out as I had planned until I was within reach of my goal, and then fate, in the unlikely shape of a highway robber, took a hand in the game. The rest you know."

"The rest I know," she repeated. "Kelvin, how long did your search last?"

"A little less than two months, but I was very fortunate."

"Two months, and in the depths of winter!" Dorothea made a little, helpless gesture, and though she smiled her eyes were suspiciously bright. "Oh, my love, what folly!"

"Never folly, since it led me to my present happiness." Kelvin took her hand, and pressed a kiss upon its palm. "Dorothea, when will you marry me?"

"When?" She rose to her feet, withdrawing her hand from his, and walked slowly across to the window. In the garden behind the inn an apple tree was shedding its frail petals across a patch of grass, and she remembered those other blossoms which had sheltered their first kisses and beneath which the truth had revealed itself to her that morning. She said quietly: "I will marry you, Kelvin, when the apples are ripe."

"In the autumn?" There was dismay in his voice. "Love, must we wait so long?"

She sighed, and turned once more to face him.

"Kelvin, I will not try to deceive myself. I know that marriage with you must result in complete estrangement from my brother, for he hates you and will never forgive me. I wish with all my heart it were not so, but if it must be, it must. But I cannot leave him, and seek my own happiness, while he still torments himself with the hope of winning Clarissa, nor can I take the risk of letting him carry her off, to save her, as he thinks, from Jevington. I alone may prevent such madness, for I have some influence with David, and Clarissa, too, is fond of me. When she is safely wed, and he has had a little time to reconcile himself to the inevitable, then I will tell him of our love and we may be married." She paused to look up at him, for while she was speaking he had risen and come to stand beside her. For a moment her eyes met his, and then she turned abruptly to the window again. "Kelvin, do not look at me so. It—it shakes my resolution."

" 'Tis what I hoped." A fleeting smile touched his lips, though the expression with which he regarded her was infinitely tender. "Dear heart, I counselled you once to let David work out his own salvation. I counsel you so again."

She shook her head.

"Lord Ardely would have their marriage set aside. No, I must do all in my power to prevent it, but it will be so hard for them. They will both have need of me."

"And I?" Kelvin was standing close behind her now, and spoke with his lips against her hair. "Have I no need of you?"

She caught her breath, and without turning put up a hand to touch his cheek.

"We have all our lives to be together," she whispered, "but they must part. Will you grudge them even such small comfort as I perchance may give them?"

"I grudge every minute of every day that keeps you from me," he replied, "but how can I deny you anything?" He turned her to face him, and kissed her. "I will wait until the autumn for my bride, if that is what she wishes."

Held thus within the shelter of his arm, her head against his shoulder, Dorothea breathed a fluttering sigh.

"It is what I wish," she murmured, "but oh, my love, I fear the summer will seem very long."

CHAPTER XI

NO IDLE FEARS

Major Rainham returned to London, and with his customary assurance took up his former place in society. Curiosity concerning his long absence was rife, but only Sally Cheriton knew what had kept him so long in the country, for to her Kelvin made no secret of the events of the past few months. He and Dorothea had kept their own counsel, and only Thomas and Janet, and now Sally, knew of their betrothal.

Soon after his reappearance in London, Kelvin gave society yet another cause for surprise by striking up a friendship with Viscount Jevington. Many wondered to see the unapproachable Major Rainham upon intimate terms with this dull-witted young profligate and his boon companions, but Kelvin had resolved to prevent, if he could, the marriage of Lady Clarissa, thus making it possible for him to claim his own bride without delay, and had sought out his lordship with that purpose in mind. At first his motive was purely selfish, but as he came to know the Viscount better he realized that David Stratton's accusations against him were well-founded, and he resolved that even if he had to resort to violence to prevent it, Clarissa should never marry Jevington. His mind revolted at the thought.

As time passed and he failed to hit upon any other means, it seemed that violence would indeed become necessary, and Kelvin knew, since they had fenced together, that his swordsmanship was so far superior to Jevington's that the outcome of a duel would not be for a moment in doubt. For that very reason he was reluctant to act upon his resolve, and although Jevington's temper, which was not of the sweetest, presented several promising openings for a quarrel, he neglected them in the hope that, even now, such measures would not be necessary.

The first days of July found him still unresolved, though with the wedding so close at hand he knew that the decision could not be delayed much longer. In this same uncertain state of mind he accepted an invitation to dine, with certain other gentlemen, at the Viscount's house, and was dismayed to learn, midway through the meal, that this convivial gathering was in the nature of a farewell. Jevington was to start for Kent the following day to claim his bride.

Throughout the rest of the meal, and the gaming and drinking which followed, his companions found Major Rainham somewhat preoccupied. They chaffed him a little, but diffidently, for not only was he older by some years than the rest of them, but the cold irony in which he commonly dealt made them wary of provoking a retort from him. Kelvin paid little heed to their jests, for he was reproaching himself bitterly for having delayed too long. Now, it seemed, it would be necessary to follow the Viscount into Kent if he wished to put his scheme into execution, for it was out of the question to challenge him tonight. He had already been drinking heavily; his usually pallid face was flushed and he showed a tendency to become excessively garrulous, and no matter what the motive, Kelvin could not bring himself to force a mortal quarrel upon a drunken man.

The evening wore on, and one by one, in varying stages of intoxication, the guests took their leave, until only

Major Rainham and his host remained. Jevington sprawled in a chair, coat and waistcoat unbuttoned and his cravat untied, the heavy periwig pushed back from his heated brow, while from where he stood by the empty hearth Kelvin regarded with distaste the dishevelled figure whose disorder was heightened by contrast with his own fastidious elegance.

" 'Tis time I, too, took my leave," he said. "It grows late."

"No, stay awhile," Jevington replied thickly. "I want to talk to you." He picked up his glass, but his hand was unsteady and most of the wine spilled, splashing in crimson stains down the front of his shirt. He laughed inanely and reached for the nearest bottle, but Kelvin stood very still, staring at those bright splashes so dreadfully suggestive of his own deadly purpose.

"We'll drink a toast," Jevington announced, filling two glasses and tipping a good deal of wine over the table in the process. "A toast to my fair bride." He laughed again, as though the words were a jest which amused him inordinately, and offered one of the glasses to Kelvin. "Come, Rainham, drink to the Lady Clarissa."

Kelvin had no choice but to honour the toast, though the wine barely touched his lips. Jevington drained his to the dregs and with a sweeping gesture cast the glass from him to shiver into fragments against the wall.

"The Lady Clarissa!" he repeated. "A sweet armful, is she not, Rainham?"

"Is she?" Kelvin's voice was even and faintly amused, but he shot a swift glance at the Viscount as he spoke. "You are to be congratulated."

"But not so sweet, you would say," pursued Jevington, "as Dorothea Stratton?"

"What?" Not even Major Rainham's calm was proof against that shock. "What the devil do you mean?"

"No harm, on my soul," Jevington chuckled, "though 'twas churlish to keep such a jest to yourself." He leaned forward to wag an admonishing finger and add with drunken gravity: "A jest, my friend, loses half its savour when there's none to share it. I speak from my own experience."

"It would appear," the Major retorted with a distinct edge to his voice, "that this one is shared already. How did you learn of it?"

"From Alfred Spencerwood, who had the tale from his brother, Andrew. 'Twould seem you fooled others besides Miss Stratton." He flung himself back in his chair and stared owlishly at his companion. "Plague on't, Rainham, but you're a queer devil! Were there not enough ripe beauties in London that you must needs go journeying into Kent after that proud, cold piece? I wonder why you did it?"

Kelvin picked up his glass again, resisted the temptation to fling its contents into the flushed and leering countenance before him, and raised it to his lips instead. When he had drunk, he said with assumed lightness:

"Let us say that 'twas to indulge a whim. I had a curiosity to know what had become of the Strattons."

"And were wise enough to seek enlightenment of the sister rather than the brother, eh? But Alfred said something of an encounter with a footpad which came near to costing you your life."

"That is true," Kelvin admitted, "and 'tis only thanks to Miss Stratton that I am alive today. Therefore, my dear Jevington, I will thank you to keep this story to yourself. I have cause to be grateful to her."

"I'll warrant you have!" His lordship was reaching for another glass as he spoke, and so did not see the flash of anger in his companion's eyes, or the sudden, dangerous tightening of his lips. "I'll say naught, depend upon't." A new thought set him laughing again. "Damme, I'm minded to bid you to the wedding. I'm told the Strattons will be there, for it seems that Dorothea has become Clarissa's closest friend. Egad, 'twould be a rare jest!"

Kelvin perceived that here was a chance not to be missed, if he sought an excuse to accompany the Viscount to Kent. He smiled mockingly, and raised a pinch of snuff to his nose.

"A rare jest indeed," he agreed. "What say you, my friend? Shall I dare Stratton's wrath, and dance with his sister at your wedding? Believe me, the situation would be piquant beyond your comprehension."

"Aye, you've a choice humour," Jevington conceded, "but I could tell you a tale, now, to set you laughing." He nodded solemnly, and, fixing a somewhat glassy stare upon Kelvin, appeared to give his consideration to a weighty problem, while the glass in his hand, tilting in his lax grip, emptied its contents on to the floor.

The silence became protracted, and Major Rainham, growing bored, was about to end it by bidding his host good night, when Jevington, apparently reaching the end of his deliberations, smote the table a blow with his fist and spoke with great decision, albeit some slurring of his words.

"Fiend seize me, but I will tell you! There's not another man in London with the wit to appreciate it, but mind! I'm trusting you to keep a still tongue, for 'twould be the ruin of me if the tale leaked out."

"In that event you had best not tell me," Kelvin replied coldly. "A secret shared is no longer a secret."

Jevington looked up at him, an unpleasant expression in his close-set eyes.

"You'll do well to remember that," he said, "or I might be tempted to tell what kept you so long in Kent." For a few seconds they regarded each other in silence, and then his lordship chuckled. "So! We understand one another, I think. Now listen!" He leaned forward and lowered his voice. "This will not be my first wedding."

"Indeed?" The Major was unimpressed. "Then, as I understand that you were betrothed to Lady Clarissa as a boy, I assume that your previous marriage took place while you were formally contracted to her."

The Viscount nodded, grinning. His amusement seemed out of all proportion to the sordid little secret he had revealed, and Rainham suspected that there was more to come.

"Was your marriage never discovered?" he prompted.

"No, nor ever will be," Jevington replied smugly. "I saw to that, depend upon't. Even if the wench were fool enough to make a claim upon me, she has not a scrap of proof to support her story."

For a long moment Kelvin stared at him, wondering

hether he had heard aright or whether his companion's
uickened speech had deceived him. At length he said
ncredulously:

"Do I understand you to say that your wife is still
live?"

"Aye, that's the cream of the jest—that, and the fact
hat the baggage is well-served, since she married me
nly for the sake of my wealth and title." He leaned
ack in his chair, shaken by a sudden gust of laughter.
She should have known better than to pit her wits
gainst mine."

For a few seconds longer Kelvin pondered him, realizing
hat all unwittingly Jevington had delivered himself into
is hands. But to obtain more definite information he
ust appear to share the Viscount's indecent mirth. He
rew forward a chair and sat down, regarding his com-
anion with an expression of amused expectation.

"You whet my appetite," he told him. "I'll warrant
his is a tale worth hearing. Who is the lady whom you
ave so signally honoured?"

"Her name," said Jevington, grinning his appreciation
f the Major's irony, "is Judith, and she is the grand-
aughter of an apothecary. Her mother, who died when
udith was born, declined to reveal the name of her
hild's father." He chuckled. "You'll perceive 'twas not
a match likely to be approved by my family."

"What I do not perceive," Kelvin retorted drily, "is
why you found it necessary to marry her at all."

"Depend upon it, I had no such intention," his lordship replied frankly. "I was betrothed to Clarissa and
I had my own reasons for not wanting that contract
broken, but Judith, curse her obstinacy, had determined
to be 'my lady.' Try as I might, she would make me but
one answer. I might marry her, or go."

He put out a wavering hand towards the wine, but
Major Rainham, forestalling him, took it up and filled
both their glasses. A cold and singularly mocking smile
curved his lips.

"My dear Jevington, you disappoint me! Surely you
could have discovered some way of attaining your object
without going to such lengths. You would be in a parlous

161

state if someone were to stumble upon the truth, as well they might. I presume that some records of the marriage exist?"

"In my possession, every one," said his lordship with simple pride. "Anything can be bought, if the price be high enough."

"But the clergyman who married you? The witnesses?"

"Harry Westbury was one, and he died last year of the smallpox. Poor Harry! He dearly loved a jest." For a moment he seemed in danger of becoming lachrymose at the melancholy memory, but another pull at the wine fortified him to continue. "The other was some ill favoured ruffian I had never seen before nor am likely to see again. We were married in the Fleet."

Comprehension dawned upon Major Rainham. The chapel of the Fleet Prison was notorious for the secret marriages conducted there without the formality of banns or licence.

"So 'twas a Fleet marriage," he said contemptuously. "I see."

"But binding, none the less, or she'd not have agreed to it," Jevington reminded him. "I told her if 'twere not kept secret my family would find the means to prevent it, and that, God knows, was true enough. If my uncle Amberstone had learned of it there would have been the devil to pay."

"I don't doubt it." The Major was at his most cynical. "What I do doubt is that any woman is worth such a vast amount of trouble and risk. Gad'slife, Jevington, were there not others less unwilling?"

His lordship laughed derisively.

"I seem to have heard that once, years ago, you deemed a woman worth far greater risks, though, to be sure, you lacked my success. I tell you, Rainham, had you seen Judith you would not wonder at what I did. Egad, what a magnificent creature! Like some damned heathen goddess."

He lapsed into silence and for a space blinked hazily at the candle flames, apparently lost in pleasant memories. At length he heaved a noisy sigh.

"Magnificent creature," he repeated. "Damme, but for

162

my betrothal to Clarissa I'd have married her openly and to the devil with my uncle. But not even Judith was worth the sacrifice of a fortune."

Kelvin raised his brows.

"I may be singularly obtuse," he remarked, "but I fail to see how marriage with Lady Clarissa can bring you a fortune. She is not, I believe, an heiress?"

Jevington displayed a hint of impatience.

" 'Tis the Amberstone fortune I mean," he said. "My uncle sets great store by this marriage, for Ardely is one of his oldest friends. If he found out about Judith he'd disinherit me."

"Would he indeed?" said Major Rainham thoughtfully. "I do trust that you have bestowed your Viscountess in some secure place—or do you not know what has become of her?"

"Do you think I'd be fool enough to lose sight of her, and so risk exposure? I sent her to live at Hampstead, and as long as she causes me no trouble she shall have a roof over her head and money enough to keep her and the child."

"What?" Kelvin looked up sharply, a frown between his brows. "You mean there is a child of this marriage?"

The Viscount laughed.

"Aye, a boy. My lawful son and heir. Poor Judith, she thought when he was born that I would acknowledge her as my wife. She's a simple creature." He chuckled again. "But I'll not neglect my duty. He shall be apprenticed to a useful trade."

Kelvin rose somewhat abruptly to his feet, and as he looked down at his companion the profound disgust he felt was for a moment visible in his face. Jevington, he knew, was genuinely amused. The crime he had committed, and the still greater one he contemplated, were to him no more than a jest, and he had as little compassion for Clarissa as for the unfortunate Judith.

He paced the length of the room and back again to the table, debating his next move. The story had so offended him that he was not now concerned merely to save Clarissa, but to help the unfortunate woman who had been so shamefully tricked and betrayed, but

163

to do that he must first obtain the proofs of the marriage, if, indeed, they had not been destroyed.

"So Lady Jevington resides at Hampstead," he said slowly. "Not, I need hardly ask, under her rightful name?"

The Viscount accorded this witticism the guffaw he thought it deserved. When he had recovered his breath he said:

"She calls herself Mrs. Barfield. 'Twas her grand-father's name."

"I see," Kelvin had halted behind Jevington's chair, one hand resting lightly on its back, "and the proofs you spoke of, the records of the marriage? You destroyed them, of course?"

Jevington shook his head.

"I kept them," he said. "I thought I might some day have need of them."

A flash of triumph lit the elder man's eyes for an instant, and was gone. When he spoke his voice was amused, but just a little impatient.

"Upon my soul, Jevington, how much farther do you intend to push this comedy? You must remember, my dear boy, that a jest unduly prolonged becomes weari-some."

"Eh?" His lordship heaved himself round in his chair to squint up at the speaker. "What the devil do you mean?"

"I mean that you have been vastly entertaining with this tale of a secret marriage, but the hour grows late and I find myself no longer diverted. Moreover, you have carried the story too far. You should have replied that you destroyed the proofs as soon as they came into your hands."

"Damme, Rainham, do you call me a liar? I tell you that Judith——"

"Is divinely beautiful and the mother of your son. Oh, I do not doubt it, but that she is your wife——" he laughed softly and shook his head. "No, Jevington! Show me the proofs you boast of and I will believe you, but as it is——" he shrugged, still laughing, and clapped the Viscount on the shoulder, "I will bid you goodnight."

"Wait!" His lordship heaved himself to his feet, staggered, and clutched at the table for support. "Damn you, Rainham, you shall see them! You'll not leave this house until you admit your mistake and ask my pardon."

The Major, who had no intention of leaving, made a gesture half-impatient, half-resigned.

"Oh, as you will, but I beg you to make haste about it. I grow weary." He stifled a yawn behind his hand.

"I'll be quick," Jevington promised. "Wait you here."

He made his way unsteadily to the door and went out. He was gone for some ten minutes, but when he returned some papers were clutched in one hand.

"There," he said triumphantly, and cast them down among the bottles and glasses on the table, "see for yourself!"

Kelvin picked them up and bent forward to study them by the light of the guttering candles, and a wave of exultation swept over him. Here, indeed, was a weapon which would put an end for ever to any thought of a match between Jevington and Clarissa, and at the same time make it possible for him to claim his own bride without delay.

"I make you my apologies," he said at length. "I was indeed mistaken." He paused, and sent a humorous, inquiring glance at his host. "I wonder why you chose to confide this secret to me?"

"Why?" Jevington dropped into his chair again and grinned up at him. "Devil take it, don't you know? Who else could I depend upon to see it for the jest it is? I've not forgotten the tale of your departure from England after the Rebellion."

"I fear that you flatter me," Kelvin retorted coldly. "Nevertheless, I perceive one thing clearly enough. Now that you are about to marry Lady Clarissa these papers become dangerous, and should be destroyed."

"Aye," Jevington, growing solemn, nodded his approval of the suggestion, and with a movement so sudden that Kelvin was taken unawares, twitched the papers from his grasp and thrust them at the nearest candleflame. Fortunately neither hand nor eye was steady and he missed the candle by some inches. Next moment the

Major's own hand had closed about his wrist.

Jevington winced and swore, taken aback by the unexpected strength of the white fingers. The papers changed hands once more, and Rainham was smiling pleasantly down at him.

"Not thus, you young fool," he said, releasing him. "Do you wish to burn the house about our ears? See, I will burn them here, upon the hearth." He crossed to the fire-place as he spoke, adding over his shoulder: "Fill the glasses again, Jevington. This seems to be a fitting moment to drink a last toast to your Viscountess."

His lordship, chuckling, reached for a bottle, found it empty, and with an oath cast it aside and picked up another. As he slopped wine into the glasses, light flared suddenly on the far side of the room, dispelling the gathering shadows for a few seconds before it began to fade again. Kelvin sauntered back to the table, leaving the papers to burn themselves out upon the hearth.

"Here," Jevington handed him a glass and grinned expectantly. "To whom do we drink, Judith or Clarissa?"

For a space the grey eyes regarded him inscrutably; the fine, austere mouth curled to a smile of infinite mockery.

"My dear Jevington," said Major Rainham reproachfully, "to your Viscountess, of course, of the present and of the future."

A short while later Kelvin took leave of his host, and when he had gone the Viscount, seated still in the chair at the head of the table, heaved a sigh and looked glassily about the empty room. The little heap of charred ashes on the hearth caught his eye and he grinned; picking up his glass he raised it mockingly in the direction of the fire-place and tossed off what remained of the wine. Then, sweeping clear a space on the table before him, he bowed his head upon his folded arms and fell into a drunken slumber.

At the precise moment when Lord Jevington was drinking to the ashes of a letter which Dorothea Stratton had written to her betrothed, Kelvin Rainham, with a link-boy to attend him, was walking briskly in the direction of his own lodgings, and in the breast of his coat, where until lately Dorothea's letter had reposed, he carried the papers he had sacrificed it to obtain. The papers which held the final, irrefutable proof of the marriage which had taken place three years earlier between Viscount Jevington and Judith, the granddaughter of one Josiah Barfield, an apothecary.

At Gallows Farm Dorothea sat in the parlour, making a small repair to the gown she intended to wear at Clarissa's wedding on the morrow. She sat in the big arm-chair with the dress in her lap, yard upon yard of richly-hued silk heavy with fringe and braid and gorgeous embroidery, and mended the little rent with tiny, exquisite stitches, wondering the while what errand had taken her brother and Michael Ashton to Ardely Place that day. Wondered, in fact, why Michael had come to the farm at all. David had come from Hampshire with Sir Edward and Lady Amberstone when they journeyed into Kent to attend Clarissa's wedding, and Dorothea knew that he had asked Michael to meet him at the farm. She knew, too, that they were bent upon some project they did not wish her to discover, and had feared at first that her brother was planning to carry off tomorrow's bride, but when she taxed Michael with this he assured her solemnly that no such madness was contemplated. That was soon after his arrival, and before Kelvin Rainham's name had been mentioned between them.

Even in retrospect she burned with shame and anger at the things Ashton had said of Kelvin, of his close friendship with Viscount Jevington and his cronies, and the excesses in which that band of wild young rakes was said to indulge. It was not that she believed him—her love and trust were too deep to be shaken by so slight a cause—but she could see that this constant dwelling upon the theme of Rainham's intimacy with Jevington was whipping David into a white-heat of anger against her betrothed. Almost it seemed that Michael must have guessed her secret and, prompted by jealousy, was doing his utmost to stir up strife between the two men she most dearly loved.

She sighed and smiled together as she sat there at her work, the busy needle flashing and her thoughts far away. How long it seemed since the day when Kelvin had ridden away to London, and yet the summer was but half gone. The apple-blossom had faded, but many weeks must yet pass before the fruit hung ripe for gathering beneath a mellow, autumn sun. How long would it be before she decked a gown for her own bridal? Her hands were stilled, and for a space she yielded to dreams of the future they were to share, as she had yielded often and often since his departure, yet now, as always, she was aware of a shadow upon her happiness, a little rankling doubt she could not name and yet which seemed to whisper that all was not well. Was it, she wondered, the thought of the estrangement from David which must inevitably follow her marriage? Surely not, for she had faced that prospect squarely long ago, and acknowledged the fact that deep as was her devotion to her brother, it was as nothing to the love she felt for the lonely, embittered man to whom she had so recklessly and so completely given her heart.

The golden sunlight of July drew the pattern of the diamond-paned window on the floor at her feet, and through the open casement drifted the scent of roses, but her thoughts went back to a wild winter's night when the wind had raved like a maddened beast around the farm-house, and love had come strangely to her out of the storm. Today only the faintest breeze was stirring, barely enough to shake the tall grasses fringing the little stream.

Hoofbeats in the lane! Could it be David and Michael returning? No, for this was but one rider, coming briskly despite the heat and the dust. A messenger from Ardely Place, perhaps. Dorothea snipped off her thread and held the gown up at arm's length, regarding her handiwork critically. The darn scarcely showed, and in any event her attire was not likely to be noticed tomorrow, when all eyes would be upon the bride.

A quick, firm tread sounded in the hall, and brought her trembling to her feet, the gown slipping unheeded to the floor. The door opened and a man entered the room, stooping his tawny head as he passed under the low lintel, and with a soft exclamation of surprise and gladness Dorothea started forward, to be caught in a strong embrace.

"Kelvin!" she murmured breathlessly. "Dearest, what brings you here, today of all days? You should not have come!"

He looked down at her, his lips curving to the rare, delightful smile she loved so well, as he answered her with gentle mockery.

"Should not have come, i'faith! Is that all the welcome I am to have after so long an absence?"

An answering twinkle crept into her eyes.

"What more do you deserve, sir, when you come so suddenly and with no word of warning? Indeed, my love, it is no jest. Did you not know that tomorrow is Clarissa's wedding-day? David is here, and Michael Ashton also, though by the mercy of Providence they have ridden to Ardely Place."

"I know. Kate Potter told me of their presence at the farm, and I saw them ride through the village while I was at the inn. Therefore I knew that I might visit my promised wife in perfect safety, nor risk being called upon to defend my life."

"Ah, do not jest!" Dorothea's eyes clouded as she spoke. "If David did return to find you here nothing less than a crossing of swords would content him. His feelings against you have grown very bitter of late, and Michael does his utmost to fan the fire. Almost it seems that he wishes to force an issue between you."

Kelvin frowned. For Ashton's hostility he cared little, even though he could make a shrewd guess at its cause, but he knew that any widening of the gulf between David and himself must inevitably cause Dorothea pain. How much did Ashton suspect, he wondered, and what was he hoping to achieve?

"Why is he here at all?" he asked, and she moved her hands helplessly.

"I do not know. David wrote to him from Hampshire, but he was delayed in London and did not join us until yesterday. David was in a fret of impatience until he me, and this morning they walked in the garden for an hour, disputing some matter which they are at pains to conceal from me. Now they have ridden to Ardely Place. Oh, Kelvin, what can it mean? Had not Michael assured me that it was not so, I must believe that David had enlisted his aid in some scheme to carry Clarissa off before the wedding can take place."

"Abate your fears, sweetheart," Kelvin replied gently. "Whatever your brother is plotting to prevent the marriage will not come to pass, I promise you. By this time all need for such desperate measures will have vanished." He laughed at the blank bewilderment in her face, and drew her to sit beside him on the window-seat. "Dorothea, I make no doubt that Ashton has told you and David of my close friendship with Jevington, but you at least cannot believe that it was prompted by liking for him, or that of my own free will I entered into the life of vice and debauchery in which he indulges."

She smiled, but her eyes were puzzled.

"That you had some purpose in what you did I have never doubted, but I own that I have no notion what it can be."

"I scarcely knew myself when I set out to make his acquaintance, save that I hoped to find some way of preventing his marriage to Lady Clarissa, but I succeeded beyond my wildest dreams. A few days since, in a moment of drunken expansiveness, he confided to me the secret of the low-born beauty he took to wife some three years ago, and who has already borne him a lusty son."

Dorothea put a hand to her head.

"A wife? A son?" she repeated dazedly. "Kelvin, you are not jesting?"

"Not in the least," he replied with a smile. "He showed me the proofs of his marriage and I obtained possession of them by a trick. Next day, while he was on his way to Ardely Place, I sought out the rightful Lady Jevington and gave the papers into her hands. I escorted her into Kent, and parted from her not an hour since, leaving her to go alone to confront the Earl, for I want no one to know of my part in the affair. I have primed her with a story to account for her sudden appearance, and the confusion into which her arrival must throw them will ⬛ the rest."

"But why are you so bent upon secrecy?" Dorothea asked. "Clarissa—indeed, her whole family—owe you a debt which can never be repaid, while the knowledge that you have intervened to such good effect cannot fail to lessen David's hostility towards you."

"Can it not?" Kelvin replied ruefully. "I have a notion 'twould increase it. Consider for a moment, my heart! There is no doubt that during the past few months David has racked his brains to discover some way of delivering Lady Clarissa from Jevington, but to no avail! Do you think 'twould please him to know that I have succeeded where he has failed? I, whose possession of the Stratton fortune is the chief obstacle to their happiness? To find himself so beholden to me would only make him dislike me the more."

She was obliged to admit the truth of this. David, particularly with Michael's rancour to prompt him, would see not the great debt he owed Major Rainham, but the humiliating fact that his enemy had delivered Clarissa from a peril which he had been powerless to avert.

"What, then, was your purpose?" she said after a pause. "Was it for Clarissa's sake you did this thing?"

"After I became acquainted with Jevington," Kelvin replied slowly, "I resolved that they should never be married if 'twere in my power to prevent it, for the idea of that child bound to such a man was too horrible to contemplate, but that thought was not in my mind when I embarked upon the venture." He leaned closer, taking her hand in his. "Dorothea, you said you would not marry while David and Clarissa had such need of you, but now the most pressing danger to their happiness no longer exists. Where, then, is now the barrier to ours?"

For a long moment Dorothea sat very still, looking not at him, but down at their clasped hands, conscious of quickened heartbeats and an odd feeling of breathlessness. There had appeared to be so many obstacles in the way of their immediate marriage, but Kelvin Rainham, it seemed, had a way of sweeping such difficulties aside. This should have been for her a moment of unoyed happiness, and yet always that ominous, nameless shadow spread and deepened, and with it grew the inexplicable conviction that such a barrier did exist, yet one so vague and intangible that she could not determine its nature.

She rose to her feet and moved aimlessly across the room until she reached the chair in which she had sat at her sewing. She paused there, her hands resting on the high, carved back, her eyes fixed unseeingly upon the bright patch of sunlight on the uneven floor, while Kelvin remained standing by the window, watching her with perplexity and growing uneasiness. At length, as the moments passed and still she did not speak, he went to her, where she stood with her back towards him, and, setting his hands on her shoulders, dropped a kiss lightly on her hair.

"Dorothea," he said gently. "What is it, my love? What is troubling you?"

She hesitated, seeking for words to explain the indefinable dread which weighed upon her, but to him her prolonged silence suddenly became fraught with sinister meaning. His hands fell from her shoulders and he drew back a pace.

"Is it, perhaps," he said in an altered tone, "that you have had time to regret the promise so rashly given two months ago?"

"Kelvin!" She turned quickly to face him, for the old bitterness had rung in his voice, and with it a note of pain which stabbed her with swift remorse. "I regret nothing," she told him quietly. "My love is yours till death and beyond, and no power of earth or heaven can change it."

He looked down into the clear eyes raised so steadfastly to his, and was shaken by a sudden humility alien to his proud, unbending nature. Happiness to him was still so strange and precious a possession that he watched over it jealously, and feared to lose it almost before it was truly his. Something of this Dorothea realized, and so she stifled her own vague misgivings, and endeavoured to make light of her obvious uneasiness.

"Bear with my foolishness awhile, my dear," she said.

"I had not thought it possible that we should be wed before the autumn, and today my heart was very heavy at the thought of the pain which David and Clarissa must endure. Now, so suddenly, their fortunes are changed." She broke off, and put out her hands towards him in a gesture almost frightened. "Oh, Kelvin, let us take our chance of happiness while we may, lest we find we have delayed too long!"

"Why, what nonsense is this?" He smiled as he took her hands in his, but then, seeing the very real distress in her eyes, drew her into his arms and held her so. "Is it that you are reluctant to break this news to David? That may soon be remedied, for I will await his return and tell him that you have consented to be my wife."

"No," Dorothea shook her head, for she feared a repetition of the scene which had taken place on the previous occasion when David had returned to the farm and found Major Rainham there. "It will be best if I tell him myself, and I will do so this evening. There is no use in pretending 'twill please him but I may persuade him to offer no active opposition to our marriage." Her eyes darkened and she sighed. "But I wish that Michael were not here. His word carries such weight with David, and he bears you such violent ill-will."

"If Mr. Ashton has any comment to make upon a matter which concerns him not at all," Kelvin replied with a hint of grimness, "he had best address it to me. With your brother I swear I will not quarrel, no matter what provocation he offers, but I cannot promise to practise a like forbearance with every gallant who aspires to your hand."

"Oh, pray do not quarrel with Michael, for he has proved himself a good friend in the past——" she broke off to look inquiringly up at him. "How did you know that he wished to marry me?"

"How can I avoid knowing of matters which are common gossip in London?" he countered, and laughed at the mingled dismay and disbelief in her eyes. "I learned of it from Sally Cheriton. There are few matters which fail to reach her ears sooner or later, and as you know it was with her help that I first learned where to search for you."

"We have much cause to be grateful to her," Dorothea said softly. "I look forward to making her acquaintance." She paused, her fingers idly rearranging the folds of lawn and lace at his throat. "I shall tell David of our betrothal this evening, at some moment when we are alone. It will be best, I am sure, if he learns of it from me before you meet again."

"Very well, since you wish it so, but tomorrow I shall come here to speak with him." She seemed about to protest, but he smiled and shook his head. "Would you have him believe that I am afraid to face him? I will go back to the inn now, lest he should hasten home to bring you the news from Ardely Place, but tell him that I shall wait upon him here tomorrow."

He spoke gently, but there was that in his voice which informed her that it would be useless to argue, and since she realized that the encounter must take place sooner or later, she resigned herself to the inevitable. Presently, after a brief talk with Thomas and Janet, which left them to suppose that Major Rainham had come to the farm in ignorance of David's presence there, Kelvin took his leave. Dorothea went with him as far as the high road, and to avoid the risk of encountering Stratton and Ashton in the lane they went by way of the apple orchard, and a path which passed through a belt of woodland to join the road a quarter of a mile away.

They went at a leisurely pace, Kelvin leading his horse, up the cool, green orchard-slope, across the strip of meadowland on the crest of the hill, and so again into the welcome shade of trees. The path wound down a gentle incline to the road at its foot, and when at length the trees thinned to reveal a strip of deserted highway Major Rainham halted and looked down at his companion.

"Our ways part here, sweetheart," he said. "If 'twould displease David to find me at the farm, his anger would not be lessened were he to come upon us here." He set a hand beneath her chin and tilted her face towards him to look searchingly into her eyes. "Child, will you not tell me what it is that troubles you? Why are you afraid?"

Dorothea's lips trembled. She cast herself into his arms, clinging to him and hiding her face against his breast.

"I do not know," she whispered. "There is a shadow upon my heart, and a furtive, half-seen thing that lurks upon the edge of vision and fades when I turn boldly to face it. I know not what it is, but something threatens our happiness, of that I am certain."

He stroked her hair, looking down at her with an expression of infinite tenderness.

"This is but an idle fancy, my heart's darling," he said gently. "Whence could such threat come? From David? Is that the thought which troubles you?"

"Perhaps. I cannot tell." She raised her head, her eyes anxious. "He is so quick-tempered. If you should quarrel, perhaps even fight——"

"Have I not sworn that we shall not? I give you my most solemn promise that, do what he will, David will not succeed in forcing a meeting upon me. Two are needed to make a quarrel, and my temper, I believe, is not ungovernable."

That made her smile, as he had intended, and so presently he succeeded in calming her fears. The shadow was not wholly dispelled, but now, with his arms about her and his kisses warm upon her lips, it dwindled to insignificance. Even when he had mounted and ridden away, when the sound of his horse's hoofs had faded along the quiet road, the comfort of his presence remained with her, and as she climbed once more the winding path towards the hill-top the light of great happiness shone still in her eyes, and played about her lips.

Michael Ashton was riding back alone to Gallows Farm. Since his arrival in Kent events had moved with a rapidity which left him somewhat bewildered, but at present he was conscious only of a deep thankfulness. He had answered David's imperative summons with no idea that he would be called upon to act for his friend in a quarrel which he intended to provoke with Lord

Jevington—for David had resolved upon this course as the only one which offered any hope of escape for Clarissa. Michael had used every argument he could think of to turn him from his purpose, but in vain, and since David had sworn him to secrecy before divulging his plan, he was unable to enlist the aid of Miss Stratton. Nor was it at all certain that Dorothea would have succeeded where he had failed. David had changed immeasurably during the past year, and his scheme, mad as it was, was no impetuous, boyish venture. He would kill Jevington or lose his life in the attempt.

So with that murderous purpose in mind they had ridden to Ardely Place, only to be met with the incredible news that the wedding was not, after all, to take place. Shortly before their own arrival a beautiful young woman had demanded speech with the Earl, and, her request being granted, had presented him with undeniable proof that she was Lord Jevington's lawful wife, and the sturdy boy she bore in her arms the Viscount's son and heir.

David had remained at Ardely Place, in the hope, no doubt, of stealing an interview with his beloved, but Michael had set out at once for the farm, to tell Miss Stratton the good news and relieve the anxiety she was undoubtedly feeling. He rode fast, for he knew how welcome to Dorothea would be the news he brought, but when he had passed through Reppington and was drawing near his destination, his eagerness received a sudden check. He had reached the crest of a long rise, and before him loomed one of the low, rounded hills which sheltered the farm. As he paused to rest his horse his attention was caught by a movement in the strip of pasture on its summit, and, wrinkling his eyes against the glare, he made out the figures of a man and a woman, the former leading a black horse, crossing the meadow towards the wood. That way led only to the farm, and the woman, he felt certain, was Dorothea; her companion was bare-headed, and even at that distance, Michael could see how the sunlight glowed upon russet-coloured hair. With an incredible suspicion springing to life in his mind, and jealousy in his heart, he rode down into the hollow where the road curved along the edge of the wood. He knew where the path from the farm joined the highway, and there he dismounted, led his horse into the wood, and concealed both it and himself amid a convenient clump of holly-trees. For good or ill, he would know who it was who walked with Dorothea.

It was an admirable hiding-place. The thickly-growing leaves, dark and shining, formed a barrier behind which he and his mount were completely hidden, and yet by parting the branches a fraction he gained a clear view of the path from the nearest bend as far as the road. Scratched hands and torn ruffles went unheeded in the tension of the moment.

He had not long to wait, for presently he heard the murmur of voices and a soft laugh, and then they came within his range of vision, Kelvin Rainham, tall and erect, with Dorothea leaning upon his arm and smiling up into his face. A short way beyond his hiding-place they halted, speaking in tones too low to reach his ears. The girl, it seemed, was troubled, the man seeking to comfort her, and presently he succeeded, for she smiled again, and when he bent his head to press his lips to hers, clasped her arms about his neck and gave him back kiss for kiss.

Michael's hands were clenched so tightly upon the holly-branches that the sharp spines of the leaves pierced his flesh, but the small, physical hurt went unnoticed amid the waves of pain and fury sweeping over him. There was a rushing sound in his ears and he shivered as though with cold, yet all the while sweat was pouring from him and his gaze remained riveted upon the couple at the edge of the wood. When at length Rainham had ridden away, and Dorothea turned to retrace her steps, the radiance in her face dealt him a fresh blow. She passed close to the spot where he stood concealed, and though it was in his mind to step out and confront her the thought took no root in his will, and he remained motionless until she had disappeared from view.

One of the branches he held had been snapped by the force of his grip and he released it, looking down stupidly at his torn and bloodstained hands. The black rage which had possessed him at the sight of Dorothea

177

in Rainham's arms was passing now, and when his horse nuzzled softly at his shoulder he turned abruptly and, flinging one arm across the animal's glossy neck, hid his face against it with a groan.

He could not return to the farm until he was calmer, nor meet Dorothea alone with the memory of the scene he had witnessed fresh in his mind. All thought of the news he brought was forgotten, for the affairs of David and Clarissa meant nothing to him if Dorothea had given her love elsewhere. Returning to the road he mounted his horse and rode blindly in the opposite direction to Gallows Farm, through the bright sunshine which for him had been transformed into the bleakest desolation of winter.

Dusk was falling when at length David returned home, and Dorothea had lit the candles in the parlour. She heard her brother's step in the hall and raised her head to listen, smiling to hear the new vitality in his movements, and the merry tune he was whistling. When he entered the room she saw again the carefree David of the old days which now seemed so far away; he caught her in his arms, swung her clear off her feet, and kissed her warmly before setting her down again. Dorothea, steadying herself with her hands on his shoulders, regarded him with an expression which she hoped expressed the blankest bewilderment.

"By my faith, you're in high spirits tonight!" she exclaimed. "What in the world has happened?"

"What has happened?" he repeated in astonishment. "Why, did not Michael tell you?"

This time her bewilderment was not entirely assumed.

"Michael has not yet returned," she said. "Is he not with you?"

"No, for he left Ardely Place hours ago, to bring you news of what has happened. Dorothea, 'tis a miracle, no less! Even now I cannot credit the truth of it."

Without more delay he poured out the story of Judith's arrival at Ardely Place, and all that it would mean to him and to Clarissa, while his sister exclaimed and questioned with an eagerness which quite deceived him. When the tale was done, however, it was she who first returned to the mystery of Michael's disappearance.

"What can have happened to him?" she asked with some anxiety. "Do you think he has met with an accident upon the road?"

" 'Tis more likely he has mistaken the way," David reassured her. " 'Twas his first visit to Ardely Place, and these lanes can be damnably confusing when one is not familiar with them. If he has not returned within an hour I will go in search of him."

This, however, was not required of him, for by the time he had recounted to Thomas and Janet the events of the afternoon, and returned with his sister to the parlour, they heard a rider in the lane, and a few minutes later Ashton came into the room. He paused just within the door, where the light of the candles penetrated but feebly, and stood there motionless while David spoke a cheery greeting.

"Where the devil have you been, Michael? Here's Dorothea fancying you killed or injured, and I about to set out to look for you——" he broke off, disconcerted by the silence of the shadowy figure, and after a moment added more sharply: "What ails you, man? Can you not speak?"

"David," Michael's voice sounded oddly strained, and still he did not move, "Kelvin Rainham is in Reppington."

Dorothea caught her breath, and David rapped out an oath.

"Are you certain?" he demanded, and Michael nodded.

"I have seen him."

"But what in the fiend's name is he doing here? Gad'slife, can it be that Jevington has bidden him to the wedding, and that he has had the infernal impudence to accept?"

Now at last Michael moved. He came slowly forward into the light and halted with his hands gripping the back of a chair, the knuckles shining white in the candlelight. His face was haggard and a trickle of moisture showed beneath his periwig.

"I think not," he said. "If Rainham is here by anyone's invitation, I fancy 'tis your sister's."

David's jaw dropped, and he said incredulously:

Michael, are you mad?"

"I wish to God I were," Ashton addressed David, but his gaze was fixed upon Dorothea, "but let her deny if she can that he was in this house today, or that they were together in the wood, with kissing and fondling and similar wantonness."

"By God, you are mad! Mad or drunk!" David was beginning furiously, when Dorothea's voice, cold and scornful, cut across his. She had risen to her feet and was facing Ashton calmly.

"So you have been spying upon me, Michael. I had not thought that you would sink to that."

"What?" David swung round to face her, mouth agape. "D'you mean it's true?"

"What of it if it is? This is not your house, David, nor is it for you to say who shall or shall not enter it. For the rest, my kisses are my own, to bestow where I choose, and I have bestowed them upon no other man." She paused, and then added more gently: "I did not wish you to learn of it in this fashion, my dear, but Michael forces my hand. I am going to marry Kelvin Rainham."

"Marry Rainham?" David repeated in a stunned voice. "Have you taken leave of your senses?"

She shook her head, smiling a little.

"Did I ask that when you told me of your love for Clarissa? Oh, David, I know that such a marriage cannot please you, but for my sake will you not try to reconcile yourself to it?"

With a supreme effort which in itself marked the profound change in him—for a year ago he would have given vent to his feelings in an outburst of petulant rage— David mastered his emotions and strove to speak calmly.

"When did you come to this decision, Dorothea? Today?"

Again she shook her head.

"We plighted our troth in April, on the day after he left the farm. We were to have been wed in the autumn, but now he wishes our marriage to take place at once, and I have agreed."

"But, devil take it, girl, why are you doing this thing?"

In spite of his efforts to control it, David's voice shook with mingled bewilderment and distress. "The man ruined us, he lied to you and deceived you, and yet you mean to marry him. In God's name, why?"

"I love him, David," she replied quietly.

"But his reputation, his shameful past! You know the crimes of which he was accused, the cause of his dismissal from the army and the years he spent in exile. Does the name you bear mean so little to you that you are willing to change it for one stained and dishonoured?"

"Those stories are untrue," she retorted proudly, "or at best are truth so garbled and distorted by those who wished him ill that they are no better than lies."

"He told you that, of course?" David spoke scornfully, and from where he stood by the table Michael uttered a short, contemptuous laugh. Dorothea paid no heed to him, but moved to her brother's side and laid her hand on his arm, raising her eyes earnestly to his.

"David," she said, "do you remember an evening in the orchard when you said that some day I should love so greatly that all else would be of no account? You spoke more truly than you knew, for if every evil word uttered against Kelvin Rainham were proved true, still would I love him, and still be willing to marry him."

"I do not understand you," he complained, covering her hand with his own. "Does it weigh with you not at all that he won your heart by trickery and deceit? That he hid his true identity under an assumed name, nor made any attempt to confess the truth until my return forced him into the open?"

"You are mistaken, David," she replied. "He had no need of trickery to win my heart, for 'twas his from the first moment of our meeting." There was a pause while she sought for words to make her meaning clear, to convey to her brother some sense of the blinding revelation which had been granted her on that storm-swept winter's night when Thomas and Will brought a wounded stranger to Gallows Farm. She moved away towards the fireplace, and David's eyes followed her with a curious intentness; Michael, standing forgotten by the table, realized with a stab of added bitterness that in this moment crisis he was of no account whatsoever either to brother or sister. At length Dorothea turned once more to face them, but it was to David alone that she spoke.

"How can I explain something which is, even to myself, inexplicable? When they brought him here he was sorely hurt, too weak even to speak, but when for a moment consciousness returned and he looked into my eyes, I felt a sense of recognition. It was as though we had always loved, but had lost each other for a while; it was something which reached beyond all worldly barriers and admitted of no denial. Had that been our only meeting, had death claimed him then as it so nearly did, the memory of it would have gone with me to my life's end; but God was merciful, and he lived, and now we are to be wed. Think kindly of us if you can, David, but do not seek to part us. You will not succeed."

There was silence for a few moments after her voice had ceased, and then David sighed and spoke very quietly.

"I do not pretend to understand," he said, "save that your love for this man is no common thing, and if he loves you in return I will not seek to come between you. Whatever right I may have had to intervene in such a matter I forfeited a year ago. I will not pretend to a liking for Rainham which I can never feel, but I will not quarrel with him because he takes you from me, nor, upon my part at least, shall your marriage be the cause of ill-will betwixt you and I."

For a few seconds Dorothea stared at him, scarcely able to credit that the dreaded moment had come and gone, and left no rift between them. Then, too much moved and too grateful to reply in words, cast herself into her brother's arms and pressed her cheek against his, and it was left to Michael to utter the protest she had anticipated from David. Astounded and shocked by his friend's reception of the news, he could not at first believe that Stratton meant to make no move to prevent such a marriage, and his incredulity found an outlet in words.

"Good God, David, you cannot mean it! You cannot permit so unsuitable a match!"

The younger man looked at him with a trace of impatience.

"I could not prevent it if I would," he retorted. "Dorothea is of an age to choose for herself, and whether or not in my opinion she has chosen rightly is of no account."

For a moment Michael stared at him, while the shocked surprise in his face gave way to fury. Racked by jealousy since that glimpse of Dorothea in her lover's arms, he had clung doggedly to the conviction that David's anger against Rainham would equal his own, and now, deprived of even that slight consolation, he lost what small measure of self-control he had until then retained. An ugly expression hardened his eyes and twisted his lips.

"I see," he sneered. "Since Dorothea discovers in herself not only a desire to regain what she has lost, but also the means to gratify it, you do not intend to stand in her way. Very brotherly, i'faith!"

"Michael, what an infamous thing to suggest!" Dorothea exclaimed indignantly. "You, of all men, should know how little worldly considerations weigh with me."

"Should I?" he retorted bitterly. "Perhaps I would have fared better had it been in my power to offer you Hope Stratton as a bridal gift."

Dorothea uttered a gasp as of sudden pain and all the colour drained out of her face. She swayed on her feet, and when David, in swift concern, caught her about the waist she leaned against him for support, though her dilated eyes never left Michael's face. His chance words had revealed at last the thing she feared, had stripped it of mystery and shown in all its hideous mockery the barrier whose shape she had been unable to define. Strangely enough, until that moment it had not occurred to her that marriage with Kelvin would make her again mistress of Hope Stratton; it was Gallows Farm that had seen the birth and flowering of her love, and it was inconceivable that any other place should shelter that love's fulfilment. Hope Stratton, and his possession of it, was the one thing she had forgotten when she had made her proud declaration that nothing could succeed in parting them.

Michael perceived that he had wounded her more deeply than he had anticipated, and took a warped pleasure in the knowledge. He proceeded to elaborate the theme with all the ingenuity at his command.

"It will seem strange, will it not, to return to your old home as Rainham's bride? To see that adventurer in your father's place, while your brother earns his bread in another man's house? But perhaps you intend him to profit also by this marriage. What say you, David? Can you swallow your pride sufficiently to curry favour with the man who ruined you, in the hope that he will prove generous? To become a pensioner upon your own estate? A unique experience, upon my soul!"

"It is not true," Dorothea whispered brokenly. "What do wealth and lands matter to me? I would marry him were he the veriest beggar."

Michael laughed, and shifted his position, setting a foot on the chair and his elbow on his bent knee. In a strangely detached way David noticed that his hands were scratched and bloodstained and his ruffles torn.

"Would you indeed?" Ashton remarked at length. "Then perhaps 'tis Rainham who seeks to profit. I was told that when he was at Hope Stratton he found himself shunned by people who accounted themselves your friends, but no doubt 'twill be a different tale when he returns with you as his wife. So Rainham wins all, and David may console himself with the thought that the next heir to the Stratton fortune will at least bear Stratton blood in his veins."

"Stop! Stop, for pity's sake!" Dorothea's voice broke, and she covered her ears with her hands. After a moment she looked up at her brother. "David," she said piteously, "before God I swear that until this moment I had forgotten Hope Stratton. You do not, you cannot believe that I was prompted by motives so base."

His arm still about her, he considered her with troubled eyes.

"I do not believe it," he replied, "and for your sake I hope that what Michael said of Rainham is equally unjust, but facts, my dear, cannot be denied. Rainham is master of Hope Stratton, and if you had in truth forgotten that, you would do well to think deeply upon it before giving yourself to him in marriage."

"Yes," she whispered, "I must think on it." She freed herself from his hold and stood upright, ashen-pale in the candle-light. "Oh, dear God, what am I to do?"

Her hands dropped listlessly to her sides, she turned, and with dragging steps went slowly from the room. When the door had closed behind her David looked across at Michael, and there was little friendliness in his eyes.

"And you profess to love her!" he said contemptuously. "Hell and the devil, did you have to be so brutal?"

"'Slife, what ails you?" Ashton retorted with a flash of resentment. "I never thought to hear you speak on Rainham's behalf. Will you stand meekly by and see her marry the rogue?"

"I'll not stand by and watch you torture her to satisfy your damned jealousy," David told him hotly, "and if I speak on his behalf—well, 'twas you who advised me to be guided by Dorothea's judgment. Why should it be at fault where he is concerned, and dependable in all else?"

"Oh, if you are to take his part there is no more to be said," Michael replied sullenly. He dropped into a chair by the table and bowed his head on his hands, thrusting his fingers deep into the curls of his periwig. "You do not know the hell I have been through today. You did not see them together as I did, see her in his arms——!" His voice was shaking uncontrollably, and he paused to gain some measure of command over it before adding savagely: "Lose her I may, but by Heaven, it will not be without a struggle!"

"You have lost her already," said David in an oddly detached voice. "You fool, do you still cherish a hope that she will turn to you?" He moved restlessly to the window and looked out unseeingly at the familiar scene, flooded now with the light of a rising moon. "Stop their marriage you may, with this talk of Hope Stratton, for Dorothea ever set great store by the place, and by our family traditions—our father was wont to say she should have been the heir—but that will avail you nothing. I know my sister better than you do, Michael, and I can tell you this. Whether or not she marries Kelvin Rainham, she will be true to him till her dying day, for hers is a steadfast heart and 'tis not in her nature to love lightly."

CHAPTER XII

RENUNCIATION

Outside the parlour, in the cool darkness of the stone-flagged hall, Dorothea dropped into a seat and crouched there with her face hidden in her hands. The fear that she had held at bay for so long had seized her in a choking grip; the lurking shadow was a shadow no longer, but a reality as tangible as the broad lands of Hope Stratton, or the stout walls her forebears had built a century-and-a-half ago. How completely she had forgotten, when she plighted troth with Kelvin, that it was to her own old home she must go as his bride. They had been happy at Gallows Farm, and Thomas had so often expressed his deep pleasure in their betrothal, and spoken of his intention to make them his heirs when they married. He, too, had forgotten that Kelvin had no need of Gallows Farm; that he was master of a rich estate and a great and noble house.

Countless memories of her childhood and girlhood flooded her mind, and she saw with the clarity of a vision the stately rooms and flower-decked gardens of her home, peopled with beloved figures. Her serene and gentle mother, whose image had grown dim with time; her father, jovial and good-natured, yet with a temper as quick as David's own; David himself, the heir to that goodly heritage, her brother whose kindness that evening had erased all recollection of wounds he had dealt her in the past. She strove with all the strength of her will to picture Kelvin in the same setting, but in vain, and the failure told her, with a bitter certainty which admitted of no denial, that the barrier she so greatly feared had indeed been thrust between them. There was one sacrifice she could not make, one obstacle not even her great love could overcome.

Yet perhaps that sacrifice would not be demanded of her. Kelvin had never spoken of a return to Hope Stratton, so perhaps he realized what she must feel upon that score. Did he realize it? The question throbbed in her mind with tormenting persistence, and she knew that the uncertainty could not be borne until he came to the farm the following day. She rose to her feet, and without pausing to inform anyone of her intention, slipped quietly out of the house into the scented summer night, and set out in the direction of the village.

She went by way of the path through the orchard and the woodland which she and Kelvin had taken that afternoon, past the clump of holly-trees where Michael had hidden to spy upon them. Beyond the wood the road stretched white and deserted in the moonlight, splashed here and there with inky shadows. The loneliness of the scene might have unnerved her had she been less preoccupied, but neither solitude nor the distance she had to traverse made any impression on her mind as she walked quickly onward, stumbling now and then on the rutted surface of the highway, but never halting until the village was reached.

A sum of country voices sounded from the tap-room of the "Brindled Hound," but the narrow passage which traversed the building from front to back was empty, and no one saw her pass along it and enter a room at its farther end. Kelvin was writing at the table in the centre of the chamber, the light of the single candle at his elbow gleaming on his tawny hair, and he glanced up with a trace of impatience as the door opened. Seeing Dorothea standing there, with neither hat nor cloak and her skirts marked with the dust of the highway, he rose to his feet in sudden anxiety. His first thought was that the news of their betrothal had led to a violent quarrel between her and David, and he blamed himself bitterly that he had not insisted upon telling Stratton himself.

"Dorothea!" he exclaimed. "What brings you here at this hour?" He went forward to lead her to the chair he had just vacated, and when she was seated dropped to one knee beside her, taking her hands in his. "Have you quarrelled with David by reason of our betrothal?"

"No," Dorothea shook her head. "I have told him, but though he did not pretend to be pleased he said that he had no right to come between us. He was so kind, so forbearing——" her voice quivered, and she turned her head away.

The answer did nothing to lessen his perplexity. Incredible as it seemed that David had received the news in so complaisant a manner, it was even more unlikely that Dorothea should have come to the inn merely to tell him of it. Her obvious distress alone belied it. He said gently:

"It is not possible that you came so far at this late hour to tell me that. If David raises no objection to our marriage, what can be amiss?"

" 'Twas something Michael said," she replied in a stifled voice, still not looking at him. "He was in the wood today—I know not how or why—and he told David that he had seen us together. When he realized that David would countenance our marriage he grew angry and made cruel, bitter accusations against us. He said that I had agreed to marry you only to become again mistress of Hope Stratton, while upon your part you desired me for your wife so that you would be accepted by those who accounted themselves my friends."

"If such accusations were true," he replied, smiling a little, "we should both be well served. My love, have you indeed allowed this farrago of nonsense to distress you? I believe I should be angry with you for such folly."

Her fingers tightened upon his.

"Ah, no, 'twas not that! How could anything so trivial trouble us?" She hesitated for a moment, almost afraid to speak of the matter which had brought her there that night, but at length she resumed slowly: "It is merely that, until he spoke of it, it had not occurred to me that I should ever return to my old home. I have been incredibly stupid, but I cannot—that is, I did not think——" her voice trailed into silence, and she sat looking down at their clasped hands.

All the amusement faded from Kelvin's face, and it was in a somewhat hard voice that he completed the sentence for her.

"You cannot think of me as master of Hope Stratton. I understand."

"But it cannot be that you wish to return there?" At last her eyes, anxious and imploring, sought his. "When you told me of your sojourn there you said you were not happy, that you could never feel it was truly your home."

"No house was a home to me then," he replied. "For years I had been a wanderer, following the red trail of war without one single tie to bind me to any place I might call home. Hope Stratton was to me then a beautiful, alien place, beloved only because it brought me knowledge of you, but now—Dorothea, will it matter so greatly if I ask you to return there with me?"

She was incapable of being anything but frank with him, and though the pain and the hopelessness were closing coldly about her heart she made no attempt to evade the question. Only the clasp of her hands slackened, and the small, involuntary gesture answered him before she spoke.

"Is it so strange, Kelvin, that it should be so? It is the house where I was born, where my forebears have lived for generations. I had thought never to leave it save as a bride, and when it passed from our possession it was the loss hardest of all to bear, but slowly I grew accustomed to the thought that I would never dwell there again. How then can I return, to sit in my mother's place when by right that place should be filled by David's wife? I have no more right to be mistress of Hope Stratton than——" she broke off abruptly, but Kelvin had little doubt of her meaning.

"Than I have to be master," he said quietly. "All that you say is true, but it was so when you consented to become my wife. Nothing has changed since then."

He rose to his feet, leaning his hands on the edge of the table and staring blindly at the flickering candle, while he strove for wisdom to deal with this crisis which had come so suddenly and unexpectedly upon them. He could not blame Dorothea for her scruples, and though it would have been pleasant to take her to Hope Stratton, to be with her in fact where he had so often seen her in fancy, it did not matter greatly to him where they lived, as long as they were together. But the trouble, he knew, went deeper than that, though he doubted whether she had yet realized it. The house of Hope Stratton was only a part of his winnings.

She was speaking now of the farm, of the plans which she and Thomas and Janet had made, believing that Kelvin acquiesced in them. Her voice held an almost pathetic eagerness, but when no response came from the motionless figure by the table her words faltered and died away. After a pause she said, very quietly:

"Is a return to Hope Stratton so important to you, Kelvin?"

"It is of no importance at all," he replied, turning abruptly to face her. "I had as lief spend the rest of my life at Gallows Farm, for I found there greater happiness than I had ever dreamed possible." She opened her lips to speak, but he continued quickly: "That, however, is not to solve a difficulty, but to evade it. Hope Stratton will still be mine, whether or not I ever set eyes upon it again."

Her stricken look informed him that his surmise was correct, that she was only just beginning to comprehend the magnitude of the difficulty. He cursed Ashton for his intervention, and yet at the same time knew that realization must have come sooner or later, and better now, perhaps, while she was free to make her choice, than after they were wed.

"Is the house then to be left empty, to fall into decay?" he resumed after a moment. "And if it is, will you be content, nor care for the fact that it is upon the wealth of Hope Stratton that we must live, for without that wealth, my dear, I am a poor man. Poor?" Mingled pain and self-contempt twisted his lips. "Little better than a beggar, a soldier-of-fortune, knight of the long sword and the lean purse."

"Do you think that knowledge would influence me?" she retorted passionately. "I would trudge the roads barefoot to be with you. Oh, why do you torment me in this fashion? Do you seek to make me believe Michael's accusations against you?"

"I seek only that which is best for you," he replied, and with a tremendous effort of will succeeded in maintaining some semblance of self-possession. She had put out her hand to him as she spoke, but when he made no move to take it returned it trembling to her lap. His own hands were gripped hard upon the edge of the table against which he leaned, for he knew that if he so much as touched her finger-tips the force of their pent-up emotions would be released and, overwhelming reason and logic, sweep them headlong into a decision which both might afterwards regret.

"Best for me?" she repeated desolately. "Is it best that my heart should break?"

"What would you have me do?" he asked unsteadily. "Rid myself of the Stratton fortune? Aye, willingly, but how? Most gladly would I restore it to David so that he, as well as we, might find happiness——"

"You could not!" Dorothea was aghast. "No man could in honour take back as a gift that which he had fairly lost."

"Do I not know it, but how then am I to rid myself of this golden incubus? To be sure, I might gamble it away as David once did, but cards and dice do not always fall as one desires; to sell the estate is but to exchange one burden for another. No, Dorothea, there is no middle course. Either you must marry me knowing that your family's wealth is mine, or——"

"Or we must say farewell," she whispered, and bowed

her head upon her hands. "Ah, how can I make such a choice? Kelvin, help me! Tell me what I must do!"

"I cannot help you, Dorothea," he said sadly. "My love, my happiness, my very life, are bound up in this—how then can I advise you? 'Tis a decision you alone can make."

She did not answer, and for a while there was silence. A burst of laughter sounded faintly from the tap-room, and somewhere in the garden an owl hooted mournfully, but the sounds fell without meaning upon their ears. He stood watching her, his face rigid with pain, and when at length she lifted her head he knew that the die was cast.

"I cannot," she said in a low, lifeless voice, and rose to her feet, looking past him into the shadows. "It is strange, is it not, when I love you so dearly, that such a thing should have power to part us? Why is it so? My mind, my heart, my will, all urge me to you, and yet I cannot obey their prompting. No other thing in all the world, not shame, nor poverty, nor dishonour, could come between, but something stronger than myself makes this one sacrifice impossible. I . . . cannot . . . marry you."

Though he had half suspected what her decision would be, the words none the less struck him with the force of a physical blow. He went white, and it was some moments before he could trust himself to speak.

"Must all our hopes and dreams then come to naught? Is our love too weak to overcome a single barrier?"

The strange, remote stillness faded from her face, and with a little cry she buried her face in her hands.

"Ah, do not speak so—I cannot bear it! Kelvin, you bade me choose! Help me now to abide by my decision."

"No!" In a stride he was beside her, crushing her in his arms. "To lose you now, upon the very threshold of happiness? I cannot, will not let you go from me."

"Kelvin, I entreat you!" She stood impassive in his embrace, but her quivering voice belied that frozen calm. "Dearest, for my sake, let me go! We must part now, for ever—ah, do you not understand? I cannot marry you . . . so let me go . . . lest I love you too well."

"Dorothea!" It was a cry of renunciation, and of heartbreak. He dropped to one knee before her, his arms still clasped about her and his face hidden against the folds of her gown; her tears fell upon the tawny hair, but for several moments neither spoke. The silence grew intolerable, taut and quivering with their anguish.

It was broken at last by a prosaic sound, a soft rap on the door which brought Kelvin to his feet and caused Dorothea to turn quickly away as though to contemplate the moonlit garden beyond the window. The door opened, and a maidservant peeped timidly round its edge.

"Please your Honour, Sir David Stratton is here, and— oh!" She broke off as she caught sight of Dorothea. "Sir David has come in search of you, ma'am, but I told him you weren't here, not having seen you come in."

"Pray ask my brother to wait, Meg. I will join him in a moment." Dorothea spoke without turning, but her voice was composed—too composed, Kelvin thought bitterly, and was racked by an instant's doubt. Then, as the servant withdrew, she turned towards him, and he saw the tears glittering on her white cheeks.

"I will go," she murmured, and moved slowly towards the door, while he watched her with a nightmarish sense of unreality. This could not be happening, here in this wainscoted parlour where they had plighted their troth in the springtime; it was an evil dream from which he would presently wake. Yet at the same moment he knew that this time there would be no awakening.

She reached the door and turned to face him again. Her lips quivered, but there was no faltering of the steadfast resolution in her eyes.

"Forgive me, Kelvin, if you can," she whispered, and the words barely reached him across the width of the room. "Farewell, my love, my love!"

She was gone. He went quickly to the door, but halted there, his hand upon the latch and his head bowed. He heard Stratton's startled, anxious question, and then Dorothea's voice, on a note which told of endurance almost at an end.

"David," she said. "Oh, David, take me home!"

There were footsteps, a murmur of voices, a pause,

and then finally hoofbeats which receded steadily and faded into the stillness of the summer night. When the last sound had died away Kelvin went slowly back to the table. He picked up the letter he had been writing when Dorothea arrived—it was to Sally, telling her of his imminent marriage—and very deliberately tore it across and across. For a space he stood looking down at the fragments, and then with a sudden, passionate gesture, a movement so violent that the candle was overturned and extinguished, cast them from him. In the darkened room Dorothea's voice, broken with tears, seemed to tremble yet upon the silence. "We must part now, for ever . . . for ever. . . ."

Michael Ashton was pacing the hall at Gallows Farm, his footsteps ringing on the white flagstones, his hands clasped behind him and his head bent. To and fro he went, between the foot of the twisting staircase and the massive door which stood open to the morning sunshine; to and fro, with a restlessness which spoke of deep mental disquiet. What had happened the previous evening, at the inn where Kelvin Rainham lodged? When Mrs. Ashe had come, in some concern, with the news that Dorothea was nowhere to be found, David had guessed at once whither she had gone, but he had curtly refused Michael's offer to ride to Reppington with him. Later, when they had returned together, he had brought her into the house and given her into Janet's care, but not before Michael had heard the sound of her desolate, exhausted weeping. He would have questioned David, but the younger man had gone straight to his own bedchamber, nor had Ashton encountered either brother or sister that morning. He knew that they were avoiding him, and resentment added itself to his already complex state of mind.

A footstep on the stairs checked him halfway to the door, and he turned quickly as Dorothea appeared around the bend of the staircase. She was wearing her blue riding-habit, with a broad sweep of feathered hat-brim above a face pale and tragically composed, and she hesitated for an instant when she saw him. Then she descended the rest of the stairs, bidding him good morning in the cool, courteous tone of a stranger. He returned the greeting, but as it became apparent that she had no intention of lingering, took a quick pace towards her.

"Dorothea," his voice was constrained, "may I speak with you? No, not here," as she paused with a glance of polite inquiry, "in private."

Without a word she led the way to the parlour, and waited while he closed the door. He could read nothing in her face, which remained calm and wholly impersonal, reminding him, with a tormenting stab of jealousy, of Rainham's own maddening aloofness. The thought did nothing to soothe his feelings, and when he spoke his voice was harsh and uneven.

"Dorothea," he said, "I have no right to ask, perhaps, but do you still intend to marry Rainham?"

Her eyes rested upon him thoughtfully.

"No, you have no right to ask," she replied pensively, "but I will answer you none the less." Her glance dropped to the riding-whip which she was gripping tightly between her gloved hands, but her voice did not falter. "I am not going to marry him."

A wave of exultation swept over him and he, too, lowered his eyes lest she should see the triumph in them. Something, then, he had achieved.

"You have discovered, perhaps," he suggested, "that what I said of him last night was no more than the truth?"

"No." Contempt flickered briefly in her eyes. "If you imagine that I went to accuse him of that you flatter yourself unduly. Do you really believe that your spite could cause such a misunderstanding between us?"

Anger was rising in him again, but with an effort he conquered it and achieved a sneer.

"Brave words, my dear, but—you are not going to marry him."

Dorothea turned abruptly away, tossing her whip on to the table, and went to stand at the window with her back to the room. Would she ever grow accustomed, she wondered, to the pain, and the aching sense of loss and loneliness? Would it lessen with time, or must she bear it till the end of her life? Now, too, the voice of doubt was whispering in her ears—had she chosen aright? To the full she realized the torment which Kelvin must have endured when, faced with a decision of great moment, he had chosen the path of duty. Yet what duty did she owe, and to whom? Not to David, for he had countenanced her marriage. To what, then? To the memory of her dead parents, and all the Strattons, back through the years to the first Sir Humphrey who had sailed to the unknown west, and brought back a fortune and a Spanish bride, and built a noble house on the site of the tumbledown manor which had been his family's home? Was it for a mere tradition that she had sacrificed so much? Wearily, like a moth fluttering about a flame, her thoughts circled the question, knowing that it could never be answered and yet unable to break free of its dread fascination.

She had forgotten Michael's presence, and when he spoke again she was startled, for the words were so closely attuned to her thoughts that they might have taken shape in her own mind.

"What is your reason, then?" he asked abruptly. "Is it merely because he is master of Hope Stratton, and because you had in fact forgotten it, as you said last night? Do you expect me to believe that?"

"What you believe, Michael, is of no consequence to me," Dorothea replied wearily. "You do not understand my feelings, nor could I, even if I wished, make them clear to you." She turned to face him, to all appearances as serene as ever. "There seems no point in pursuing this conversation. David is waiting to go with me to Ardely Place—Clarissa wishes to see me. Will you go with us?"

He ignored the question, but continued to watch her with sombre eyes. At length he said:

"If that is indeed so, you should be grateful to me for opening your eyes to the truth before it is too late."

"Grateful?" Dorothea paused as though considering the point. A little smile more sad than tears quivered about her lips. "Perhaps I should be more so had you let me remain blind to the truth—until it was too late."

He frowned.

"I do not understand you. To have left you in ignorance would scarcely be conduct worthy of a friend."

"So you still account yourself my friend?" Dorothea's voice was gentle, but something in its tone brought the colour to his cheeks.

"Your truest friend, you once named me," he retorted. "Have I not given proof of my friendship in the past, both to you and to David?"

"We have cause to be grateful to you," she admitted, smoothing her gloves over her hands, "but I cannot refrain from wondering how much of your concern for us a year ago was prompted by self-interest. Your actions yesterday scarcely suggested friendship."

"To the devil with friendship!" Michael, his self-control wearing thin, strode forward and halted close beside her. "That was never what I wanted from you, and well you know it. Flout me as you will, I have not abandoned hope——"

"Then do so," Dorothea broke in coldly. "I shall never marry. My love is given wholly to Kelvin Rainham, and no other man can ever take his place in my heart. Now I pray you, Michael, have done with this folly, nor persist in conduct which makes it difficult for me to remember your past kindnesses."

She had picked up her whip and was turning away as she spoke, with the intention of going past him towards the door, but he grasped her arm and swung her round again, none too gently, to face him.

"So 'tis folly, is it?" he said between his teeth. "My only folly has lain in the patience I have used, and too great a reverence in my dealings with you. Until yesterday I deemed your cold prudishness sincere, but what I saw then taught me the way to win favours from you. 'Tis the adventurer's way, is it not, the way of the soldier-of-fortune—thus, and thus!"

He gripped her by the shoulders and his lips came down fiercely upon hers. She struggled wildly to free herself, broke from his hold at last, and in the same instant her right arm rose and fell. Michael uttered a cry and sprang back, with the mark of her riding-whip reddening across his face.

The pain of the blow sobered him and he realized the enormity of his offence. Dorothea's cheeks were scarlet, her eyes flashing—for the first and only time in their acquaintance he saw her really angry—and yet when she spoke, her voice, in curious contrast to her looks, was quiet and controlled.

"Neither that way nor any other," she said contemptuously. "You are aware, I suppose, of what would follow if either David or Kelvin learned of your conduct towards me?"

"Plague take them both!" he retorted savagely, a hand against his bruised cheek. "I am not afraid to meet them!"

"There will be no meeting," Dorothea's voice was cold. "I would not have either of them risk his life for so paltry a reason. No, Michael, this matter rests between you and me. Be good enough to leave this house, and do not approach me again."

He realized then what his brief recklessness had cost him, and though he knew his conduct to have been unpardonable, ventured a plea for forgiveness, offering as excuse the jealousy which tortured him and ending with an avowal of his undying devotion. She heard him to the end in unyielding silence, and then turned once more towards the door.

"We shall remain all day at Ardely Place," was her only reply, "and so you will have ample time to take your departure. I will make some excuse to David, for it will be best if you and I do not meet again."

The door closed behind her, and Michael was left standing in the middle of the room, listening to her retreating footsteps. After awhile he lifted his hand and touched the scarlet weal her whip had scored across his cheek, his face hardening to an expression which might, had she seen it, have caused her to regret the blow.

David was waiting in the yard, and to his query as to whether Ashton meant to accompany them she returned only a brief negative. He raised his brows, but made no comment until they had left the farm behind them and were approaching the village. Then he said:

"What is amiss, Dorothea? Why did Michael not come with us?"

"We quarrelled," she replied, choosing her words with care. "You will not, I think, need to ask me why. Suffice it to say that he will have left the farm before we return, nor do I wish to see him again."

David sighed.

" 'Twas to be expected, I suppose," he said resignedly. "I told him last night that he had no hope of prevailing with you, but he would pay no heed." He paused, studying the calm profile presented to him. "Dorothea, are you certain that you have acted wisely? Last night you were in no case to consider any matter calmly, and if Michael's words swept you into a decision you have since regretted——"

"He said nothing to influence my decision," she said unsteadily, "but his words did reveal to me a truth which I had overlooked. Cost me what it may, I cannot marry Kelvin while so much stands between us."

He shook his head.

"Heaven knows I never thought to find myself Rainham's advocate," he said with a wry smile, "but that anything stands between you is in some sort my responsibility, and you have already suffered too much upon my account. I would I might repair the harm."

They had entered the village street now, and were approaching the "Brindled Hound," where Jonas Potter stood in the doorway, puffing at his pipe and surveying the sunlit morning with a benign expression. He touched his forelock as they came up to him, and on a sudden impulse David drew rein and addressed him.

"Is Major Rainham within, Jonas?"

He heard Dorothea's faint gasp of alarm and protest, and with his free hand reached out and grasped the bridle of her horse, forcing her to halt with him. The innkeeper removed the pipe from his mouth and shook his head.

"No, Sir David," he said regretfully. "The Major was away off to London nigh on two hours ago."

David nodded his thanks and they moved on. He did not know what he had intended to do, what he would have said to Rainham had he been still at the inn, but the sadness in his sister's eyes had prompted him to make some effort to help her. Now he stole a covert glance at her face, and was surprised to see there an expression almost of relief. He was not to know that to her Kelvin's departure seemed an indication that her decision had been the right one. Regret now was of no avail; he was gone, and all was over.

CHAPTER XIII

SHADOWS FROM THE PAST

For the second time Major Rainham returned to London from Kent, but now instead of joy he carried black despair in his heart. He spent his time in the company to which Lord Jevington had introduced him, and sought in wild excesses forgetfulness of all he had lost. Sally Cheriton watched him and grew anxious, but when she sought to reason with him he met her protests with mockery, and told her, with a hard, sneering laugh, that he was but fulfilling her own prophecy in riding to the devil as fast as he could. To rebukes and warnings alike he paid not the slightest heed, for he had ceased to care what became of him—had ceased, in fact, in that dark hour when he realized that Dorothea was beyond his reach for ever.

David Stratton was also in London at this time, still, it seemed, with little hope of attaining his heart's desire, for though Clarissa was safe from Jevington there was no possibility that, even had he known of David's hopes, Lord Ardely would bestow his daughter's hand upon a penniless secretary. Sir Edward had removed to the capital from Ardely Place at the same time as Jevington and his grudgingly-acknowledged Viscountess, for he knew his nephew well enough to deem it prudent to keep a watchful eye upon his lordship's treatment of his wife and son.

The affair had naturally given rise to a great deal of talk, but thanks to Amberstone's presence Lord and Lady Jevington contrived to dwell together, if not with amity, at least with an outward show of complaisance—and this in spite of the fact that her ladyship's name was presently linked, quite unjustifiably, with that of Major Rainham—until the day when in a fit of shrewish temper she disclosed to her husband how she had obtained the proofs of her marriage.

Jevington's first impulse was to call to account the man who had betrayed him, but courage was not one of his outstanding virtues and, remembering Major Rainham's formidable swordsmanship, he determined upon a more tortuous revenge. Sally was one of the first people to hear the story he spread about, and, hearing it, she sent at once for Kelvin.

He came, immaculate and unhurried as ever, but his air of leisurely calm was soon dispelled.

"Well, Kelvin," Sally greeted him, her shrewd brown eyes appraising him somewhat grimly, "I presume you have not yet heard this tale the whole town is laughing over?"

"No, I have not." The Major produced his snuff-box, and took a pinch with an elegant turn of the wrist. "Is it particularly amusing?"

"You are not likely to consider it so," she retorted. "It concerns you."

"My dear Sally," his smile was ironic, "notoriety no longer discomposes me."

"You," Mrs. Cheriton repeated deliberately, ignoring the flippancy, "and Dorothea Stratton."

"What!" The air of languid indifference vanished as though it had never been, and his hand closed about her wrist in a grip which made her wince. "What are they saying?"

"A deal of nastiness," she replied frankly. "It seems

that the story of your stay at Gallows Farm has leaked out, or rather, a lewdly-distorted version of it. The tale runs that for a jest you sought out Miss Stratton at her rural retreat, and under an assumed name wooed and won her, but that the jest recoiled upon your own head when Sir David returned home unexpectedly to avenge his sister's honour. Your defeat, we are told, was complete and ignominious, and the injury you were nursing when you returned to London, sustained at his hands. So much for the story; I leave you to determine its source."

"Jevington!" said Kelvin bitterly. " 'Tis not difficult to distinguish his hand in this. He must have discovered my part in his discomfiture at Ardely Place, and chosen this way to repay it." He released her wrist and stood drumming his fingers on the table, a frown between his brows, while Sally watched him curiously.

"What do you mean to do, Kelvin?" she asked at length.

"What can I do, except call him to account? 'Twill do little to repair the harm, but at least 'twill silence his poisonous tongue. I would to God that I had done it long ago."

With that he left her to go in search of the man who had maligned Dorothea. Left alone, Sally looked down at her wrist, marked still by his bruising grip, and thoughtfully pursed her lips. Viscount Jevington, she felt certain, was a doomed man.

In another part of the town, Michael Ashton heard the slanderous tale with emotions so violent and conflicting that for a while he scarcely knew what he was doing, but when he had regained some measure of composure he betook himself without delay to the house of Sir Edward Amberstone. David, when Ashton was ushered into his presence, was engaged in transcribing a letter, and looked up in surprise at his visitor.

"God's death!" was Michael's unexpected greeting. "What manner of man are you to sit driving a quill while your sister's name is bandied about every tavern and coffee-house in London? Have you been a damned clerk for so long that you have forgotten what is expected of a gentleman?"

"What the devil——" more in surprise than anger, David came to his feet. "Have you taken leave of your senses?"

For a long moment Michael looked at him, and then he came farther into the room and spoke more calmly.

"So you know nothing of it," he said. "I ask your pardon."

"Never mind that," David brushed the apology aside. "What is this about Dorothea?"

Michael told him, sparing none of the details with which Lord Jevington's fertile imagination had embellished the story. David listened in tight-lipped silence, and at the end of the tale swept his papers together and thrust them into a drawer.

"It seems that Lord Jevington and I are fated to cross swords after all," he said quietly. "Where are we likely to find him?"

Since Sir David Stratton and Major Rainham were diligently searching the town for the same quarry, whose elusiveness led them to suspect, quite erroneously, that he was deliberately avoiding them, it was inevitable that eventually their paths would converge upon the same point. This, by an odd chance, proved to be Mrs. Cheriton's gaming-house, whither the Viscount had gone quite openly, with two of his boon companions.

This was by no means a proof of courage—he simply did not perceive that he was in danger. In Major Rainham's place he would have dealt with the story, as he had dealt with the tale of Kelvin's intrigue with the Viscountess, by ignoring it altogether, and he was quite unprepared for any swift, decisive action on Rainham's part. The presence in town of Miss Stratton's brother he had completely forgotten.

There were others, however, less confident of his immunity, and when Kelvin entered the gaming-room, and paused just within the door to cast a searching glance over its occupants, the hum of conversation faltered a little. His tall figure, elegant in dull yellow brocade, with glowing hair framing the stern, pale face, was one to

command attention, and the faint smile which ho
about his lips was neither pleasant nor reassuring
bowed slightly to two gentlemen of his acquaintance
were standing nearby, and as they returned the gre
one murmured to the other:

"Egad, Rainham's in an ugly mood! I'd not car
cross him tonight."

His companion nodded agreement, and they tu
to watch him as he passed on. Mrs. Cheriton, at a
for once in her life, started forward to meet him,
tated, and was favoured with a glance of mocking
prehension as Major Rainham went past her to the
where Jevington sat.

He halted close beside it, and the Viscount's two
nanions, quick to heed the menace of cold eyes
smiling mouth, rose hastily to their feet, but his lord
remained slouching in his chair, looking up at K
with an unpleasant sneer on his face. He had
drinking, and his glance was a trifle hazy but still wi
intelligent.

"I fear I interrupt you," Kelvin said smoothly,
cating the cards scattered on the table. He had alr
determined upon the course he would follow, allo
Jevington no chance of escape, but before he
say more he was interrupted in his turn. Hasty foot
sounded on the stairs, and the door was unceremoni
flung open.

Every glance turned in that direction as Sir D
Stratton strode into the room, paused to locate his qu
and moved purposefully forward. Kelvin saw Sally
herself directly in his path so that he was oblige
stop and reply to her greeting, and took imme
advantage of the respite thus gained. There was no
now for finesse; he must act, and act quickly.

"My lord," he said, turning back to Jevington, "pe
me to observe that you are a liar and a villain," an
struck him lightly across the face with his open han

There was an instant of utter silence and then
fusion as the Viscount came furiously to his feet,
the other men moved quickly to restrain him. I
found Mrs. Cheriton clutching his arm.

"Quickly," she whispered, in a voice so soft that only he heard the words, "if you wish to crush this scandal once and for all, offer to act for him in this affair."

"For Rainham?" He stared at her in blank bewilderment, and she shook his arm impatiently.

"Of course for Rainham. Would you make such an offer if the story were true?"

Comprehension dawned in his eyes, and without a word he turned from her and thrust through the group surrounding the two men. Michael, disconcerted by the turn events had taken, remained in the background.

"Major Rainham," David spoke distinctly, drawing the attention of all present upon him, "may I ask a favour of you? I should be honoured to act for you in this affair."

For a moment the cool, grey eyes met his inscrutably, and then passed beyond him to Sally. There was an infinitesimal pause, and then Major Rainham inclined his head.

"The honour, Sir David, will be wholly mine," he said. "I accept your offer."

The duel was over. Lord Jevington lay coughing out his life on the stained and trampled turf, while the man who had dealt his death-blow unhurriedly resumed the coat and baldrick he had laid aside. Presently his second detached himself from the little group about the fallen man and came across to him.

"The surgeon can do nothing," he said. " 'Tis a matter of moments only."

"Indeed?" Major Rainham's voice was completely indifferent. "Then our continued presence here is totally unnecessary. My carriage is at your disposal—let us go." The other appeared to hesitate, and Rainham's brows lifted. "Permit me to point out to you, Sir David, that for the present it will be well for us to preserve an outward appearance of amity."

David agreed, flushing a little, and so together they made their way to the coach which waited a short way off. In silence they entered it, nor did they speak for several minutes after they had left the scene of the encounter.

Leaning back in his corner, David covertly studied his companion's face and wondered what thoughts were passing behind that impassive mask. The fact that he had just killed a man had made no visible impression upon the Major, nor could the younger man recall, as he looked back over the events of the morning, a single instant when Rainham had departed by so much as a fraction from his normal self-possession. He had faced the Viscount's furious onslaught contemptuously, and delivered the final thrust with a cold precision which even David, who would willingly have slain Jevington himself, found singularly unnerving. What qualities, he thought wonderingly, did this strange, cold-natured man possess to have won the love of such a woman as Dorothea?"

"I fear, Sir David," Rainham said suddenly, "that your part in this morning's affair will place you in a somewhat embarrassing situation. Jevington was, I believe, Sir Edward Amberstone's heir?"

"That is so," David's manner was constrained, for he found his present situation embarrassing enough. So far their conversation had been limited to formalities concerned with the arrangements for the duel, and he was uncertain whether or not this opening gambit was a subtle form of mockery. "Considering his lordship's offence, however, I do not think Sir Edward likely to blame me for acting for you."

The Major's unfathomable gaze rested upon him pensively.

"Do you know," he remarked, "how Jevington came by his knowledge?"

"When he was at Ardely Place he would have heard of your sojourn at the farm," David replied curtly. "Others knew of it, of course, but all have too much regard for my sister to slander her." He broke off, frowning. "What I do not understand is why he delayed so long in telling his story."

"I fancy that he discovered a sudden grudge against

me, for it was against me that his malice was directed, and not your sister."

"Because of Lady Jevington?" The question was asked without thought, and as quickly regretted, but the Major's calm remained unimpaired.

"Because of Lady Jevington," he assented, a glint of humour in his eyes, "but not, believe me, in the way that you suppose."

"I ask your pardon." David, annoyed at his own indiscretion, spoke stiffly. "The question was impertinent."

"Not in the least," Kelvin assured him equably. "Since I aspire to your sister's hand you have every right to ask it."

"Do you still aspire to it, sir? Forgive me, but I understood from Dorothea that all thought of your marriage was at an end."

"And, understanding that, you were relieved?" Kelvin countered. "Be easy, Sir David, Dorothea will not marry a usurper."

Startled by the bitterness in his voice, David spoke impulsively and with more warmth than he had yet used.

"I will be frank with you, Major Rainham. It is by no means the marriage I would have chosen for my sister, but when I realized how deeply her heart was engaged the last thing I desired was to prevent it, and because I know she suffers I have regretted your parting. I shall regret it still, and not for her sake alone."

Kelvin smiled. Hitherto David had seen only a cold mockery playing about his lips, and he was struck by the singular charm of that rare smile, intensified now by the wistfulness which invested it.

"You are generous, Sir David," Kelvin said quietly, "and I thank you for it. Had matters fallen out differently I believe we might have become tolerably good friends."

The coach stopped with a jerk at the gates of Sir Edward's house, but David did not immediately move; he was engrossed in the conviction, startling in its novelty, that had nothing stood between them he could have liked Kelvin Rainham very well. Perhaps some day— but no, they were too deeply enmeshed by the snare laid for them by their own heedlessness. He sighed, and becoming aware that he had arrived at his destination, descended slowly from the coach. Framed in the doorway, he turned and looked Rainham full in the eyes.

"I believe we might," he said, "and I am sorry that matters did not—fall out differently."

The news of Viscount Jevington's death at the hands of Major Rainham created less of a sensation than the astounding fact that the Major had been supported in the affair by Sir David Stratton—a fact which, as Sally had foreseen, left no doubt at all that Jevington's infamous story was false. A less widely-known result of the incident was that it marked the end of David's dislike of Rainham, and since Michael Ashton's hostility towards Kelvin increased as Stratton's faded, the erstwhile friends drifted ever farther apart. In Ashton's nature there was a streak of unsuspected vindictiveness which Dorothea's contempt had roused to malevolent life, and now he made no secret of the hatred he bore the Major.

On a certain day early in October Ashton received a visit from a stranger who gave his name as Miles Latimer. He was a man of some forty years, with a lean, brown face disfigured by a scar which twisted his mouth into a perpetual sneer, and he informed Michael that he had only recently returned to England after years of exile. In conclusion he surprised his host by adding: "I am informed, Mr. Ashton, that you are a close friend of Sir David Stratton."

Michael laughed shortly.

"It would be more correct, sir, to say that I was a close friend of Sir David Stratton."

"I see!" Latimer frowned. "Nevertheless, Mr. Ashton, I take it that you would not be averse to doing him a service if it lay in your power?"

"That, my dear sir, would depend upon the manner of the service. What have you in mind?"

A smile twisted the scarred mouth yet further.

"One, Mr. Ashton, which might possibly enable him to regain the fortune he lost to Kelvin Rainham a year ago."

"What!" Michael came abruptly to his feet. "Are you serious?"

Latimer nodded.

"As I told you, sir, I have been a soldier, and for some years served in the army of France. It was during that time that I met Major Rainham, who was, like myself, an exile. Five years ago he was found guilty of cheating at cards. It was an unsavoury affair, and out of it arose a quarrel which led to Rainham killing a man named Dacres. Dacres, Mr. Ashton, was my closest friend."

"I understand," Michael was frowning, "but because Rainham cheated then, Mr. Latimer, it does not necessarily follow that he did so when he played against Stratton last year."

"You think not?" Latimer's voice was sceptical. "They played, I believe, on five consecutive nights, and not once did Rainham lose. A remarkable run of luck, surely? One might almost say—incredible?"

"That is very true." Michael took a turn about the room, apparently deep in thought. Suddenly he said abruptly: "Why did you not carry this tale to Sir David himself? He is in London."

"So I discovered, sir," Latimer replied promptly, "but I did not wish to raise in him hopes which may never be fulfilled. From those who were present at the time I learned that you, Sir David's closest friend, were with him each night he gambled with Rainham, and that you sought to restrain him. It seemed best to come to you."

Michael nodded, and again fell to pacing the room. Excitement was rising in him, and he strove to dissemble it. Here at last were the means to be revenged upon Rainham for taking Dorothea from him, to ruin him utterly and irretrievably. David and his fortune he dismissed from his mind; it would be almost impossible to force Rainham to give up Hope Stratton, but once the shameful truth was made known he would not dare to show his face in London again. To be discovered cheating at cards was an unforgivable sin.

Nor, if he, Ashton, were any judge of men, was Latimer much concerned with Sir David Stratton, in spite of all his specious talk. He bore Rainham a grudge, whether because of the death of the man Dacres, or for some other reason, Michael neither knew nor cared. The Major was undoubtedly a man who made enemies more easily than he made friends.

"Tell me, Mr. Latimer," he said at length, "is Rainham aware of your presence in London?"

The other shook his head.

"No, for I have been at some pains to avoid him, lest he should seek to put a quarrel upon me. I trust I am no coward, but now that my fortunes are mended I wish to live to enjoy my inheritance. Rainham is an exceptional swordsman, and when he fights, he fights to kill. That, I believe, was discovered to his cost by a certain nobleman not long ago."

"Young Jevington?" Michael nodded. "Yes, I am told it was no more than a polite form of murder. Take my advice, Mr. Latimer, and continue to avoid Rainham for the present. Meanwhile I will discuss the matter with Sir David Stratton, and we will determine how best to proceed."

On that they parted, and in the mind of neither was there any doubt that, no matter what became of the Stratton fortune, both would be satisfied to bring about the ruin of Major Rainham. Michael lost no time in carrying the story to David, only to meet with stronger opposition even than he had expected, and a blunt announcement that whatever action was taken, Dorothea must first be consulted.

Accordingly David wrote to his sister an account of Latimer's strange accusation, and she, concluding at once that this was a plot of Michael's contriving, sent back word by the same messenger that she would come to London without delay. The desire to be with Kelvin in this crisis was purely instinctive, but at the back of her mind was the thought that she alone might have the power to persuade Ashton to abandon his schemes of vengeance. In conclusion, she informed David of the part played by Rainham in Clarissa's deliverance, hoping that this would strengthen his resolve to make no move against the Major.

It so happened, however, that when Dorothea's letter reached Sir Edward's house David was absent from London on business for his employer, and did not receive it until late upon the following evening. By this time a second letter had joined it, but David's first thought was for that inscribed in his sister's hand. Its contents inspired in him a variety of emotions, though resentment against Rainham was not among them, and it was somewhat absently that he broke the seal of the second letter and glanced at its contents. It was a curt note from Latimer, informing him that Major Rainham would be accused that night at Mrs. Cheriton's house, and that if Stratton hoped to recover his wealth he had best be there.

David read the missive twice, incredulously at first, and then with swiftly mounting anger at Michael's duplicity. For a moment or two he stood irresolute before realizing that his only hope of preventing a scandal was to go with all speed to Mrs. Cheriton's house. If he could reach the conspirators before any accusation was made, Rainham might yet be saved.

He was already at the door when he recollected that his sister might arrive at any moment, so, turning back, he scrawled a hasty message, folded it about Latimer's note, and left both in charge of a servant, with orders to deliver it at once to Miss Stratton should she arrive during his absence.

Michael Ashton's resolve to use his weapon against Major Rainham in defiance of David's wishes had taken shape as soon as Stratton announced his intention of seeking advice from his sister. It never occurred to Michael that after what had passed between them Dorothea would come prepared to plead with him, to beg him to abandon his scheme. Her intervention, he thought, would inevitably strengthen David against it, and since the prospect of ruining Rainham grew more enticing the longer he contemplated it, the only thing to do was to keep the younger man in ignorance of it.

He took counsel with Latimer, and found him a ready

tool—though had his natural shrewdness not been overwhelmed by his desire for vengeance he might well have wondered which of them was in fact the tool, and which the guiding hand. It was Latimer who had the happy inspiration of challenging Major Rainham at the house which had been the scene of his triumph, and Latimer's inquiries which informed them when the Major intended to pay his next visit to the establishment. Michael, finding the path of conspiracy beguilingly smooth, gave thanks to the good fortune which had sent him so gifted a confederate.

On the day which was to witness the end, in ruin and humiliation, of Major Rainham's triumphant career, the plotters dined together at Ashton's lodging, and at a suitable hour of the evening made their way to the gaming-house. The big saloon seemed unusually crowded when they entered, and Michael was able to congratulate himself that his rival's downfall would be witnessed by a large number of influential persons.

The Major they presently discovered where the crowd was thickest. He sat at cards with the swarthy, saturnine Lord Pencannon, but at the moment when Ashton and Latimer approached, the game was at a standstill and a good deal of raillery being exchanged by the gentlemen grouped about the table. Rainham's level, faintly mocking voice fell clearly into a momentary pause, the target for his barbed wit being Sir Walter Maddox, florid and self-important, who uttered outraged spluttering noises as he sought in vain for a suitable retort.

The press parted, and the two conspirators had a sudden clear view of their quarry. He was leaning back in his chair, one long, white hand holding a gold snuff-box, a slight smile playing about his lips as he contemplated Sir Walter's discomfiture; a satin coat of an unusual colour between green and blue set off to great advantage his tall, vigorous person and tawny hair, and a jewel, half hidden in the folds of his cravat, glinted in the candle-light. Ashton, regarding that striking figure, dwelt with satisfaction upon the thought that he surveyed a sun about to set for ever.

"Gad'slife, Rainham, Maddox is no match for you,"

Pencannon put in, laughing. "Let him be, and we will continue our game."

"A moment, my lord!" Latimer, quick to seize his opportunity, stepped forward to the table. "May I venture to predict that you will regret this game? Those who play against Major Rainham customarily do."

Kelvin looked up quickly at the speaker's face, and just for an instant his eyes widened. He recovered himself at once, but not before others besides Latimer had seen that flash of dismayed recognition. Pencannon favoured the newcomer with a glance of haughty inquiry.

"I do not think I know you, sir," he said coldly.

"You do not, my lord, but Major Rainham will present me. We are old acquaintances, are we not, Major?"

Kelvin had not moved. He studied Latimer's scarred face deliberately, his grey eyes calm and wholly indifferent once more. Mrs. Cheriton, who had heard all that passed, moved forward a little to set her hand on the back of his chair, but he did not turn his head; he seemed as oblivious of her presence as of the stares and whispers of the company.

"I fear you are mistaken, sir," he said at length, with sardonic courtesy. "It is not possible that I should have forgotten so felicitous an association."

"It's possible you'd wish to forget it," sneered the other, "but allow me to refresh your memory. Our last meeting took place five years ago in France, and you stood exposed for the cheating scoundrel that you are."

He had raised his voice a trifle, and the words were clearly audible to the farthest corners of the big room. Sir David Stratton heard them as he thrust open the door, and knew that he had come too late; Rainham's only hope now lay in offering undeniable proof that his accuser lied, and as David shouldered his way through the press he found himself hoping that such proof would be forthcoming.

Latimer's challenge had provoked an outburst of talk. Some of the gentlemen were demanding that he be instantly ejected, others insisting that he should be allowed to enlarge upon his words. Only the accused man sat silent and faintly smiling, while Pencannon's voice, on a new note of gravity, broke in upon the babel.

"So serious a charge, sir, cannot be ignored, but I must ask you to be more explicit. And tell us, if you please, who you are and by what right you make such an accusation against Major Rainham."

"My name is Latimer," the other replied promptly. "Miles Latimer, at your lordship's service. I am a soldier, sir, until lately in the service of the King of France, and now returned to England for the first time in many years to take possession of an inheritance. Mr. Ashton, whom I think is well known to you, will confirm the truth of what I say."

His lordship's frowning gaze transferred itself to Ashton, who nodded.

"That is so," he said curtly. "I will vouch for Mr. Latimer, and I pray that you will hear him. Many of us here tonight have sat down to cards with Major Rainham in the past, but few, I think, can boast of winning from him."

"We will hear Mr. Latimer," Pencannon assured him, and glanced across at Kelvin. "In justice to you, sir, we can do no less."

"Oh, proceed, my lord, I beg of you!" Rainham's voice was mocking. "I have no objection, provided that I am given an opportunity to reply to his charges."

"Upon that, sir, you may depend," Pencannon assured him. "Well, Mr. Latimer, we await your pleasure."

"A moment, sir, before you begin," Sir Walter Maddox put in pompously. "I think I perceive Sir David Stratton yonder. He, surely, is deeply implicated in this matter."

Made thus the focus of attention, David came reluctantly forward, studiously ignoring Michael's dismayed and astonished gaze. Lord Pencannon regarded him sternly.

"This is a privilege we have not enjoyed of late, Sir David," he greeted him, and looked from him to Ashton and Latimer. "Upon my soul, this begins to savour of a conspiracy."

"Your lordship is mistaken," Latimer put in before David could reply. "It is at my suggestion that Sir David is here tonight. Most of the company present have lost

216

paltry sums to Major Rainham, but Sir David lost a fortune."

"Give me leave, sir, to speak for myself," David said sharply. "I am by no means convinced that your accusation against Major Rainham is just."

Kelvin had been looking down at the snuff-box which he was balancing between his hands, but at that he glanced up quickly. For a few seconds his eyes rested upon David with an inscrutable expression, and then returned once more to contemplation of the trinket he held.

"Of that, Sir David, these gentlemen shall judge," Latimer retorted, and turned to address the attentive company. "Upon the occasion to which I refer, gentlemen, there were but four persons present. Rainham and myself, and two other Englishmen, Ralph Dacres and Anthony Forrest."

At the mention of the latter name David stifled an oath and looked sharply at Kelvin. Anthony Forrest was the name which Rainham had assumed when he went to Gallows Farm, and later he had told Dorothea that it was the name of his dead friend. Could it be that, after all, Latimer spoke truth? With a sinking heart he gave his attention to the other man's story.

He told it well, briefly and yet with a vividness of phrase which conjured up for them the scene he described. The game, the sudden challenge flung down by young Dacres, and the accused man insolently admitting its truth but replying to it with a blow across the mouth.

"I cannot offer you proof of what I say, gentlemen," Latimer concluded bitterly, "for in exchange for the gold he had stolen from him Rainham gave Ralph Dacres steel—a foot of it through the poor lad's vitals! He knew that Dacres was no match for him at swordplay, and for the same reason no one else ventured to challenge him. But he could not silence the truth that murdered boy had made known, and I give thanks that Fate has granted me the chance to unmask him here in London, for Dacres was my friend."

There was a pause after he had finished speaking, and then Pencannon asked gravely:

"What of the other man, Forrest?"

Latimer shook his head.

"He, too, is dead, my lord. He died a soldier's death on the field of battle."

"I see." His lordship pursed his lips, looking from one to the other. "Then it would seem, sir, to be Major Rainham's word against yours."

At that, another buzz of conversation broke out, and under cover of it Sally leaned forward to whisper urgently in Kelvin's ear.

"The letter! Anthony Forrest's letter to me! You cannot, for the sake of a quixotic ideal, refuse to make use of it now, when 'tis your only hope."

A glimmer of triumph crept into Rainham's eyes, and he replied in the same tone:

"You have it?"

" 'Tis locked away. I shall need five minutes at least to come at it."

"You shall have them. You are right, my dear, I have need of that letter now as never before."

She nodded and withdrew unobtrusively from the room. Lord Pencannon turned once more to Kelvin.

"You have heard the accusation, sir. What answer do you make?"

In leisurely fashion Major Rainham rose to his feet and stood to look round at the assembled company, dominating them by his height and the cold self-possession which never failed him. One man there, he knew, hated him with jealous intensity, and the rest regarded him with varying degrees of dislike; even Pencannon, despite his determination to be just, cherished no kindly feelings for him. Of those present, only one man would be glad to see him clear himself, and he, ironically enough, was the one man who stood to gain by his downfall.

"As his lordship so truly says," he remarked at length, "no proof exists either of my innocence or my guilt. It is indeed a case of my word against Mr. Latimer's. So now I tell you, gentlemen, in all sincerity, that the story he has told you is in every detail completely—true."

The words, spoken in the level, dispassionate voice they had come to know so well, struck them all into astounded silence. They stared at him in amazement, each wondering whether he had heard aright or whether Major Rainham had taken leave of his senses.

"Do you realize what you have said?" Pencannon asked incredulously at length, and the familiar, cynical smile crept once more about the Major's lips.

"My dear sir, I am still, I trust, responsible for my words and actions. I said that Mr. Latimer's story is true, as indeed it is. What further assurance do you desire?"

"Upon my soul!" Sir Walter Maddox spoke explosively. "Such effrontery, such infernal impudence, passes all bounds! Stap me, sir, if I ever heard the like!"

Kelvin waited courteously for the interruption to come to an end, and then resumed as though Maddox had not spoken. He seemed to be faintly amused.

"To say that I am happy to renew my acquaintance with Mr. Latimer would be to strain your credulity too far, but since he is here I will not trouble to deny his accusation. The incident to which he refers was unfortunate, but I do not believe that it gives me any cause for self-reproach."

His cool insolence nonplussed them, and all the righteous emotions they felt were for the present held in check by astonishment. Ashton was frowning, for though his plot had succeeded beyond his wildest dreams, Rainham's bearing somehow robbed vengeance of its savour. David's thoughts were in confusion, regret, disbelief and anger so intermingled that he did not know which prevailed. It was Lord Pencannon who broke at last that heavy silence, in a voice eloquent of contempt.

"The admission, sir, is not one which does you credit. Your attitude is, I confess, beyond my comprehension, as I believe it is beyond the comprehension of every man here."

"Perhaps, my lord," Miles Latimer broke in, "since Major Rainham has used such frankness concerning one affair, he will tell us also whether or not he acquired the Stratton fortune by the same means."

Once again all eyes turned towards Rainham, where he stood with one hand resting lightly on the back of the chair from which he had risen. He met them with that aloof indifference with which he had learned long ago to cloak his feelings.

"But of course," he said lightly. "Is it possible that fortune would smile so consistently upon any man unless he brought skill to the aid of luck? I am astonished that no one suspected it ere this."

"You admit it?" Pencannon's face had hardened to an expression of haughty distaste. "You have the effrontery to confess that you have consistently cheated at cards ever since your arrival in London?"

"Your lordship mistakes me," Kelvin retorted mockingly. "I admit that I cheated Sir David Stratton out of his fortune, but after that my improved circumstances rendered such action unnecessary."

He paused, his glance drifting to a nearby clock, and then once more addressed them, still in that level, ironical voice.

"I have learned, however, that there is much truth in the saying that riches do not bring contentment. For more than a year now I have supported the burden of great wealth, and found it well-nigh as wearisome as I have found the life of a man of fashion. Therefore, gentlemen, I formally withdraw all claim to the fortune and estate of Hope Stratton, and I trust that Sir David will not hesitate to take back his wealth. When all things are considered, it never really passed from his possession at all."

For a moment Pencannon considered him in silence, a sneer on his swarthy face.

"Very fine, my friend," he said unpleasantly at last, "but do not think that by making a grand gesture you can blind us to the vileness of your conduct. Certainly, Stratton will regain his fortune, but I think you realize that he would have done so even had you not withdrawn your claim to it. I speak for every man here when I say that you would not have been allowed to remain in possession."

There was a murmur of agreement; someone clapped David on the shoulder and another shook his hand, but he paid no heed to them. He stood staring at Rainham, conscious of a feeling of bitter disappointment which not even the sudden, immense change in his fortunes could dispel, until he was roused by Pencannon's voice.

"It is my belief, Sir David, that it would be possible to order this man's arrest. If you wish it——"

"No!" David spoke so sharply that his lordship was distinctly taken aback. "That is not possible, my lord, for private reasons. I beg you to say no more of it."

"As you wish!" Pencannon looked at him rather hard for a moment, and then shrugged and addressed himself once more to Rainham. "You hear, sir? I own that in Sir David's place I should be less forbearing, but since he wishes it you should go unpunished. A word of warning, however! Do not seek to prevail now as you did five years ago in France, for if you so much as issue a challenge in regard to this affair, before Heaven I'll have you thrown into prison! We want no bully-swordsmen here. Now in God's name get you hence, lest I am tempted to summon my lackeys to give you the flogging you deserve."

David was still watching Rainham. There was no smile now about the austere lips, and the fine, stern face was so rigidly pale that it might have been carved from stone; his expression, and the slender hand gripped hard on the back of the chair, suggested a tremendous effort at self-control. Just for an instant, to Stratton's somewhat over-wrought imagination, he had the look of a man crucified. How much of what he had said was true, and how much false, David did not know, but he remembered suddenly that it was the Stratton fortune which stood between Kelvin Rainham and his heart's desire, and wondered whether, faced with Latimer's accusation, he had taken this way of ridding himself of it. Yet, even for Dorothea's sake, could any man of his own free will face dishonour so public and so absolute? Could he himself have done it, to win Clarissa's hand?

These questions, and many others, echoed confusedly in his mind, and before even one of them could find an answer Rainham moved at last from his position by the table and walked unhurriedly in the direction of the door. He did not look at David as he passed, and though the younger man opened his lips to speak he could find nothing to say. For the whole length of that long room Rainham was obliged to run the gauntlet of contemptuous eyes and hostile murmurs, but his calm bearing never faltered. At the door he turned, and before passing out of the room he bowed with ironical ceremony to the staring company. For almost every man present that parting glimpse of the elegant, soldierly figure was the last they were ever to have.

CHAPTER XIV

THE HOMECOMING

When the door of the gaming-room had closed between him and the men who had witnessed his humiliation, Kelvin bowed his head and covered his eyes with his hand. For a moment he stood thus, then, looking up, found that he had withdrawn only just in time, for along the broad corridor towards him Mrs. Cheriton was hastening, one hand holding up her trailing skirts, the other grasping a folded paper. He went quickly to meet her, took her arm, and in spite of her protests and anxious questions urged her irresistibly in the direction of her own sitting-room. When its door had closed behind them he said:

"You have the letter?"

"Yes, it is here. Kelvin, what has happened? Why did you not await my return?"

"May I see it?"

She put the letter into his outstretched hand and he turned aside to where a branch of candles stood upon a nearby table, unfolding the paper and bending his head to read it, while Sally watched him anxiously.

"This is some plot of Ashton's, you may depend," she said after a little. "He would like nothing better than to see you discredited in the eyes of the world. Oh, but he has had the devil's own luck! What evil chance brought him and Latimer together, and how did Latimer know that you had once been accused of cheating? He lied when he said he was present that night, did he not?"

"Yes, he lied, but doubtless he heard the tale from one who was present." Kelvin came to the end of the letter and stood for a moment looking down at it. "You were right, Sally, this offers conclusive proof of my innocence. Therefore——" he broke off and with a deliberate movement thrust the corner of the paper into the candle-flame. Mrs. Cheriton started forward with a gasp of horror, but Kelvin dropped the blazing paper into the fireplace and caught her by the arm, holding her so until nothing was left of the precious letter but a crumpled piece of black ash, glowing faintly along its edges.

"Kelvin, what have you done?" Sally's voice was horrified. "The only proof——! You must be mad!"

He shook his head.

"I had not the least intention of using it," he said, "but somehow I had to trick you into giving it to me that I might destroy it. Forgive me, my dear."

Released from his grip, Sally leaned against the table, staring at him while an incredible suspicion took shape in her mind.

"Kelvin," she said, in a tone little louder than a whisper, "who told Latimer that story?"

He shrugged and turned away.

"You had best ask him that question. A number of people knew of it, and any one of them might have told him."

"No," Sally said slowly, "no, it was not chance which brought Ashton and Latimer together. I see it all now! It was you who told him the story, was it not?" He did not reply, and she caught him by the arm, shaking it a little. "Was it not?"

He frowned, looking down at her with an expression half-impatient, half-rueful.

"You are too damnably shrewd, Sally," he complained. "Yes, it was I."

"You mean you planned this, your own disgrace? Merciful Heaven, you are mad!"

"Not in the least," he replied levelly. "I wished to restore to David Stratton all that I had won from him, but I knew he would not accept it as long as he thought I had won it fairly. So I bribed Latimer to carry the story to Ashton, whose hatred of me by this time exceeds David's. The rest followed naturally enough, and though he will never know it, Ashton has been my tool throughout, for it was I who chose the time and setting for tonight's denunciation. It had to take place here so that I might possess myself of the letter."

"You knew they would come tonight?" She spoke incredulously, remembering his easy bearing, the casual way in which he had taken part in the light-hearted conversation which had preceded Latimer's arrival. Was there no limit, she thought wonderingly, to the demands he would make upon himself?

"Do you realize what you have done?" she asked him, and flung out an arm towards the hearth. "'Tis your honour lies in ashes there."

"My dear Sally, you are being quite needlessly dramatic. My honour was forfeit long ago, and when my tarnished reputation is remembered my confession of guilt will be more readily believed than if it had been made by a man whose past was blameless. 'Slife, I believe I have cause to be grateful to Catherine for the disgrace she brought upon me years ago."

The words, and the sardonic, slightly amused tone in which they were uttered, might have deceived her had her judgment depended upon hearing alone, but in his face she could read something of what it had cost him to immolate his pride and assume a burden of shame which he had done nothing to deserve. She leaned forward and placed her hand on his arm.

"So you have rid yourself at last of your golden burden," she said gently, "but the cost, my dear, the cost! I think this was the hardest thing you have ever done."

A spasm of pain crossed his face; he shook his head.

"The hardest thing is yet to do," he replied in a low voice. "Good God, Sally, do you suppose that I can go to Dorothea now and ask her to be my wife? Now, when by my own confession I stand convicted of so despicable a crime?"

"She will not believe it!" Sally's voice was shocked.

"Whether or not she believes it is beside the point. In the eyes of the world I am a man dishonoured beyond hope of redemption—do you imagine that I expect her to share my shame? Moreover, with her brother's recovery of his wealth she becomes again a lady of fortune, and what have I?" He laughed mirthlessly. "My sword, my training as a soldier—there is no market for them in England. If I am not to starve I must set forth on my travels again."

"Many years ago," Mrs. Cheriton remarked reflectively, "I left my home and family to go adventuring with the man I loved. We were poor, our life was by no means easy, yet I never regretted it."

Kelvin did not reply. He stood staring at the steady, golden flames of the candles, remembering a wainscoted parlour in a country inn, and Dorothea's voice saying quietly: "No other thing in all the world, not shame, nor poverty, nor dishonour, could come between . . ." A wave of temptation swept over him. He had sacrificed so much of wealth and pride and honour, why should he cast away also the love which had brought him the first real happiness he had ever known? Then he remembered the hardship and squalor of his roving life, and knew that the thing he contemplated was impossible.

"No, Sally," he said in a hard voice, "that is a dream which can never be realized. 'Twas not with the intention of dragging her down to shame that I duped Ashton into accusing me tonight."

"Then why?" Mrs. Cheriton demanded exasperatedly. "In the name of Heaven, Kelvin, why go to such lengths to rid yourself of the Stratton fortune, if not because it was the one thing which stood between you and Dorothea?"

He turned to face her, moving his hands in an impatient gesture.

"The situation was intolerable," he replied. "It had to be ended somehow, and what better way than that which gives David back his fortune? He and Lady Clarissa may marry now, Dorothea's future security is assured, and I——"

"And you?" Mrs. Cheriton repeated as he paused. "What of yourself, Kelvin?"

"Oh, I still ride alone, my dear—to the devil, no doubt." The tone was light, but this time the cynical manner did not quite ring true. "Do not suppose that my plans are not made. A ship to France, and thence wherever my sword may command the highest fee. The old life, Sally, for a time. I've a notion 'twill not be for long."

She looked at him sharply, her brows drawing together in a frown, but made no comment upon his last remark. Instead she said:

"I do not understand you, Kelvin. If by your own deed a fresh barrier has been raised between you and Dorothea, why did you do it? Did you not realize until too late what it would mean?"

"Oh yes, I realized it," he replied with a hint of bitterness. "For weeks I had racked my brains to discover some way of ridding myself of the fortune that stood between us, and at last perceived that there was indeed a way—the only way—to achieve my object. The only way, which even as it removed one obstacle set another in its place." He paused, regarding her beneath lifted brows. "I fear, Sally, that the exquisite irony of the situation escapes you. A pity, for this is Hell's own humour, my dear. You should not let it pass unappreciated."

The bitter, mocking voice broke suddenly, and he bowed his head. Sally felt unaccustomed tears rising to her eyes, and blinked them irritably away; when she was certain that she could control her voice she said:

"Has it not occurred to you to consult Dorothea before making your plans? It is possible that she may take exception to this arbitrary ordering of her future."

He frowned, looking down at the snuff-box which he had taken once more from his pocket.

"Dorothea will know nothing until after my departure. The ship on which I have taken passage lies now at Rotherhithe, and sails for France tomorrow."

"You will go without seeing her again?" Amazement and disbelief struggled for supremacy in Sally's voice. "Kelvin, what an infamous thing to do!"

His lips tightened, and there was an appreciable pause before he replied.

"If you will consider the question in the light of reason, my dear Sally, you will perceive that it is nothing of the kind. By Dorothea's own wish we parted, and though her reason for that decision no longer exists, another has taken its place. Why then reopen wounds which time should already have begun to heal? I take the course which is easier for both of us."

"Is this your reasoning?" Mrs. Cheriton retorted scornfully. "Do not try to deceive me, my friend, for we have known each other too long and too well. You go thus because you dare not face her."

"Confound you, Sally, you see too much!" he said with a sigh. "You are right, of course. I have set my feet tonight on a path I cannot ask her to tread with me, but so great is my need and my desire that I dare not tarry in England lest, seeing her again, I have not the strength of will to say farewell."

"So you take refuge in flight? I never thought to see you play a coward's part, Kelvin."

He turned abruptly away, saying over his shoulder:

"Which is the greater evil, to be a coward or to be a knave? What if I let myself be guided by you, and took Dorothea a-roving with me? A soldier's life is a hazardous one at best, and if any mischance befell me she would be left alone and friendless in a foreign land. That one danger alone makes such a course unthinkable."

The argument was unanswerable, and Mrs. Cheriton could find no means to counter it. Reason and logic were both upon his side, and yet she knew instinctively that the decision he had made was wrong; but because she knew him so well she was equally certain that only

Dorothea herself had power to alter that decision, and she was far away in Kent. Desperate calculations flashed through Sally's mind. If she sent at once to fetch her, could she arrive in time to prevent Kelvin's departure? It was scarcely possible, even if the journey could be accomplished without any kind of delay, and yet somehow that departure must be prevented. Argument had failed. She knew that, and wasted no further time upon it. Could she use force? Her servants would obey without question any commands she chose to give them. She eyed Major Rainham speculatively, while he, unaware of the thoughts of violence in his companion's mind, stood lost in a reverie which set haggard lines upon his face.

The door opened to admit a footman, and so much in tune with her thoughts was his arrival that Mrs. Cheriton started guiltily. With an apologetic glance at the Major he crossed to where she sat and bent to whisper in her ear. Sally shot him an incredulous glance and then rose to her feet, saying briskly:

"Forgive me, Kelvin, but there is a matter I must attend to below. I shall not be long, for we must discuss this matter further."

"As you please," he replied wearily, "but I assure you that no amount of discussion can alter my decision."

"We shall see," Sally retorted cryptically. "Wait here."

She went out, and Kelvin walked slowly across to the fire-place, where, leaning one arm on the mantel, he looked down at the ashes of Anthony Forrest's letter. He did not regret what he had done. The lands and riches he had won from David Stratton had become a hollow mockery which he was glad to lay aside, and since the only road of escape had demanded the sacrifice of his honour, he had taken it with the same steely fortitude which years before had enabled him to survive an ordeal in many ways more grim than this. But when for the first time he went into exile it was only lost ambitions and a ruined career he left behind him; immeasurably greater was the loss he faced today. He thought of Dorothea, and was shaken by a storm of loneliness and longing so violent that with a groan he bowed his head upon his arm.

He had not moved from his position by the hearth when the latch clicked and he heard the whisper of a woman's gown across the floor, but even then he did not look up. Only when a hand was laid upon his shoulder did he raise his head, to find beside him, not Mrs. Cheriton, but a slender girl whose face was pale and weary in the shadow of a wide-brimmed hat, and whose riding-dress showed dusty and travel-stained.

"Dorothea!" he whispered. "No, it is not possible. How have you come here?"

"Does it matter?" she replied softly. "Does anything matter save the fact that we are together again, and the one barrier that stood between us swept away?"

With a sudden abrupt movement he turned from her and moved away towards the table; with his back to her he said curtly:

"Do you know what has taken place in this house tonight?"

"I know that when Michael faced you with his trumped-up charge of cheating you admitted its truth so that you might restore to David all that you won from him." Dorothea's voice was tranquil, but her hands were clasped tightly together and her eyes were anxious. "What else is there to know?"

"One thing only," he replied in a hard voice. "The tale happens to be true. I did cheat Dacres five years ago, and in the same way I cheated your brother of his fortune."

She shook her head.

"No," she said, "you knew that only in this way could you restore Hope Stratton to David, and if you took the guilt upon yourself on that other occasion, you had a good reason for it."

"Who told you so?" He swung round to face her, and both eyes and voice were stern.

"My own heart, Kelvin," she replied gently. "I need no other counsellor."

"On this occasion it has played you false. The charge is true, but even if it were not, in the eyes of the world I stand stripped of the few poor rags of honour I still possessed. I think you do not yet realize what an outcast I have become tonight."

There was a pause. Dorothea moved slowly to the chair which Mrs. Cheriton had lately occupied; she sat down, and for the sake of something to do took off her wide-brimmed hat and smoothed the feathers that adorned it. Her hands were not quite steady.

"Kelvin," she said at length, without looking up, "when David first heard Mr. Latimer's story he sent me a very full account of it, for he thought I had a right to know. I understand that there was no proof upon either side, that 'twas merely Latimer's word against yours." She glanced up inquiringly, and he nodded without speaking, wondering whither the question led. "It is well known," she continued, "that Michael dislikes you and would possibly scheme to discredit you. Had you pointed out this fact, and denied Latimer's story, is it not possible that you would have been believed?"

He shrugged.

"Perhaps, though 'tis not very likely. Ashton is not my only enemy, and my friends are few."

"But with so much at stake, surely it would have been worthwhile to put it to the test? When you won so much from David, to cheat him over so long a period must have entailed great danger of discovery, and yet, little more than a year after you risked so much to possess yourself of Hope Stratton, you surrender it without making the least attempt to defend yourself. Why, Kelvin?"

The question took him unawares, for until that moment he had overlooked this glaring inconsistency in his conduct. He hesitated, and could find no better explanation than that which he had offered a short while ago to the company in the gaming-room.

"I found the burden of riches and fashionable life less to my taste than I had anticipated. I grew bored, and would be off on my travels again."

Her eyes were frankly incredulous; almost she seemed amused.

"I imagine that one might travel farther, and find a quicker relief from boredom, with the resources of a large estate to draw upon at need. That does not answer my question."

It did not, and he knew it. Another explanation offered, but one so brutal that at first he hesitated to use it, even though he knew that if he succeeded in speaking the words convincingly, pride alone would prevent her from pleading with him again. She was still awaiting an answer to her question, and with a supreme effort he forced himself to assume his most cold and mocking manner.

"I had hoped to spare you the true answer," he said in a level voice. A faint, cynical smile hovered about his lips. "However, if you must have the truth, pray hold me absolved of any desire to wound you, and believe me sincere in this at least. For your care of me when I lay ill at Gallows Farm you have my most sincere gratitude."

"Only gratitude, Kelvin?" she asked softly, but there was no answering smile in his eyes.

"Only gratitude," repeated coldly. "For the rest, the situation seemed apt for dalliance, and though it pleased you to assume the guise of a simple country maid, I supposed you familiar with the kind of delightful comedy we played." He produced his snuff-box and took a pinch, noting with faint satisfaction that his hands were perfectly steady. "That you considered it anything more I did not realize until too late. Pleasant dalliance had suddenly become something far more serious, and there you have my reason for wishing to be rid of all suggestion of responsibility. You had saved my life and I did not want to hurt you, but there is one thing I value above riches, or influence, or even honour, and that, my dear Dorothea, is my freedom."

He closed the box with a snap and brushed an imaginary speck of dust from the sleeve of his coat. Dorothea's head was bowed and he could not see the expression in her eyes, though her lips were trembling; he thought she wept, until, quite incredibly, she laughed.

"And so you flung away the one sure guardian of your freedom—the Stratton fortune," she said. "Oh,

Kelvin, 'tis a wonder they believed you tonight, for I find you a most unconvincing liar."

He raised his brows.

" 'Tis natural, of course, that you should be unwilling to believe anything so unflattering to yourself. For the rest, to restore your wealth was the least that I could do, since I had no further use for it."

The laughter faded from Dorothea's face. She rose to her feet and, coming to his side, laid her hands on his shoulders, looking up into his face.

"Kelvin," she said quietly, "can you swear before God that you never loved me, that all you told me of the portrait and your search for me was false? Swear it— thus—with your arms about me and your eyes on mine, and I will believe it, and all else."

"I swear——" he began lightly, and then stopped, unable to speak the monstrous lie she demanded. "The hardest thing is yet to do" he had told Sally, but how hard it was to be he had not known when he spoke. "I swear——" he began again, but once more the words died upon his lips, and with a sudden gesture of defeat he bowed his head. Dorothea smiled, and reached up to press her cheek against his.

"My own dear love," she whispered, "why are you so determined to send me from you?"

"Do you not understand?" he said sadly. "I am poor, and now that the Stratton fortune is restored to its rightful owners——"

"I want no part of it," she interrupted. "David may keep it all."

"I am by my own confession utterly dishonoured——"

"In London, perhaps, but what does that signify? We have no need to stay in London."

"The life to which I must return is not fit for you. Poverty, and hardship, and no home to call our own——"

"In that you are mistaken, Kelvin. Gallows Farm can be our home, if you will return there with me. Thomas and Janet wish it, as well you know."

He shook his head.

"They did so once, but when they learn the depths

233

to which I have sunk they are more likely to close their door against me."

"Do you think them such fair-weather friends?" she asked reproachfully. "They know what errand brought me to London, and they bade me tell you that they know such story cannot be true of you. See"—she fumbled in her pocket and produced a crumpled letter—"Thomas is no scholar, but he made shift to write this to tell you as much. They are your friends, my dear, do you not realize that? Change of fortune does not mean to them a change of heart."

Kelvin took the letter and stood looking down at it without breaking the seal, seeing in his mind's eye the honest, ruddy face of the man who had penned it. Seeing, too, the huge farmhouse kitchen and the oak-panelled parlour, the walled garden and the orchards embracing the ancient house. There was kindness there, and comradeship, as well as the love which had so miraculously been granted to him; a life such as he had never known; not the life of high ambition and worldly glory to which he had dedicated his youth, nor the idle pursuit of pleasure in which his days had lately passed, but one more full and rich than either. A wife, a home, true friends, and the rich earth yielding a goodly harvest. For a space he contemplated it, the goal he had sought so long in vain, and then he remembered that twice his fortunes had crumbled into ruin and disgrace, and fear touched him with a chilly hand, lest this fair prospect should find a similar end.

Dorothea was watching him anxiously, knowing what it was that troubled him and desperately afraid that upon this new barrier he saw between them the frail bark of their happiness would founder anew. She laid her hands over his, which still held the unopened letter.

"Kelvin," she pleaded, "come home with me."

He looked down at her, the trouble in his eyes deepening.

"And bring shame with me?" he questioned bitterly, but she shook her head, and her fingers tightened upon his.

"We shall leave it behind us, as we shall leave all else

belonging to this empty, idle existence. When we go forth from London it will be to a new life, one which will atone in full measure for the grief and suffering of the old." She smiled, and put up her hand to touch his cheek. "I think you are afraid of happiness, Kelvin, or you would not hesitate to grasp it."

He caught the caressing hand in his, and turned his head to press his lips against its palm.

"Perhaps I am," he said with a sigh, "for how can true happiness follow in the path of shame and ignominy?"

Before she could reply the door was flung open to admit Sir David Stratton. Startled, Dorothea and Kelvin drew apart, but at first David paid no heed to his sister's presence. As Mrs. Cheriton followed him into the room he said impetuously:

"Rainham, you cannot do this thing! Do you seriously imagine that I will permit it?"

"David!" Dorothea spoke in bewildered protest, and he swung round to face her.

"Do you know what he has done? Deliberately he has sacrificed his honour in order to restore Hope Stratton to me. I tried to prevent it! I came here as fast as I could, but Michael and Latimer were too quick for me."

"I know, my dear," she replied. "Your letter told me of that, and I was glad."

"That is another thing!" David exclaimed obscurely. "Why was I never told that 'twas Rainham saved Clarissa? Fiend seize it, surely I had a right to know that?"

Kelvin and Dorothea exchanged glances.

"Would it have pleased you to know?" inquired the former. "I fancied 'twould but increase your ambition to cross swords with me if you learned that I succeeded where you failed."

For a moment David glared at him; then the engaging grin flashed across his face.

"I dare swear it would—at the time," he agreed cheerfully, "but now I know you better I no longer cherish that ambition—save in regard to what happened tonight. Oh, I have the whole story, never fear! Thanks to Mrs. Cheriton, I have been granted a private interview with our friend Latimer."

"David," Dorothea exclaimed eagerly, "did he admit 'twas Michael who concocted this fantastic charge against Kelvin?"

"Michael!" David stared at her. "Devil take it, do you still not know the truth? 'Twas Rainham who was the real author of the plot! When he admitted to Latimer's story I suspected something of the truth, but as God's my witness I never guessed the full extent of it. He bribed the man to make this accusation, and trick Michael into believing it, and even told him to be certain that I was present when the charge was made. That is why Latimer sent me that message this evening."

"Had I known that you would seek to prevent him from telling his story," Kelvin put in drily, "I should have been less eager for your presence. I wished to be certain, however, that you took advantage of your opportunity to reclaim your birthright."

"Kelvin!" Dorothea was looking at him wonderingly. "Then it is true? You did indeed send Latimer to Michael?"

He bowed his head.

"I did, but the story he told was true enough. I did kill Dacres five years ago, and I was convicted of cheating."

"You were unjustly convicted," David broke in swiftly. "It was your friend Forrest who cheated, but you chose to shield him. There was written proof of your innocence in Mrs. Cheriton's possession, but you persuaded her to give it to you tonight, and then destroyed it. See"—he pointed triumphantly to the hearth—"the ashes lie there yet."

"Indeed," Kelvin's glance passed to Mrs. Cheriton; there was an edge to his voice. "There was a time, Sally, when you knew how to keep a secret."

"I still do," she retorted, unabashed, "but I also know when to share one. Good lack, Kelvin, he has a right to know!"

"I am very grateful to Mrs. Cheriton," David announced, "and permit me to tell you, Major Rainham, that I do not intend to let this preposterous story go unchallenged. The truth must be made known."

Kelvin raised his brows.

"I wonder," he said pensively, "how you propose to accomplish this? Since I myself confessed to cheating you, no one is likely to believe that I did not."

"They will believe me," David replied firmly, "for my word must carry conviction, the more so when it is seen that I refuse to accept the return of that which I lost to you, and when I give you my sister in marriage."

For a space Kelvin considered him in silence, a more kindly expression in his eyes than David had ever seen there. Then he shook his head.

"You forget, I think, that your sister will not marry me while I am master of Hope Stratton. I want no part of it."

"Kelvin," Dorothea turned quickly to face him, her eyes very bright. "Oh, my love, what mean you?"

He took her hand and looked down at her, and for a moment it was as though they were alone in the room. He said quietly:

"Have you no fear, Dorothea, that some day you will regret the choice you make tonight?"

"Never," she replied, and her voice was joyous and unafraid, for she knew now that the struggle was over. The ship of which Sally Cheriton had told her would sail lacking a passenger, and in the fullness of time Gallows Farm would gain a new master. "Never, Kelvin, while life endures."

"But I cannot take back Hope Stratton," David was protesting. "Dorothea, do you not understand?"

His sister, becoming aware of his presence again, turned to face him.

"I do not understand one thing," she said quietly. "Do you realize, David, all that you must sacrifice to such a course? 'Twould mean the end of all your hopes of winning Clarissa to wife."

David nodded.

"I know," he said in a low voice, "but I know also that nothing, not even her happiness, must be allowed to prevent it. Hope Stratton belongs to Rainham; he won it fairly, and I will not take it back at the price of his honour."

"David," Dorothea's voice was not quite steady, and she took both her brother's hands in her own, "I believe Clarissa would be as proud and happy as I am to hear you say such a thing, but Kelvin is right. Hope Stratton has stood too long between us, and we want no part of it. Take it, my dear, and go ask Lord Ardely for his daughter's hand. I do not think he will refuse you. As for us, we shall be more than content with Gallows Farm."

David looked doubtfully from her to Rainham, and then to Mrs. Cheriton. It was Kelvin who broke the silence, and though he spoke to David his eyes were upon Dorothea.

"Hope Stratton and all its wealth," he said quietly, "are as nothing to the infinite riches brought to me by your sister's love. When I knew that the fortune I had won stood between us I desired nothing so much as to be rid of it for ever. Now there is only one thing I would have of you."

"What is it?" David asked eagerly, and at last Kelvin looked at him. The rare, transfiguring smile was in his eyes, and softening the sternness of his lips.

"Your friendship, David," he said simply, putting out his hand, and with an answering smile Stratton grasped it in his own.

Kelvin Rainham and Dorothea Stratton were married in London two days later. It was no ordinary wedding, for the bridegroom went to the altar booted and spurred, and the bride in her shabby riding-dress. There was no feasting to follow the ceremony, no drinking or dancing or vying for bride-favours, for horses stood saddled at the church door, and after taking a fond farewell of Mrs. Cheriton, Major Rainham and his wife mounted, and with David to bear them company, set their faces towards Kent. Once free of the town they made a good pace, and since the marriage ceremony had taken place at an early hour they had every hope of reaching the farm by nightfall.

It was a day such as only October could show, with bright sunshine to temper the coolness of a keen wind, and yellow leaves blowing against a cloudless sky of deepest blue. Hedgerow and woodland glowed like a herald's tabard with scarlet and gold, so that it seemed as though the whole countryside had put on festal attire to honour the merry party as they rode southward through the bright autumn weather, on into the heart of Kent.

Darkness was falling, and a full moon already sailing low over the wooded hills, when they came at length to the point where the road to Ardely Place branched away from that which led to Reppington and Gallows Farm. David, who had fallen silent some minutes before, reined in his horse.

"We part here," he announced. "I am for Ardely Place."

"David, at this hour?" Dorothea protested laughingly. "They will think you mad."

"So I am," he agreed promptly. "Mad with impatience to tell Clarissa of the change in my fortunes, and to ask her father's leave to marry her. Has there not been delay enough?"

"So much that a few hours more can make no difference. Wait until tomorrow, and present yourself in a more seemly fashion."

"That comes oddly from you, my dear, who were in such unseemly haste to wed." He caught her hand to his lips, and then looked up, laughing, to meet Rainham's amused gaze. "What say you, Kelvin? Do you also counsel delay?"

"You would not heed me if I did," Major Rainham replied, smiling. "Let him go, Dorothea. Mad or no, I cannot find it in me to blame him."

"My thanks to you," David said with a grin, and looked once more at his sister. "You hear, Dorothea? Go with your husband, child, and leave me to fashion my affairs as best I may."

He wheeled his horse and, with an airy flourish of his hand, set off at a brisk pace along the road to Ardely Place. Dorothea laughed and shook her head.

"He is incorrigible," she said. " 'Twill be no more than he deserves if Lord Ardely shows him the door."

"I trust," replied Kelvin, "that his lordship will not

be guilty of so gross a piece of folly."

"No, I fancy that when his mended fortunes become known, David will be warmly welcomed. His lordship, I believe, was beginning to despair of finding another rich bridegroom for Clarissa. Her dowry is small, but David cares nothing for that."

They rode on again, passed through the village of Reppington, and so came at last to the lane which led to Gallows Farm. In silence they followed its winding course, until at last the house lay before them and their journey was over. They drew rein before the door, and Kelvin, dismounting, came to lift Dorothea from the saddle. For a moment he held her close against his heart, but presently she freed herself gently from his embrace and mounted the time-worn steps. Beneath the pressure of her hand the heavy door swung slowly open, letting forth a shaft of light, for candles were burning in the empty hall. Faintly from the direction of the kitchen came the murmur of voices and the homely sound of Janet's spinning-wheel. Dorothea turned and put out her hand to her companion.

"Welcome home, beloved," she said softly.

For a moment or two Kelvin stood in rapt contemplation of a picture which would never fade from his memory. The kindly old house between its sheltering hills, with the full moon, round and golden, above its steep-pitched roof; the open door and the candle-lit hall, and Dorothea smiling at him from the midst of that welcoming radiance. A great peace descended upon his spirit; the last lingering doubts were swept away, and with them the burning memory of his self-sought dishonour, and he knew that at last, after bitter sorrow and many troublous years, he had indeed come home.

He took his wife's outstretched hand and raised it to his lips, and so drew her again within the shelter of his arm. Together, they passed into the house.